UNDRALAND

BOOK ONE IN THE UNDRALAND SERIES

MARY E. TWOMEY

ISBN-13: 978-1508634546
ISBN-10: 1508634548

http://www.maryetwomey.com

For Saxon

"What is desired in a man is loving kindness."
Proverbs 19:22

PROFESSOR VIN DIESEL

"Think I can get away with a sore shoulder again? I'm seriously sick of weightlifting class." I stuffed my too-thick hair into a lopsided ponytail that swooshed when I walked. The blonde curls brushing against my neck in cadence with my steps made the songs I sang in my head more entertaining to listen to while I tuned out the professor. The fact that the instructor had the nerve to make us call him a professor was ridiculous. He was a glorified gym rat, himself being the one doing the glorification. I slammed the locker door shut and popped my gum. *Professor* Hamilton hated when I chewed gum in class, though he never said anything directly about it. It was his slight cringe when I popped it that felt like payback for scheduling a gym session so early twice a week.

I groaned through a stretch my torso wasn't ready for. "This was supposed to be a blow-off class, like gym was in high school. This whole nine in the morning nonsense? Not cool."

Tonya's laugh was loud, even when the jokes were not laugh-worthy, which made them all the better. Her mocha-colored skin always looked prettiest when she smiled, which she made sure to do often. "You can't use the same excuse twice in a row. You gotta mix 'em up. Twisted ankle here, death of a family member there." She stopped short and placed her hand over her mouth. I could tell by her intake of breath that she was mentally kicking herself. "I'm sorry, Loos. I wasn't thinking."

The stabbing pain in my chest dissipated as soon as I reassembled my grin, which was a task at the stupidly early hour, let me tell you. "No sweat." I popped my gum again. "Which is what I hope to say about the next three hours."

Having a best friend and roommate like Tonya made the last year less of a horror than it would've been without someone to cry to. Losing my twin brother was one thing. His leukemia had been in remission for almost a whole year before the disease issued him a Do Not Pass Go ticket. But the real obliterator was when my parents' bodies were found by the cops later that night. Our old red clunker had been hit by a semi, no doubt seconds after they heard the awful news. The officer in charge told me I couldn't see them or even have their bodies to bury. Apparently when your entire car gets crumpled like a piece of tinfoil in an accident, the remains are pretty horrific.

No, my parents hadn't been there for Linus's passing. Just me.

No, I hadn't seen them that entire day.

No, I didn't want to talk about it. Still don't. I told the police as much when they sent me to a social worker to deal with the mess that was my shattered life. Yes, please, stranger. Let's chat all about it.

A few months later, and the University I was attending pulled my scholarship because, let's face it, I flaked on all my finals after that blast of awful. Then I took some time off to pick my jaw and smashed heart up off the floor.

Hello, community college. Let's be best friends.

Whatever. I'm pretty much done talking about it. There are much better excuses for not doing all twelve reps during class today than playing the whole "dead family" card.

Tonya apologized seven more times before it started to get irksome. She's such a sweet one; it's hard to get truly annoyed with her. "It's fine, Tonya. Now let's give these jocks a run for their money."

"Do it to it," she agreed with the best serious face she could muster as we walked to the gym door. "I totally thought this would be a great way to stay in shape and meet cute guys. Complete bust on the last part."

"At least we're staying in shape," I said with a shrug as I strolled into class a whopping two minutes early. "Good morning, Mr. Hamilton."

He cringed at my greeting, like he'd been waiting for it since his alarm went off. "*Professor* Hamilton, Miss Kincaid."

I'd never seen a professor wear spandex pants and one of those stretched-out string tank tops for men from the eighties. "Mm-hm." I grabbed a spot to stretch in the corner away from the manly competition to see who had the biggest penis, er, I mean, muscles. It didn't dawn on Tonya or me that Weightlifting 101 would be all freshmen guys, and not the juicy upperclassmen. Guess the University was right to renege on the whole higher education for Lucy Kincaid thing.

I felt someone staring at me, but couldn't identify the source of the creeping discomfort. I rolled my neck from side to side and glanced over my shoulder, confirming the wall was the only thing behind me.

Paranoia. It's my sexiest quality, for sure.

Tonya tempered her laugh since we were in class, taking it down a whole decibel, thank God. "You know, he's kinda cute when he's aggravated."

I blanched. "He's a little old."

"You think? I dunno. Kinda reminds me of an older Vin Diesel."

My eyebrow rose involuntarily, I swear. "And that's a turn-on? Isn't Vin Diesel old enough? Like, on the outer edges of being disgustingly too old for your twenty-year-old booty?"

"This one?" Tonya shook her butt like she was in a club, drawing many a male eye, but not Professor Vin Diesel's. "Nah. He's a classic. Like Campbell's soup. You never truly outgrow him."

Laughter was always easy with Tonya. We'd been good at that since we met almost two years ago. Longest I've ever stayed in one place. My parents were obsessed with finding the perfect home, moving us at least twice every grade. With them off in Heaven-cloud-angel land, I get to stay in one place for as long as I like. The small town just outside Sandusky, Ohio isn't the greatest place in the world to plant one's roots, but it's as good as any other, so I'm not repacking another box. I even bought return address labels, so you know it's official. You can't just undo address labels. They're printed in actual ink.

Tonya opened her mouth, I can only assume to add a snarky comment about Vin Diesel's backside, but blushed and shut it before she could teenager all over the place.

"What?" I turned to follow her line of vision, noticing a few of the soccer team members entering the gym on the opposite end. Tonya was a bit boy-crazy. Her blush was the dead giveaway that one of them would soon become Mr. Tonya Weeden for exactly one week before she got bored. She was easily distracted by a handsome face (using whatever messed-up ruler she used to judge handsomeness. I mean, Vin Diesel. Let's be real, here. Girlfriend needs her head checked). Tonya made a beeline for the nearest lifting bench, knowing I preferred the ones closest to the wall so no one could sneak up behind me.

Tonya fluffed her thin, spindly black braids. "You think any of them go for non-jock girls?"

I responded with some noise that meant, "How should I know?" Tonya spotted me while I benched the exact same weight as when I started in the class. I'm a selective over-achiever.

"You can bench more than that," she said just low enough so Mr. Hamilton didn't hear.

"I have no interest in hulking out. I'm going to be a doctor, not a bodybuilder. I just need a way to blow off steam from Orgo and Bio." Oh, and the stupid filler classes they make you take your first two years. I mean, didn't we get enough English Lit in high school? Honestly. When I become president, that'll be the first thing to go.

"He's watching me!" Tonya squeaked between her teeth, in case Professor Diesel was a lip reader.

"Maybe it's because you're in a sports bra and we're the only women in the room." I put the bar on the rack and shook out my puny arms. I stood and gave her the bench. "Or maybe it's because he's the teacher, and he's responsible for us not killing ourselves in here."

"Here, put more weight on. I'm feeling like I'm ready for the next level." Tonya sucked in her ebony stomach and laid back, taking on more weight than she normally did during her reps to impress the old dude.

My breath cut short and the hairs on the back of my neck stood up. For the third time that morning, I got the distinct impression I was being watched. That eerie feeling of someone standing too close made me whip my head around like a lunatic, only to find nothing. Again.

That same paranoia crawled up my veins, but I tried to push it back down. *At least I'll have something good to tell the shrink when I inevitably go insane.*

I shook off the unexpected tension and focused on the boring task of making sure Tonya didn't decapitate herself trying to impress her married gym teacher. Oh, the joys of almost adulthood.

Tonya yammered throughout the entirety of the class and most of the way home. I did my best to listen, honest. It was that nagging clenching feeling in my gut that someone was watching me that divided my attention. It wasn't a foreign feeling, but the intensity of it was increasing out in the openness of nature (you know, the coupla bushes by the side of the road and the weeds clawing their way through cracks in the sidewalk underfoot). It was like I could actually feel someone staring at me. My brother and I lived with some form of social discomfort our whole lives. It comes with the territory, perpetually being the new kid. People always stare. Like they've never seen twins before. Linus and I used to joke that our parents must've witnessed a crime or something, and that we were all in witness protection. With how often we moved, it wasn't too far a stretch. Dad was not amused.

Yeah, our parents named us Lucy and Linus. Insert some lame joke about the Peanuts characters here. Do your worst; I've heard them all. I bet in Heaven-cloud-angel land, God has a rule that no one can make quips about our names ever again, per Linus's request. Lucky duck. He's probably up there, yucking it up whenever I have to fake laugh through the cringe down here.

I miss him.

When Tonya looked at me like she was waiting for some kind of response, I grabbed for my usual. "Whatever, T. He's old."

This seemed to be the right thing to say, and had been my standby in many a situation where my mind wandered.

"Old is using a walker to get around. Professor Hamilton is distinguished." Tonya kicked a pebble with her hot pink Chuck Taylor as she strolled next to me, fumbling with her keys a few feet from the apartment. The main entrance was supposed to require a code to get in, but it was a quaint town, so when it broke no one bothered to fix it. This caused me no small amount of discomfort. Tonya and Danny didn't see the problem.

Danny greeted us in the state we'd left him earlier that morning. Forearm slung across his eyes, shirt climbing up his pudgy midsection and left leg hanging off the futon. He groaned and threw his pillow at us when Tonya turned on the light. "Turnitoff!" he whined.

"It's noon!" Tonya argued. "Time to start your day."

Danny frowned, not having thought through the forfeiture of his pillow. Sweet little Danny. So in love with Tonya, but will never have the grapes to make a move. At least we get a third of the rent paid out of the deal. He uttered some incoherent curses that only made us laugh. I flung his pillow back at him. "This is what you get when you're a valet for a nightclub, dude. You turn into a vampire. Up all night and hissing at the sight of daylight."

I kicked my shoes off on the mat. There were six pairs of size seven Chuck Taylors there. Tonya and I were the same size, so we mixed and matched at will. This morning I was feeling black and neon green. But I sensed I'd be feeling sky blue and a cheery yellow after lunch.

I walked over to the window and rubbed a stalk on my green bushy fern that sat on the sill. I pretty much had a black thumb when it came to houseplants, but my fern took pity on me and did most of the work required for survival. He was a determined little guy. You had to admire that.

Danny left us for the bathroom, which was near the back of our one-bedroom slice of suburban heaven. This gave Tonya and I free reign of the mostly unfurnished living room and our pathetic excuse for a kitchen. Tonya began flipping through the channels at random, dancing on autopilot and adding to Danny's torture as he peeked his head out of the bathroom to ogle her gyrating hips.

I moved to our closet kitchen and rummaged around in

the fridge for the shredded cheese to confirm that I had the necessary ingredients to assemble a pan of enchiladas after work. "Where's the cheese, guys?"

Danny was finally ready to welcome humanity, rounding the corner with a toothbrush in his mouth, thank God. He stepped into the hallway to be heard. "I finished it off when I got home last night." Or at least I think that's what he said around the toothbrush.

"Seriously? It was a full bag!" My shoulders deflated, and I reevaluated my shoe color choice to include one dismal black one.

Danny shrugged, which was his way of asking what I expected, living with a twenty-year-old guy.

Touché, Danny old boy. Just to piss him off, I grabbed one of his fancy man granola bars that cost, like, two dollars apiece and exited for work before he could protest. "See you, guys. My shift ends at ten." Leaving the two of them alone in the apartment when they were both awake was my other way of getting back at him. He felt the sexual tension between him and Tonya, but she did not, which only compounded it on his end. *Let him listen to her old man fetish for a while.*

2

STRANGER THINGS

*W*orking as a cashier in a small town is a lost art. You have to look interested in your job while being totally bored out of your skull. Luckily my boss wasn't under the impression that I needed to act like my life's ambition was bagging and checking, so he let me do my homework when the store hit its inevitable lulls.

I'd been so nervous for college, thinking it would be infinitely harder than high school. But as most things in life, the buildup was bigger than the thing itself. Bio was boring after looking at the syllabus, so I spent the first two weeks doing all the homework sections in the book just to be done with the busy work. This was the way of most of my classes, with the exception of English Lit. There was little structure to the way Professor Branson did things, so homework in her class was anybody's guess. This is how I got stuck reading *The Hunchback of Notre Dame* like a pretentious poser at the end of my shift. I talked to Tonya about it on my cell during my lunch break. "I honestly don't understand classic literature like this. I mean, this would never get published today. A billion pages on the architecture of the city? Boring!"

"You want me to rent the Disney version?" Tonya suggested.

She's a sweetie. "Something tells me it won't be as close to the original as Branson wants it. You know what's next on the chopping block? *A Tale of Two Cities*. And after that I get treated to the heartwarming tale of *Love in the Time of Cholera*. I swear, the woman's a masochist."

I heard a telltale clatter of pots that told me Tonya was trying to cook again. It was a thing of mercy I wasn't home for it. She burns everything and makes a huge mess doing it. Then she grins with this expectant cutie face when she serves you the slop. I have to be all cheery and eat the gruel with gratitude, using my best acting skills. I just don't have that in me today. *Stupid Danny eating all the cheese.* "Hey, T, are you cooking something?"

"Yep! Just finished making us a hot dog casserole, Little L." Oh, the pride in her tone. I never had the heart to blanch to her face, so over the phone worked just fine. "It's in the fridge, so just heat it up when you get home. I've gotta leave for work."

"I'll bet you a dollar Danny eats it all by morning," I groused. My phone chirped to let me know my battery was a piece of crap, and was currently crapping out on me. Like a big giant piece of crappety crap. I hate my phone. I hurried to end the call. "Sounds awesome. Have a good night at work. Wait those tables like a wildebeest."

"That's the plan. Waitress extraordinaire."

"See you soon," I said.

On my walk home after work, my stomach rumbled and churned at the same time. The creepy feeling that someone was watching me always amplified at night. Out in the open. By myself. I looked over my shoulder, but again saw nothing.

Stupid overactive imagination. I'll never let Danny talk me into an all-night marathon of the Evil Dead movies ever again.

I picked up my pace, knowing that if Linus was watching, he'd be laughing. I wished he were still here. Nothing was all that scary when he was around. That's before the chemo wiped out his high school jock build. Linus got the height and the outgoing personality. I got the figure no one looked at and the ability to make two whole friends since moving to the area. I shouldn't even count Danny, since I got him by default. He comes with Tonya, who never seemed bothered by my melancholy moments or my disinterest in sneaking into the club Danny valeted at. She's a treasure, hot dog casserole and all.

A rustle in the distance made my heart jump. I scolded myself immediately. *Of course there's movement in the woods. Probably a raccoon.* I squinted at the thick wall of trees, but saw nothing to explain the tightening knot in my gut. Well-lit street to the right, dark bands of trees on the left. I'd take the noises of busy city life any day over the quiet of nature, luring you into a false sense of security.

The movement became more patterned, and I could tell the raccoon or person or zombie or whatever was ambling with more purpose toward me.

Okay, seriously. Too much rustling to be the wind. Not caring that my messenger bag was banging my thigh, I picked up my pace to a jog, my heart rate increasing when I heard the movement in the woods following me. The hairs on my arms stood on end, and not to be superstitious, but my arm hair is never wrong.

Dread jolted my heart when I heard uneven running coming toward me from the trees. I broke out into a full on run, trusting my Chucks to make up for my natural lack of sprinting skills. I'm pretty sure there was something in the commercials about that. Nature whipped by me, and though I still saw nothing, I heard it charging at full force, crashing through bramble and crushing stray branches underfoot. I ran with all my might, turning my head to the side at the sound emerging from the woods to find… a bear?

I swear, I was so shocked, I nearly stopped running to gawk at the beast barreling toward me from my left. It was such an odd sight. A giant brown bear. In Ohio. On the sidewalk.

Chasing me.

I screamed like the girl I am, alerting no one. I stumbled once as I turned from the beast and pumped my legs for all they were worth in the direction of home.

Then the chase stopped, quick as it came. The pounding steps ceased, and were replaced by animal howls and roars, reaching their crescendo when a horrific ripping sound cracked through the night. I slowed my flight and turned to see the largest bear that ever was. He was easily over ten feet tall, hulking in musculature, with massive paws and rabid foam clinging to its fangs. The bear was wrestling an olive-skinned man… and losing.

I still don't understand it, but somehow the tall and muscular Atlas of a man, crazy enough to wrestle a bear, bested the beast. He knocked the furry mass onto its back and put the bear in a chokehold like a professional wrestler in a Lycra onesie. Only this guy wore jeans and a black t-shirt, which really, professional wrestlers should've adopted a long time ago.

"Run, Lucy! Go home!" the man shouted in a deep timbre.

"What?" I said stupidly. Shock is the only way I can think of to explain why I needed to be told to get the smack out of Dodge.

"Run!" he repeated, his expression wild as he wrestled the bear, who was putting up quite the fight. The bear clawed at his face, leaving a gouge I screamed at the sight of.

I wanted to help. I mean, who was I that this Good Samaritan should die because of me? With one more command from his angry mouth, I obeyed. I think we both understood how little help I could actually be to him in this scenario. I mean, seriously. It's a bear. Some kind of a rabid giant brown bear who was gunning for Kincaid girl ribs and barbecue sauce for dinner. I ran away from the two, fishing through my bag for my phone and cursing loudly when the battery failed me. This was my punishment for texting Tonya while on the job.

Half a mile left, and the stitch in my side was begging me to join track next semester to replace weightlifting. Seriously. What a useless skill. What was I thinking? I ignored the discomfort and bolted to the apartment in record time, not stopping until I was safely tucked away inside. One bedroom, one bath, no dishwasher, three locks.

Good enough. I bolted all three, then pushed a chair in front of the door for good measure.

Tonya was waitressing, and Danny was at work driving Cadillacs in the parking structure, so there was no one to freak out to. I let out one tearless sob to the empty apartment. I plugged in my phone and left Tonya a breathless message to watch out for bears on her drive home. I worried she would think I was joking. Visions of Tonya getting mauled by the beast plagued me until a fist slammed on the front door not five minutes later.

Bears don't knock, but neither does someone with a key. I moved the chair and peered through the peephole, gasping at the grisly sight that greeted me.

It was him. Six and a half foot tall Samaritan Sam with a large cut bleeding through the arm of his grimy black t-shirt. My stranger danger alert went up, but knowing his injuries were my fault moved my fingers to open the door. "Come in. Oh! Your shoulder! Oo! The bear got your face!" The blood was far thicker up close than through the comfort of the peephole, seeping down from his high cheekbones and painting red streaks into his five o'clock shadow.

He didn't need introductions, but barreled through to the bathroom without a word. Like he knew where it was. Like he'd been here before.

I knocked on the door lightly. "Are you okay? Do you need anything, guy-I-don't-know?"

"I got it," he answered gruffly. "Where'd Danny put the antiseptic?"

Danny recently sustained a life-threatening injury of scraping his elbow in a game of touch football. Two days, and we were still hearing about his heroic moves. "It's probably out here. Hold on." Danny was always leaving things in unexpected places. I once found the jar of peanut butter on top of the rickety bookshelf and the jelly under the duct tape-patched futon next to the remote. He's lovely to live with.

I scanned the living room, fished under the futon, rifled through the pantry and finally found the antiseptic in the laundry basket. "I got it!" I called through the apartment. I was gripping the handle before it dawned on me I should probably never barge in on a man in the bathroom. "Can I come in?"

"It's your place."

With that warm welcome, I let myself into the narrow space. It was small with one person using the facilities; introducing a huge-chested hulking guy into the bathroom made the walls feel even closer together. "Here, let's wash that and see what the damage is." I put on my best professional voice, hoping it fooled him. If I really wanted to be a doctor, flinching at a gushing flesh wound was not an option. "You can borrow one of Danny's shirts. Yours needs a washing." *Or a trash can.* It was torn in three places and drenched in what I hoped was mostly the bear's blood.

He nodded and pulled his shirt over his head. I tried not to look at his perfectly cut abs or his entire torso that looked straight off the covers of Tonya's skeezy meet/cute-flowers-dinner-handcuffs romance novels. He had a rope around his neck with a pouch on the end, resting against his bare chest. Blood streaked the counter and pooled on the floor. One of his hands was shaking as he washed off his broad shoulder and too-large bicep in the sink, bending at odd angles to get under the wimpy flow. The two biggest culprits for his pain were the gash on his shoulder and the one on his cheekbone.

"I got it," I offered, pulling a rag from under the sink and wetting it. I gently dabbed at his skin, aware of our close proximity and the discomfort that came with it. Aside from the assumption that he was Danny's football buddy, I really knew nothing else about the guy. He made no effort to break the building tension, so I kept quiet, praying the wounds would not be super deep. I pressed the rag to the seeping gash on his shoulder, noting that he did not make his soreness known.

"You... there was a bear. He was chasing me, and you stopped him." He said nothing to this, which for some reason made me feel relieved that at least I had not lost my mind and imagined the whole thing. "Thanks for that."

His green eyes landed on mine, a million questions flickering between us. He swallowed. "Yup." He reached for the antiseptic and removed the cap with his teeth, looking savage. Like, you know, a man who wrestles with bears. His thick black hair was messy and matted with blood that dripped down his forehead and touched the ornate diamond-shaped gold tattoo under his cheekbone. I'd never seen a metallic tattoo before, and didn't even know that kind of ink existed. It blended into his olive skin, and I only noticed it when I was uncomfortably close to the stranger. I fought with the urge to touch it, feeling foolish as I moved my gaze to his very naked shoulder.

Occasionally Danny would walk around without his shirt on. With his pooched belly hanging over his boxers, it was hard to tell if he was trying to impress Tonya or if he'd given up on showing off for women altogether.

This was not the same. The guy looked like, well, a man who wrestles bears. He even had scarred-over violent slashes across his chest and one that wrapped in a downward swirl across his abdomen.

Why did we get an apartment with such a tiny bathroom?

I examined the fresh cuts on his face and his shoulder with a frown. "Why was there a bear?" And then the questions started tumbling out of me. "How did you survive a fight with a bear? How did I get away? Where were you going this time of night?" Then the most obvious question of all came to me, and I was chagrinned how turned around I'd gotten that I hadn't asked it before opening the door in the first place. "Who are you?"

"You shouldn't let strangers into the house." His eyes hardened at my accusatory tone. "And I'm the guy who kept the Were from eating you."

"The what?"

"You heard me."

"Did *you* hear you?" I left the rag on his shoulder for him to put pressure on if he wished. "Who are you?"

"Jens." He glanced toward the door. "And we should get out of here. Pack a bag."

"Huh?" I shook my head, as if that might make sense of the night's events. "We? Look, I appreciate you fending off the bear. Really, I do. That was some legit Ultimate Fighting Champion stuff, for sure. But I'm not going anywhere. I don't know you."

He leaned toward the door. His neck muscles were tensed, and he seemed to be listening for danger. It was then I realized his Spidey sense was tingling, and he had not let down his guard even in the solid bear-proof apartment structure. He spoke in a low whisper, grabbing my arm in a firm manner I did not appreciate. It didn't hurt, but the I'm-bigger-than-you implication was clear. "Look, I don't have time to explain the way of the world to you. We have to get out of here. If one Were found you, more are coming. I can handle one, sure, but a whole pack? You'll have to trust me on this."

"You?" My voice was shrill. "Who are you? Trust you? That may work in the movies, but I don't trust on a dime. You can patch yourself up." I pointed to the door. "Get out."

Instead of arguing, he said the one thing that stopped my brain. He looked at me to make sure I heard him and said, "Salmon Seesaw."

3

FIVE MINUTES

Salmon Seesaw. There it was. The secret family password. When our parents couldn't pick us up from school or practice or whatever and they sent a neighbor, they had to use the secret family password, or Linus and I didn't budge.

Jens smirked at my dropped-open mouth, which pissed me off. I did my best not to let it show.

"Well, that changes things. How did you know about that?" Not like my parents were sending him to pick me up from school. A dagger of pain shot through my heart, and I swallowed it down like a compartmentalizing champ as I began to bite my nails. My parents would never know about my schooling ever again. I never thought I'd hear the secret password after that. My heart warmed and hardened simultaneously. "Spill it, John."

"Jens," he corrected irritably. "And I know it because it's my job to know it." He pointed to the bedroom. "Pack."

"Well, that's nice and vague," I grumbled, spinning on

my heel away from him. "Tell me to pack. Like I'm not allowed to ask questions of the guy ruining my bathroom rug." I stomped into the bedroom Tonya and I shared and grabbed a duffel bag. "Pack for a day, or longer?" I inquired, dreading the answer.

Jens turned on the shower to rinse the blood off his shoulder and called out, "Pack everything you don't want burned to the ground in the next five minutes." He sniffed the air like a dog. "Or less. I say go, and we run with whatever's in your green backpack."

I could feel my pulse banging in my cheeks. My green backpack. Not my school bag or overnight duffel, but the bag our parents made us keep packed and ready that had essentials in it in case whatever it was that made my parents up and move us around the country time and time again caught up with us. I got it out without thinking and shoved more clothing and a few keepsakes into the sack, praying it was not happening all over again.

No. Not this time. I was the only adult left, so the decision to leave or stay was mine. I wanted a home – was desperate for it. Sure, the tiny apartment wasn't exactly the white picket fence I was dreaming of, but it was mine. I wasn't leaving unless I was ready, and a stranger yelling at me didn't make me antsy to follow him anywhere. The instinct to run away from him was stronger than the secret family password in that moment. "How... how do you know about my green backpack?"

Jens harrumphed, as if I was the one being a problem. "Just do it!"

I marched back out into the hallway and shouted at the bathroom door, "Don't you think you can tell me what to do without giving me answers! I make the decisions now, and I say I don't have to leave!"

"Dammit, Lucy! This isn't the Fourth of July! I won't fight with you about this. I don't care if I have to pick you up and take you myself. We're leaving in four minutes!"

My head whipped around in his direction. Fourth of July? It was my least favorite holiday ever since Linus and I got the grounding of the century from my parents for hotwiring the teacher's car and moving it to the strip club parking lot. We even called a local news tip hotline to report the car's whereabouts just for good measure. Like Mr. Morris didn't have that coming. He was our Chemistry teacher who referred to Linus strictly as "chemo kid" and even chuckled at the nickname. He had wiry gold caps on his browned teeth and cigarette stains on his fingertips that were so filthy, I didn't like touching the papers he graded. When Linus had to run out of class to throw up during a test, Mr. Morris failed him, even with the doctor's note. I usually don't retaliate, but you cross my brother, I go for blood. Our parents demanded to know why we hadn't involved them, insisting they would have scheduled a conference with the principal.

We didn't want a conference. Linus deserved Mr. Morris's career on a silver platter. Maybe that's overboard to some people. Really, we just did what a principal with a smackhole teacher on tenure couldn't. Linus's stellar defense to our parents' tirade was that we wouldn't have had to hotwire Mr. Morris's car if his keys had just been in his jacket when I'd tried to pickpocket him earlier that morning. Linus had never been great at feigning contrition.

My cheeks reddened that Jens somehow knew about the third biggest fight our family ever had. "How do you know about that?"

"Ah!" His outburst of pain stayed my next argument. I rushed into the bathroom, knocking him in the rear with the door by accident.

I swear it was by accident.

"What's wrong?" I asked, compassion tempering my rage. He held his head, rubbing the bloody spot on his left cheekbone. His fingers came away doused in red, so I sat him down on the edge of the tub and prodded his face with my fingertips to judge the depth of the two-inch-long cut. He flinched and batted at me like a child. Taking advantage of his seated position, I kept my fingers poised over the painful spot just in case I needed to convince him to behave. "This needs stitches. Like, needs them bad."

"It'll be fine."

I looked at him, hoping to convey how idiotic I deemed his judgment. "No, it won't. You need stitches now. Let me at least take you to the hospital." Under his nose, my eye caught on a shimmer of purple glitter. It was nowhere else on his body, just a few pinpricks to distract me.

"No hospitals. Just give me a Band-Aid or something and let's run."

I shook my head and reached for the first aid kit under the sink. *Thanks for this at-home lesson, Dad. We'll see how well I was paying attention.*

I ran to the kitchen and heated the needle at the stove, ignoring Jens calling from the bathroom that we were down to three minutes. "Would you shut up?" I yelled back. When I reentered the bathroom, his cheek was all bloody again, despite him having rinsed it twice. His aggravation at me was not as adamant, which was the first time I saw blood loss as a positive thing. "Close your eyes," I ordered, wishing someone would let me close mine. When he jerked his chin away petulantly, I yanked it back, aiming the diluted rubbing alcohol over his head. "Close your eyes or go blind."

Okay, I'm not sure he would actually go blind from rubbing alcohol, but it accomplished my goal. He closed his eyes as I dribbled a bit of the clear liquid over his angular cheekbone. "It looks like the bear did you a solid and missed your face tattoo. Now, hold still." I threaded the needle and exhaled what I hoped was the last of my nerves. With a shakier hand than I would've liked, I swallowed the girlish scream in my throat and gently wove the needle through his tanned skin.

Jens huffed. "Could you not make that face, doc? You're scaring me."

It was then I realized I had my horror movie expression on. I tucked that away, too, along with my revulsion. I was going to be a doctor someday, so I'd have to get used to this. I had no idea what I was doing, so I completed the task as fast as possible, with Jens hemming and hawing the entire time, commenting that we needed to leave.

"Really? Really? We need to leave? Well, why didn't you say so in the first place?" I snapped. "I'm not exactly a pro at this! I'm doing the best I can!"

His badgering grew less insistent, which was a relief, until I saw his eyelids drooping.

"Hey!" I barked, tying off the knot and snipping the thread. His hands pushed through the air like weighted paws, finally landing on my hips. I brought his head to rest on my chest and held it steady, permitting him a few balancing breaths. "It's okay. You're all done."

Instead of a bratty quip, he held tighter to my waist. This was how I found myself participating in the bizarre, yet still tender, hug with the half-naked stranger. When my irritability finally broke, I held him tighter around the neck, not sure how to make sense of a bear attack that was almost fatal.

Jens smelled like sugar cookies. I couldn't tell if it was coming from a girly body spray or from his actual skin, but it made my mouth water, despite the situation.

When it dawned on both of us that we were of the opposite sex, Jens loosened his grip on me. I lowered myself slightly and tapped him under the chin so I could look him directly in the eye. "Look, thanks for the save. I don't know why there was a bear or how you escaped, but thanks." When he nodded once, I continued. "But I'm not leaving. This is my home, and I decide when I leave it. And I'm not going back out into the night with a stranger when I know for sure there's a wild animal out there. I don't care how much you yell. I'm not going."

I ran my thumb across the space above his upper lip, brushing away the lavender shimmer I couldn't make sense of. His intake of breath and wide eyes told me he had no idea he'd had glitter on his face.

I showed him the remnants. "Rave much?" I asked.

Jens touched his neck, tugging at the pouch that rested against his bare chest. "Wash your hands!" he demanded, trying to bolt upright, but not having the space to do so without knocking me over. He pointed to the sink. "Right now. I'm serious."

"Sheesh! I was just going to." I turned on the hottest water I could stand and scrubbed until the glitter and the blood smears were gone. I displayed my clean hands to him, and watched him deflate by a degree.

Slowly, without breaking eye contact, Jens raised himself up so that he once again towered over me. I'm a solid 5'7", so I didn't often feel dwarfed, but Jens was nearly a foot taller than me. I would have shuddered at his intimidating form, were he not clinging to me like a child seconds before.

Without a word, Jens slapped a bandage over the cut on his shoulder and exited the bathroom. I exhaled, relieved at my tiny victory. Now he would leave, and I could be alone to try to make sense of the night. I could ponder it all while I cleaned the macabre bathroom that had blood on the floor, the sink and streaking down the bathtub. I needed to find a way to quadruple-bolt the door shut, too.

Before I could make a solid plan for that, Jens pushed one of Danny's old black shirts over his head and jerked me out of the bathroom. "That's six minutes. You're done." He hefted me up over his good shoulder and marched out of my apartment with my green backpack and my messenger bag in his free hand. Though I screamed and flailed, he and the closed doors we passed paid me no mind.

4

FLEEING THE SCENE

"Isn't it common courtesy for the kidnapper to tell the kidnappee where he's taking her?" I groused, trying to keep my fear hidden so he didn't snatch that up too, and throw it over his shoulder like a caveman and then shove it into the backseat of a car. I kept a tight hold on my body with my left arm, leaving my right hand free so I could bite my fingernails.

"Shouldn't the kidnappee be afraid I might slit her throat and dump her body in a river?" He looked in the rearview mirror to make sure I was behaving. I inched further into the corner of the stolen vehicle's backseat. He shook his head in a somewhat contrite manner. "I was only kidding. I'm not going to kill you."

"Love your sense of humor. I'm sure I'm the first to tell you that."

"Second," he corrected me, though I can't imagine why. "Quit biting your nails. It makes me anxious."

I banded both arms around my ribs. The beige leather of the Buick smelled like old people and too many pine-scented air fresheners, which did nothing to relax me. "You want to talk to me about what happened back there? Why we're in a stolen Buick instead of calling the cops or animal control? Why there was a bear you conveniently happened to stumble across tonight?"

"Is this you thanking me for saving your tail?"

"I'll thank you to keep your hands off my tail. I don't appreciate being thrown around like a rag doll." That was one of my pet peeves. After I passed the age of crawling, I did not relish being carried. By family, friends or bear-slaying strangers with face tattoos. "And I already said thank you."

"You're welcome."

"Man, you're arrogant. When can I go home?"

"First off, we're in a Buick because it's an older person's car. Less of a chance we'll get pulled over." He adjusted the mirror so he could look at me while he spoke. I let childish defiance take over and turned my head to stare out the window. "Would her majesty prefer something newer?"

"Shut your mouth. You don't know the first thing about me."

Jens chuckled, and the sound sent shivers down my spine. "I bet you're asking yourself right now how I knew the family password, or about the green backpack. Maybe how I knew where you lived. I know you a lot better than you'd guess, Loos."

I did my best to keep my tone clipped and not let him know I was shaking inside. If this would be my last night on earth, I wouldn't spend it breaking down like a child. "Let's start with that. How do you know my name?"

"I check in on your family from time to time."

"How long have you been doing that?" I swallowed with great difficulty, not really wanting the answer.

"About five years."

I gulped and debated jumping out of the car, even at the highway speed we were traveling. I took a few deep breaths and tried to come up with a better, less maiming plan. "Check in on us? What's that supposed to mean?"

This was it. This is where he drops the bomb Linus and I always feared. Mob boss. Witness Protection. Government conspiracy.

Jens tapped his thumb on the steering wheel as if we were going for a midnight drive to an ice cream parlor. "Nothing shady. Your parents requested me specifically. I keep you safe."

"Bang-up job you're doing," I grumbled before I could stop myself.

A moment of respect for my pain was permitted before he spoke. "Sorry for your loss."

I rolled my eyes. If I had a dollar for every time I heard that asinine phrase, I would've been able to bury my family in gold caskets. "You don't know anything about loss." Yes, I was being bratty, but to be fair, I had just been kidnapped, and it was somewhere around one in the morning.

"You done sulking?" he asked. When I scoffed, he shifted in his seat and turned his attention back to the road. "I guess not. Take your time. We've got a long drive ahead of us."

Through clenched teeth, I muttered, "I hate you so much."

Jens laughed. It was a loud, bitter sound, which only made me more furious. "Aw! That's cute, you thinking your big, bad feelings matter. Say it again."

I bit my lip to keep from screaming at him, drawing in several long breaths. "Where are you taking me against my will?"

"To someone you'll listen to. If I explain the way of the world to you, you'll argue the whole time. If he does, there's a chance you'll hear it."

"Where?"

Jens cracked his neck. The sound was horrible, like he'd been through about seven too many bear fights. "A few states south. The Werebears have been migrating closer to your area for a while, but none ever got this close. Now that one's dead so near you, it'll send the other Weres swarming for a nice juicy piece of Lucy Kincaid."

"Don't be gross," I scolded him. "Werebears? Like were-wolves but bears?"

"Sort of. Pesta's bears. They're really just vessels for..." He scratched at the cut on his shoulder, and then waved his hand to brush me off. "I'll let him explain it all to you. Like I said, you'll take it better from him."

I bit at my thumbnail. "Wait, you said one's dead. You killed that bear?"

Jens scoffed, as if any other outcome was a joke. "Of course. Do you think I'd really just leave the job undone?"

"Being that I don't know what the job is? Sure. And I think you can probably guess how high my opinion is of you."

He snorted, as if I was joking. "You know, I always knew you were funny, but I wondered if you'd be like that around me. You do that quiet blending in thing whenever you're the new kid. Always going from moxie to mouse inside a minute."

"Glad I could amuse you, Jack."

"Jens."

I threw my arms out in exasperation. "How about Jackass?" I snapped my fingers as brilliance came to me. "No, Jens the Lumberjackass!"

I rock so hard at nicknames. Being dubbed "Lucy Goosy" until the second grade brings about a desperation that tends to make a girl get creative.

He let out a full-bodied laugh that would have been endearing, were it not directed at me. "Sure. You can call me your Lumberjackass. I'm decent with an axe. Already got the boots for the job." He stomped his heavy black boot to the floor of the car. "Plus, I like pancakes."

"Huh?"

He glanced at me in the rearview mirror. "Don't lumberjacks eat pancakes?"

"That's not a thing. Lumberjacks eat whatever they feel like."

"Does the same rule apply for the jackass variety? That's my main concern. I'm not switching vocations unless I get pancakes." His green eyes danced with the joy of a good tease in the dimly lit rearview mirror.

Despite myself, I cracked a smile at the pleasure he took in my insult. "Maybe you could have flapjackasses."

Jens pumped his fist in the air that the joke had come full-circle. "That was awesome."

31

"If you like that so much, I got a million more."

"Let it rip. We've got hours ahead of us."

"Who's got two thumbs and likes to…" Then my eye caught on the stitches I'd given him across his cheekbone when I saw bits of him reflected in the rearview mirror. My brain skipped a beat and I lost my momentum, frowning. "Forget it. I'm not playing with you. Don't want to get Stockholm syndrome."

He peered at me with skepticism. "Whatever. You've got nothing."

"Nothing but a headache from your mouth."

"That was weak. You can do better. I saw you tear that boy from Jersey a new one when he messed up your science project."

I blushed, embarrassed that the little-known debasement had been witnessed. "You don't know what you're talking about."

"Poor Kenny. He had a little thing for you, you know."

"He did not. It doesn't matter. I'm not engaging." I looked out the window and tried to guess how long we had been driving. Probably somewhere between twenty minutes and a billion hours.

He took one hand off the steering wheel to gesture about the car with it. "I personally don't see it, but to each his own. You two would've been so cute together, safety glasses bumping as you reach for the microscope. The scent of formaldehyde in the air while something geeky plays in the background."

"When do I get to go home?" I asked, switching tracks. I didn't want to spend my time talking about a tenth grade science project.

Jens sobered, sitting up straighter. "You can't go back there, Loos."

"When do I get to go home?" I repeated. He did not answer this time, and my heart began to sink. "Jens? Why can't I go home?"

"I told you. We burned it to the ground. Same as every time you and your family had to move. I was assigned to watch you. Tucker's in charge of cleanup."

I mouthed something, but I don't know what. Were there words for this? My childhood. My adolescence. The pink stuffed bunny my parents got me that one Christmas had been left behind at one of the houses in the chaos of a fly-by-night move. I stupidly thought it might magically reappear someday. All of it. Gone.

The air became unbearably thick, impossible to breathe in. The stale scent of old people soaked into my skin and threatened to take me under. I was being chauffeured by an arsonist with a superhero complex who apparently stalked me.

I would not die in this car.

My brain went into planning mode to keep a panic attack at bay. I flipped through my mental Rolodex, trying to recall all the rental cars and clunkers we'd gone through, cataloging where exactly the buttons near my headrest were. I looked out the window and stretched my arms behind my head, fumbling around for the right spot. I used the window's reflection as my spyglass, making sure Jens saw nothing suspicious. There wouldn't be much time once I found the button, and even after that, there was no telling it would actually work. Either way, I was done dealing with the fire-happy lumberjack kidnapper.

I found the lever, but it was old and would not budge without coercion. "Could you turn on the radio, Lumberjackass?" I requested as politely as I could. Really, really didn't want him to hear the click and put it together.

"There's that moxie again," he grinned, turning on an earful of static. "You went all quiet for a minute. I was worried you ran out of ways to make this car ride even longer." Jens fished around until he found a hard rock station.

I clicked the button, but held the seat in place, scooting over to give myself room for the final move. I waited until the singer with issues he could only scream about hit a particularly high note. Then I slammed the right side backseat forward and scrambled into the trunk, wrestling my way past a tarp, a bunch of plastic grocery bags, and who knows what else. I rolled myself into position as the car swerved and began to slow. I tried to find the latch to pop the trunk, but I couldn't locate it. My heart pounded, and I kicked as hard as I could at the taillight, praying it would actually work. Linus had taught me this trick when he went through his I-want-to-be-a-mechanic phase. If he was getting his information from the Dukes of Hazard or something equally unrealistic, I was going to be in a tough spot as soon as Jens stopped the car.

Three more kicks, and the light pushed out onto the road, shattering as the car slowed on the shoulder. Turns out the Dukes were right. I scrambled away from the damage, knowing I could not fight my way past him, but hoping he might keep driving and not notice the hole in the back carriage once he yelled at me. In my sparking and fizzing imagination, a cop would pull him over for having a taillight out. Then I could escape for real.

This would work. TV would never lie to me.

The trunk flew open, and Jens grabbed at me, dragging my flailing body out and dumping me on the pavement. "What's the plan, Loos? Huh? Give me a heart attack? Cause a car wreck that'd kill us both? Brilliant idea!" He glanced at the car and saw the missing taillight. He threw his head back in frustration. "Great! Now I've gotta steal another car. Do you think I like screwing unsuspecting people over?" He looked around toward the road. "We don't have time to switch cars. You'd better cross your fingers we don't get pulled over for this. You have no idea the kind of danger you're in."

Sweat began to bead on my forehead, and for the life of me, I couldn't swallow. My chest started to feel tight, and I knew I wouldn't last long in the land of sanity. "I... can't! Let me go!"

His tone calmed, but it did nothing to soothe me. "Breathe, Lucy. It won't do for me to save your life, and then you do something stupid like this." He leaned over and patted me awkwardly on the back, which was so patronizing; I wished I'd taken weightlifting more seriously so I could've made my opinion on his close proximity perfectly clear.

"Get away from me!" I wheezed, clambering to my feet and stumbling for the road like a drunken sorority girl. I waved my hands in the air to catch the attention of anyone on the freeway, but at this late hour, we were the only ones on the road. "Help! Somebody! Anybody?"

He stood next to me, arms crossed over his chest, his

expression a mixture of irritation and amusement. Finally he joined in, adding to my shouts for the abandoned freeway to enjoy. "Help!" Then he turned to me, speaking as if I was an idiot. "Humans don't stop to help each other. Give me a break."

Humans?

When I did not back down, he continued making fun of me. "Help her! She's being 'taken against her will' from wild Werebears who were trying to kill her! Life's so unfair! She's blonde and beautiful, so her loud mouth must be right."

"You shut up!" I yelled, unconcerned that I sounded like a child. My breath was shallow, but my fury was unswerving. "You set my life on fire! There's no trace of me anywhere but where I stand right now!"

He turned to face me, using his height to appear much older and wiser, though he only looked to be about mid to late twenties. "Better that than you disappear altogether."

I sneered at his calm calculation of such a hurtful thing. "Like you care what happens to me. So you get demoted or whatever happens to you if, God forbid, I get to stay in one place longer than a year and die happy."

He squinted his left eye at me, sizing me up. "People would care if you died. Your Uncle Alrik is the one who recommended me to your parents."

My mouth hung open until Jens reached out and moved my chin upward to shut it. I batted his hand away, which for some reason made him smile in that charming punch-me-in-the-face kind of way. "How do you know Uncle Rick?"

The corner of his mouth twitched. "That's who I'm

taking you to." He motioned to the car in a sweeping gesture made to mock me. "Are you ready to get going, your highness?"

I showed him a choice finger and snarled, "Don't you talk to me." Then I stomped to the Buick and shut myself inside, staring resolutely out the window.

5

WEREDOGS AND GNOMES

I thought not speaking to each other would be more peaceful, but Jens responded by turning on the radio to a country station and blasting the most overly emotional song I'd ever heard. He sang along, like we were on a Sunday afternoon cruise just to kill time. "Don't you just love the twang of it?" he asked, switching his cadence to that of a good old country boy. "The whole singing about your problems thing. It's so... what's the word? Emotionally balanced." He took a bite out of a greasy hamburger that stank like it was fried on the same surface as day-old fish and grinned in the rearview mirror at me.

I knew he was baiting me, but I refused to ask him how he knew my Uncle Rick.

It was seven hours of remaining firm in my silence before Jens turned off the freeway and onto a side street. I was proud of myself that I'd remained strong in my vow that I would no longer speak to him. I was reintroduced to life without country music when he shut off the radio to better focus on the nighttime driving down the residential streets. Oh, how sweet the sound. I swore off cowboy boots and rodeos right then and there.

We motored slowly past the burned-out shell of a commercial building. Jens gasped and swore as he peeled into the abandoned parking lot. He flung his body out the door and stood outside, taking in the damage that was apparently news to him. "No!" he yelled to the remnants of the building. His hands were in his hair, taking his stress out on the black, messy tresses. His thick eyebrows bunched together as he tried to make sense of the char-broiled destination.

His angst worried me. As I knew nothing of his plan or our destination, I couldn't offer any help. I had to look to him to know when I should feel alleviated or scared.

Holding tight to my vow of silence, I got out of the car and stood beside him. Parts of the roof had caved in, letting us and nature peer straight in to the guts of the wreckage. The building was blackened on the inside and barely standing on the outside. I had questions, sure, but Jens was too preoccupied to offer any answers. He walked around the rubble, reading the damage to see where the fire started. His eyes fell on a smattering of something that looked like gold dust on bits of the blackened wreckage. He slid his phone out of his pocket and punched in a number. "Hey, Tuck. Did you hit Alrik's bowling alley?" Jens exhaled, a relieved smile surfacing. After a few more perfunctory comments, he hung up. "It's okay. It's one of our fires," he confirmed, as if I was supposed to know what that meant. I couldn't tell if he was talking for my benefit or just thinking aloud. His shoulders relaxed and rolled back, the defensive stance mutating to mere observation. "No one died. It was preemptive. A cover-up."

I nodded uncertainly and left him to his search for whatever and walked around the parking lot to stretch my legs. I was uncertain of what to make of Jens, and even more unsure of our environment. Even though we were in the middle of an urban city, the night felt empty, and the world vast with its void. The normal rustle of nature seemed hushed either out of respect for the broken building, or in fear of something else lurking under the sparse expanse of stars.

I made an executive decision right then and there to nix scary movies out of my life. Reality was getting a little too harrowing on its own.

Dry and dead bushes were at the outer edges of the lot, so I kept myself occupied picking the trash out of them and tossing it all in the plastic bag Jens had gotten fast food in a while back. I hate the stink of sliders. It's like he was purposefully doing all the things that irritate me.

I reached for a mangled shopping bag in the bracken, but stopped when I felt eyes on me. I could still hear Jens stomping around in the rubble, and the itch felt like it was coming from the street. I looked up slowly and saw a glowing pair of yellow eyes. As the body stepped forward, I made out the shape of a large dog. I'm terrible with breeds. What was Scooby-Doo? Well, the dog was as big as Scooby was next to Shaggy. So, you know, pretty friggin' big.

Only this pup was nothing like Scoob. His brown fur was matted in parts, with a chunk on his left flank missing altogether. My breath felt too audible when his foaming maw snarled at me. I swallowed, and the sound seemed to echo, alerting him to my apprehension. A childish whimper caught in my throat when he decided to go for the big meal – me. Only he didn't charge. It was like he was watching to make sure I stayed where I was, like he was waiting for backup.

The yellow eyes glowed with a predator's precision as he stepped toward me, his snorting exhale like a boar's. I froze, wondering if movement would make things worse.

And then there were three. Three sets of glowing yellow orbs found me, all belonging to Great Dane-type dogs. Their hackles were raised, their teeth bared and dripping with white foamy saliva that made me equally afraid and grossed out. Their bodies were pure muscle, and the angry marks on their fur from other fights only added to their intimidation factor.

"Jens!" I whispered. I meant to call for him, but my voice decided to wuss out on me.

I took a step backward toward the car, trying not to breathe in a way that might tip off the dogs that their next meal was a flight risk.

On the second step, they charged.

I am not ashamed to admit that I screamed like a child with three rhinos chasing her in an abandoned parking lot. I am also not ashamed to admit that I run like a Muppet, only slower.

I'm a little ashamed that I called out for Jens, hoping he forgave me enough for my silent treatment to come to my aid. In hindsight, there was some small part of me that was warning him to get in the car. The larger part of me was hoping he had some of that bear-whooping ninja action on tap I'd seen him unleash earlier.

I thought he'd heard my warning and was running for the car, but he raced passed me and collided with the dogs, meeting two mid-air. There was a crash of barking, growling, ripping and snapping. I turned around, afraid when I heard an ominous crack of a neck that could only mean a swift death.

For the dog. It started as three on one, and Jens was winning, reducing them down to two. He was primal, as he had been with the psychotic bear. Despite my distrust of him, in that moment I marveled at his beastly fervor. He was both man and monster, and it was a beautiful thing.

And also a little terrifying. Jens wasn't afraid of getting bitten. He went straight for the head, grabbing one of the giant Great Danes and bashing its cranium against a concrete barrier. The Franken-dog yelped like a baby, and my heart lurched as he twitched and went limp. Maybe the dogs weren't as dangerous as I'd thought. Did Jens have to be so brutal?

"Lucy, what are you doing?" Jens yelled as he wrestled the last dog to the ground. His arms and legs were wrapped all the way around its torso, and he squeezed the thrashing mutt in his vice grip, making it look smaller and somehow less threatening. For a second, as it thrashed against Jens, I could almost imagine the whimpers were directed at me, begging me to save him from the hulking man.

My heart went out to the poor baby, and before I could stop myself, I cried out, "Well, don't hurt him!"

"Get in the car!"

Oh, yeah. I spun around and bolted for the car, shutting myself in and sinking to the floor of the backseat. I rolled myself in a ball against the door furthest from the last of the mongrels. I hugged my knees in the fetal position, trying hard to think of the lead singer's name from the Polyphonic Spree. His happy hippie songs always calmed me down when I was scared. I could change my train of thought from panic to a life where all my problems were gone because I was a carefree musician who wore flowing colorful robes and sung songs about clouds. Maybe I'd play the panpipes in his merry traveling band of nomadic musicians.

I screamed when Jens flung open the door and slumped down into the driver's seat.

"It's alright, Loos. It's just me. What? Did you expect a dog could open the door?" I could see a hint of that same purple glitter I'd dusted off his upper lip in my apartment back under his nose again. Just a few specks, but eye-catching nonetheless. His forearm was bleeding, but he paid the injury no mind.

I tried to muscle past the panic and play the adult. I let the grip on my body go slack and slid up into the backseat as he started up the car. "Have you ever seen Tom and Jerry? Animals are capable of exceptional cruelty," I informed him in all my sagely wisdom. He gave me a one-note obligatory laugh as he peeled out of the parking lot. "What were those things? Weredogs?"

"I honestly don't know. There's no such thing. Alrik warned me it would happen, but I guess I needed to see it to believe it. Weredogs. Never thought I'd see the day."

"Werebears are no big deal, but Weredogs blow your

mind?" The car swerved onto the left side of the road and then back, knocking my head on the car door. "Hey! Jens, are you doing alright?"

"Uh-huh."

Real reassuring. His blood was dripping in a line down his elbow and pooling on the seat below. "You need to pull over and let me look at that."

"Wanting to be a doctor and actually being one are two different things."

"Wanting to stay alive and driving off the road because you're stubborn are two different things, too."

He paused before answering. "I can't stop yet. Weres found you by your house, and now these dogs all the way out here? You're being tracked. Not wise to stop until we've put more distance between us and them."

I threw up my arms, my adrenaline beginning to ebb. "Fine. Bleed to death. You're so manly. Just pull over before you do, so I don't die in here."

Jens huffed, as if I was the one making his arm bleed. "Well, it's not like you can't be helpful in the car. Come on up here and take a look at it. I can't do anything about it right now, and it's getting annoying."

"But I'm not a doctor," I sassed him, taking in his eye roll with pleasure. I climbed with care into the front passenger's seat, collecting the excess napkins that had fallen on the floor from the fast food. I blotted the injury, holding a wad of napkins to his arm until the wound started clotting. "How's that?"

"I'm magically cured."

His chest was moving slowly, and I wished aloud that

he would just pull over. "I can drive, you know. If you pass out, we both die."

Jens pretended my words had no validity. "I'm fine. Just get it to stop bleeding."

I cocked his arm up above his heart to get the blood to stop flowing out of him so quickly. "Let me know if you're going to faint. I'll ready the smelling salts and prop up a pillow for you to land on in your delicate state."

"Shut up." The corner of his mouth twitched, and I could tell he was trying not to smirk at me. I lowered his elbow to rest on the center console between us.

Twenty minutes later, I was still holding the napkin to his wound, which had long since clotted. Kinda forgot about it in my preoccupied state of staring out the window. I had questions and he had answers, but neither of us wanted to break the truced-out silence that had fallen between us. When his arm stiffened for whatever reason, I rubbed it without really thinking. In the silence, we were almost friends. It was when either of us opened our mouths that we ran into trouble.

"I can feel that, you know. You asking a million questions in your mind," he pretended to grouse. He wouldn't admit we were getting along, but I knew he could feel the tension abate by millimeters every few miles we drove down the highway. He leaned back in his seat as he drove.

"How about just one?" I made sure to keep my voice quiet and non-confrontational.

"I don't believe you. I tell you what, if you can ask just one question, I'll give you a dollar."

"A whole shiny dollar all for myself? Take it easy, Moneybags." I permitted a small smile, and one appeared on his lips, as well. He was devastatingly handsome, and I immediately chided myself for noticing. "Challenge accepted. And I'll raise you one. If you can answer my question to the point where I'm satisfied, I'll throw in my left shoe."

He raised an eyebrow, glancing at me sideways in a playful rhythm we managed to fall into. There were Werebears, fires, Weredogs and who knows what else, but in the quietness of the car, the urgency of my fear began to fall to the wayside. Jens smirked at me. "What am I going to do with your left shoe? It doesn't even have a match. Pass."

"Okay. If you can answer me till I'm happy, I'll answer one question of yours. Help you out with your girl troubles and whatnot."

"What makes you think I have girl troubles?" he scoffed.

"Something about the way you stuff a girl in a car. Just a hunch."

Jens sighed, gearing up for truth time. "Fine. For the record, I don't have girl troubles, so I'll pass on the prize of your left shoe and love advice." He gripped the steering wheel, rubbing his thumb on the curve as he thought of where he'd best like to begin.

I kept the napkin pressed to his arm and waited patiently to see if he'd spill his guts without me having to actually use up my limited questions quota. My fingers gave his wound a gentle hug to let him know I wouldn't interrupt.

"Okay. Where to start? I'm not from here. From your world." He rolled his eyes at himself. "This sounds so cheesy and melodramatic." He shook his head. "I'm a Tomten, Lucy. Here, grab my phone. I'll show you."

He leaned his hip toward me, so I tried to be the least amount of intrusive as I slid the device from his jeans. He still smelled like freshly baked sugar cookies.

"Just hit the button to light up the screen. I want you to see my screensaver."

I obeyed and saw his screensaver was a garden gnome. I swallowed my inner grimace. I really hated those lawn ornaments. They looked creepy, like overly happy children's toys that came to life at night and hacked villagers to bits. Perhaps I'd seen one too many horror movies with Linus.

Linus. He loved a good scare, which to me seemed an oxymoron, as there was nothing good about being afraid. If a movie really freaked me out, that night he would wait until I was almost asleep and then whisper creepy lines from the movie into the darkness. My retaliation? A cigarette lighter to the underside of the DVD. That way no one could be haunted by the movie ever again.

"That's a Tomten," Jens explained, clarifying nothing.

"Oh," I said lamely. I held up the screen to his face and nodded. "Striking resemblance. I mean, the old man face, the Santa Claus hair, dunce cap, cheery little cheeks, two feet tall. Totally you." I paused and then shook my head. "Oh, wait. He's smiling. Nope. I don't believe you're a lawn ornament, Jens. Man, you almost had me there." I slipped the phone back in his pocket, my knuckles accidentally brushing his toned abdomen. My cheeks pinkened, and I retracted my hand guiltily, though I knew I'd done nothing wrong.

"Those lawn ornaments are protection charms left by guardian gnomes when they retire. I'm a guardian gnome. I was hired to protect your family. If I ever retired, one of these would be left behind to provide you with some sort of safeguard. The reason they all look like the same guy is because that mini Santa Claus was the first gnome ever. He's the first Tomten our race sprung from. So we leave a little tribute behind to watch over our charges."

Jens didn't give the vibe of trying to trick me. He seemed pretty sincere. But, you know, garden gnomes. I decided to stick with suspending my disbelief in the spirit of seeing where the rabbit trail led. At worst, I'd get a good bedtime story out of it. "Okay. But you're so tall. Maybe it's a guard versus guardian thing," I reasoned.

"Nope. Most Undrans are taller than humans. Our average is over six feet tall. Seven, in some parts. Except dwarves, obviously."

"Obviously," I commented, rolling my eyes at him. "Why is it common knowledge in my world that gnomes are smaller, then?"

He cast me an innocent smile and batted his thick eyelashes at me. "Why is it common knowledge that blondes are dumb?"

I flicked the gash on his arm in retaliation. "You deserved that," I said of his intake of breath. "So you smell like sugar cookies, but you're not Santa Claus? I gotta warn you, any story that doesn't end in me getting presents is pretty lame. I may need you to tell me the rest in song."

Jens relaxed by a degree, just enough to get more of his story out. "I've got a nice lump of coal all picked out for you."

"Oh, you spoil me." I rubbed his arm to soothe it. "Go on."

"It's my job to keep you safe. Back there with those Weredogs? Not safe. I know you don't like it, but I really did have to get you out of there."

"Thanks for that," I offered, realizing how selfish I'd been not saying anything sooner. "I'm sorry you got hurt."

Jens pfft'd. "I'm not hurt. That's nothing." His volume quieted when his pride finally did. "But thanks. Anyway, Tomtens come from Undraland, not here. There are two worlds: here and Undraland. We call this the Other Side. I'm taking you to Undra right now, in fact."

"Do they have Chinese food in Undraland?" I asked after a long pause.

"No. Mostly farms. Nothing like your world. Get ready for a culture shock."

"Do they have mocha milkshakes?"

"No. Think Amish, Loos."

"Do they have burgers and fries?"

"Not how you like them. Ours have real beef."

I glanced wistfully out the window at the billboard advertising a taco so gorgeous, I wanted to move in and make myself a blanket out of the refried beans. "Can they take a hint in Undraland? I'm starving."

He chuckled. "Sure. Give me a couple exits to put more distance between us and our Were tail, and we can stop somewhere and grab a bite real quick. I gotta refuel anyway. Now where was I? Oh, right. Undraland. I'm from Undraland, which is made up of different countries. Some of us get along, some not so much. All the races have different abilities and limitations, but Tomtens are best known for guarding and farming. Tonttu, the tribe I'm from, is mostly farmers. Not many guards left, actually."

"How'd I get so lucky?" I teased.

"You'll have to ask Alrik when you see him. He can explain the rest better than I can."

I really hated that there was this whole other world my uncle knew about, but I didn't. I cleared my throat and tried to keep everything light so Jens wouldn't turn and see my gaping emotional wound. "How can that be possible? You've told me so much. I feel like I'm eating Chinese food in Undraland as we speak."

"You're doing shtick," he observed. "I freaked you out. Did I say too much?"

I kept my expression cool and did my usual conversational dance to avoid talking about things that made me anxious. "You know, every time I meet a guy who kills bears, steals cars and burns down homes, I wonder if it's the garden gnome figurines sneaking out at night to do nefarious deeds. You just confirmed it all. The world makes sense again."

"Double shtick? Now I know you're upset. Just wait. Alrik can explain everything better. I suck at this. I shouldn't have answered your question."

"I didn't actually ask my question yet, you know. That was all free information."

Jens frowned, flipping over the conversation in his mind to try and find the spark that started his information spill. "Whatever. I knew what you were going to ask. And I changed my mind. I decided I do want your left shoe."

"Not a chance. I was going to ask if you happened to know of any elves up at the North Pole, or any reindeer who needed a job pulling cars." I pointed to the dash. "You're almost out of gas, Saint Nick."

"Whatever. I earned your left shoe. That blue one would look fetching on me. Don't you think?"

"Ravishing," I agreed. "I guess I get that dollar. You didn't answer my one question."

He took his eyes off the road to look at me, sizing up my level of commitment to our strange conversation. "I do know an elf. A great many of them, actually. That's one of the countries in Undraland. Elvage is on the other side of the mountain from Tomten, but our countries don't get along all that great. Not many of us travel back and forth, but I've done the trek before." He paused, steeling himself to say his next piece. "Your uncle lives in Elvage."

I said nothing to the blast of information that made my boat of reality rock back and forth on tumultuous waves I wasn't ready to trust just yet. Inside, I was a jumble of questions and doubt. Oddly enough, my burgeoning distrust wasn't directed toward Jens, but rather my uncle, whom I couldn't believe kept such a big secret from me. "Uncle Rick's an elf? And you're a garden gnome." I shifted in my seat, my discomfort only increasing.

"Actually, I'm a *guardian* gnome, but I'm from a tribe that's mostly garden gnomes. All gnomes, just different professions."

I began tapping a rhythm on the door. "So when a bear attacks me in the middle of suburbia, I should be glad you're the guardian kind, and that you won't try to stop him by growing him a tomato plant and making him a salad?"

"Exactly." Jens pulled over to a rest stop, looking every bit as exhausted as I felt. The early morning sun was making me a mixture of tired and jittery.

When I came out of the restroom, Jens handed me a leathery beef stick from the vending machine. I looked at it, wondering when the last meal he'd eaten with a woman was. I gave him back the non-food. "Thanks, but I'm not hungry." *I'd rather eat those disgusting orange circus peanuts than chomp on leather dipped in bouillon,* but I decided to keep that to myself.

"There's other stuff in the half-empty vending machine, but you wouldn't like any of it. Potato chips and candy bars mostly with fake peanut butter in them."

I pursed my lips together to keep from letting my anxiety surface that he knew my quirks so well. I nodded, trying to appear pleasant and not like I was having a mini freak-out.

He led the way back to the car and leaned on the hood. "So, that bowling alley's where we were supposed to meet Alrik."

I tried to keep my voice even and my questions to a minimum. "He's... he's okay, right? You said no one died in the fire."

Jens waved his hand to quiet my fears. "It was one of Tucker's fires, so Alrik's fine. Tucker's the best. I'd be able to sense if it Alrik was dead."

"Well that's nice and cryptic." I tugged at the hem of my shirt, fighting off my sleepiness with movement.

"The plan's to get you to Alrik, and he's crossed over to Undraland, so I'm taking you home." When my chin lifted hopefully, he shook his head. "Home to my people, not yours. Think you can manage another few hours?"

"Sure." I needed something normal. Something mindless to reset my spinning brain.

What's the name of the lead singer from the Polyphonic Spree? I knew if I didn't look it up it was really going to bother me. I pulled out my phone and did a search for the band to waste time while Jens chewed his hunk of boot leather that was posing as food.

Jens snatched the device out of my hands, earning a frown. "Nope. No contacting anyone from beyond the grave."

"I wasn't. I was just looking something up."

Jens turned it off and stuck it in his back pocket. "I'm serious."

"So am I. I was looking up the lead singer's name from the Polyphonic Spree. It's bugging me." I scratched my forehead. "That's the thing about humans who aren't garden gnomes. We like information when we want it. Gimmee my phone."

"Oh, sure. That guy? His name is…" Then Jens smiled in that superior way I was growing to hate. "I'll let you guess for a while. It'll keep you occupied till we get home. And I'm not a garden gnome. *Guardian* gnome. Big difference." He pulled out his own phone and punched the screen a few times, bringing up the band's homepage. He flashed it to me, showing me the lead singer's face, but not his name. His grin turned wicked, like a schoolboy who desperately needed slapping.

All my things now fit into a backpack, and he was stealing from my meager possessions. "Give it back. I'm serious."

"Oh, you're serious? That changes everything." His levity shifted to authority. "No. Now get in the car." When nothing brilliant came to mind to spew at him, he arched his thick eyebrow at me. "What? You don't have any quippy comebacks? Nothing about where I can take a flying leap?"

I answered by getting in and slamming the door. I wanted to thrash him, but that would involve me speaking, and I decided I was against that. Truce over.

Being silent for long periods of time was a gift of mine. Most may not see it like that, but it actually takes a strong will to cultivate said talent. There was one year Dad moved us in the middle of the night to a motel three states away. Linus had been a month into his first relationship ever, and I actually kind of liked her. Melissa wore an old pink sweater every day and had braces to match. Sweet girl who went out of her way to be nice to me. Made ninth grade not too shabby for that small span of time.

Linus and I knew better than to question our parents on the constant moves. We never got straight answers from them anyway. But this move went too far. Linus decided to dig his heels in and protest. His fight wasn't loud or emotional; it was cold and silent. When the verdict didn't change even after he'd made his opinion known to Mom and Dad, Linus went on strike. He sat in that crappy motel facing the corner for a solid week. He didn't speak, not even to me. I knew better than to try and make him. We were united in everything, so I took up his mantle and shut my mouth, too. We sat on the floor facing the wall, barely moving for seven days. Linus only ate or drank with me, shutting out the world in his quiet way. I learned a lot that week, listening to our parents slowly lose their minds as they tried everything to get us to talk, except for moving us back to Linus's Melissa.

Sometimes you reach a point where you realize no

one's listening when you talk. Most people get louder. Ever since Linus's lesson, I like to evaluate the situation and turn inward when I hit a wall like that. Then I know at least one person cares about my viewpoint – me. So that's how Jens and I drove another three hours without speaking.

6

STINA

We ended up at the entrance to a rickety amusement park I'd never heard of, and were greeted by a clown trashcan that had been tipped over onto its side, cigarette butts spilling out of its painted smile. The faded and splintered arch over the gate was missing all the vowels in the word "carnival", making the sign kinda pointless. When I glanced beyond the gate to the tall rides, I noticed none of them were moving, and several were missing cars or whole bits of track.

I had no idea which state we were in. Details mattered, but so little of everything Jens had done made any sense to me, I guessed that even if I knew every detail, I'd still be in the dark.

He parked the car and got out, stretching from head to toe and then shaking like a dog kept in a cage too long. I made no effort to join him, though I was terribly stiff. Jens opened my door and popped the trunk, taking out a red backpack. He jerked his head toward the lackluster park.

"Out you go. You'll be safe with my people while we figure things out."

I obeyed, but only because I didn't want him to carry me again. I'm sure Tonya would've been thrilled to be tossed around by the older, rugged-looking man. I frowned, my melancholy stamping itself on my shoulders and weighting them. Memories like those would have to do, being that I would never see her again. Only solid girl-friend I'd ever had, and just like that she was gone from my life. I tucked that despair away and kept my expression neutral as I followed Jens to the entrance.

I heard organ music piped in from the center of the park, but it had that terrifying serial killer clown feel to it – too slow and clunky to be classified as cheery. Despite my dislike of Jens, I didn't stray too far from him. I'd never been terribly fond of clowns ever since Linus downloaded every clown slasher movie in existence and made me watch them all in a single weekend. That was his retaliation for me making him watch all the seasons of my favorite girly show, which he declared was far more scar-ring than his horror movies.

We didn't go to the open ticket booth, but to a closed one. He banged on the plexiglass, waving a gold badge from his pocket. An elderly lady looked up from her knit-ting and greeted him. She wore an orange cardigan and had thick creamsicle bifocal frames to match. Her sweater reminded me of the one my Uncle Rick wore like a uniform with his Dockers. If you've never seen a tall black man in an orange cardigan, you're missing out. Somehow he rocked it. "Good to see you, Jens. It's been positively boring without you around to entertain me."

"Now, now. You can't have me all to yourself, Mattie. But I came back for you, so the world's right again."

"So it is." She uploaded his badge information with a digital scanner and read the pertinent information to him through her thick lenses. Her eyes and lips were framed in accordion wrinkles as she read aloud. "The Kincaid girl's place was terminated. No casualties. An imprint of her dental work was left where the authorities could find them in the rubble. She's been identified and declared dead. Well done, peach pie, as usual."

Jens nodded, ignoring the fact that my heart plummeted in my chest and my nerves were showing themselves in the form of cold sweat beading on my forehead. It was hot out, but I was chilled through to the bone. I would never see Tonya again. My life had been yanked out from under me.

"Peach pie. Are you flirting with me, Mattie?" Jens pocketed his badge and leaned on the sill.

"Oh, I'm always flirting with you, and you love it." The woman whose blue faded nametag read "Matilda" slid open the window and reached forward at the same time he leaned in. She pinched his dimpled cheek, and then slapped it lightly.

"Is Alrik still here? I couldn't find him."

"Alrik came back early. Said he ran into some trouble with Weres entering civilization too close to humans, not that anyone except for you and me would believe him. Three of them were tracking him, so he had to get Tucker to burn his favorite place down. Then he came back to Undra just to throw off the scent." She shook her head.

"Such a shame. He loved stocking the shoes at that bowling alley. Alrik crossed over earlier this morning."

Jens rolled his eyes. "Must be nice to port places. Just pop from state to state whenever you like. Elves are such cheaters." He jerked his thumb in my direction. "I'm taking my charge to see him."

Matilda handed him a clipboard with her thick, wrinkled fingers. "Sign her in, dear." She looked me up and down appreciatively. "Thanks for bringing this one in without making a scene. Did you get a Huldra to spell her to make her so calm?" She gave a visible shiver to indicate she did not care for Huldras.

Something in the recesses of my brain pinged when I heard the term, but I couldn't place why it sounded familiar.

Jens glanced back at me and frowned. "Nah. Just used my awesome people skills."

Matilda made a huff of disbelief and took back the clipboard, her chubby fingers winding the pen's chain back around the clip. "Boy, you're lucky you've got the face of every mother's nightmare."

He grinned in a churlish way that made me want to puke on his black boots just to take him down a notch. I pretended to accidentally brush against him as I reached past to check he spelled my name right. I smiled through my irritation, loving how easy he was to pickpocket. I'd picked many a pocket in my day – not to steal cash, but usually as part of one of Linus's harebrained schemes that *never* (always) got us into trouble.

"Go ahead on in, kids. Give Alrik a hug from me and

remind him he owes me $3.25 from our bridge game last week."

"I can pay off his high-stakes gambling debts." Jens's thumb touched the edge of his empty pocket. My victory was ill timed and therefore, short-lived.

Matilda smiled, her cherubic cheeks moving her glasses up on her face. "Oh, you're a sweet boy, Jens. I don't care what King Johannes says about you."

His thick eyebrows pushed together as he patted both his back pockets. "Left my wallet in the car. I'll be…"

He stopped talking when a red sports car pulled in at a speed not considerate of pedestrians. It parked at the entrance, which was not actually a parking spot. A black-haired beauty in her thirties stepped out, revealing…well, just revealing. She wore a purple dress that was kind of a dress and kind of a butt-length form-fitting shirt. Her black heeled boots up to her knees and red lips to match her car made me feel like a kid still in pigtails.

My toes clung to my mismatched sky blue and black Chucks as I leaned against the ticket booth, waiting for Jens to put his tongue back in his head.

"Jens!" Matilda's voice turned sharp in that way elderly women have of shaming you by simply saying your name. "Everything on this side of the gate is property of Undra-land. Huldras aren't allowed past it. Not a toe. I don't care how short her skirt is."

"I know the rules, and so does she," Jens assured her. "We're not together, Mattie. She just helps me out on jobs sometimes." He pointed an adult finger in my face, and I despised him for it. "Don't move from this spot. I'll be right back." He called to the woman, "Stina, what do you want?"

Short Skirt Stina's eyes glossed over me like I was a sea urchin, or you know, something that doesn't belong in a picture with Jens.

Matilda slammed the sliding window shut, a clear look of fear on her face. "Huldra," she mouthed, shuddering, staring with dread at Stina.

Then I remembered. When Mom and Dad went out on their rare date nights, Uncle Rick would stay with Linus and me. We straight up begged like gypsies when it came to avoiding bedtime. We put on puppet shows with our socks for Uncle Rick, sang songs, and pled for story after story.

Uncle Rick was a great storyteller. He made up all sorts of goofy tales, one of which was about a people called the Huldras.

I studied Stina, suspending my disbelief for the moment that the world was in fact, a more bizarre place than I realized, and that Huldras were real.

Huldras were women who had magic in their whistle that could be used to control people. They could enchant people to do their bidding for hours, which would explain Matilda's self-inflicted booth isolation. I began to feel very exposed.

Jens needed no mind-controlling whistle to scamper toward Stina. Their conversation was too far off to eavesdrop on. I turned and leafed through his wallet, bummed at the lack of useful information he'd stashed inside. I expected some top-secret intel or direct orders or something.

Instead I found a few receipts for nothing damning, a black card I tried not to be impressed by, and a few pieces of paper I began thumbing through to gain more information on Jens to be used for nefarious purposes later.

One folded piece of paper had a list of cities, all with a line drawn through them except for my latest address. My intake of breath was not noticeable, but my upset probably was. There, in perfect geographic order were the past five years of my life. It was the list of cities my family had moved to on our run from Weres or whatever it was my parents were always hiding us from.

The next piece of paper was a note to someone from Linus. My heart banged in my chest like an alarm as I read it.

YOU ATE THE LAST BAGEL, *you jag. The ransom's set at 2 dozen donuts if you ever want to see your precious knife again. You have until I get home from school.*

I COULDN'T STOP ASKING the note over and over and over whom it had been written to. Linus didn't know about Jens and Weres and all that. He's my twin brother. I would've felt it if he had. Maybe someone from his soccer team? "Jag" didn't exactly narrow anything down. Which of his jock friends carried around a knife? And why did Jens have a piece of my brother in his wallet?

I tugged at the thin braided rope around my neck, twisting through the material the heart-shaped vial that hid under my shirt. It was Linus, literally. He'd been cremated, and I got a vial of his ashes. The cop who'd found my parents in the car wreck gave me some crap reason why I couldn't see or have my parents' bodies, so I didn't have a piece of them to take with me.

It was just Linus and me.

I kifed the note from Jens's wallet and shoved it in my back pocket. My brother. My note.

I was too upset to go through the rest of the wallet's contents. I dropped it next to me for Jens to find when Stina was done flirting with him, if a timeframe existed for that. She was trilling her red fingernail down his arm. She was over six feet tall, which was a nice match for him, height-wise.

Jens shook off her advance, but she paid his subtle signals no mind. She reached out for his hand, tracing a design into his palm as she spoke.

Boys are so dense.

She followed him to his car while he fished around for the wallet he would never find, chatting all the while as she checked out his butt none too subtly. That, I couldn't blame the girl for.

When he went to search the trunk, I took pity on him. "Jens, your wallet," I called, making a show of picking it up so he could see how clumsy he was in dropping it in the dust.

He rolled his eyes at himself and trotted toward me, ignoring Short Skirt Stina as she prattled on about something very important to her that Jens couldn't have cared less about.

"I'm talking to you, Jens!" she shouted.

Jens stopped and turned, an eyebrow raised almost comically. "I'm working, Stina. Why don't you just keep dialing up the crazy? Nothing sexier than that."

"A blonde? Really?" she directed toward me. "You're such a cliché! I can't believe you'd take her to your house when we were together not a month ago!" She said it to me like she was announcing some scandal, as if he'd been cheating on me with her last month. I didn't really have a convincing gasp in me, so I leaned against the ticket booth while I waited for their very mature fight to finish up.

"Ignore her," he called to me.

She shouted to me in a high-pitched screech of desperation, finger jabbing like a threat. "If you think he's only sleeping with you, you're dead wrong, honey!"

Jens met my wary gaze with one that was mildly embarrassed, then he turned to bark at the long legged beauty. "Leave her alone, Stina."

I thought Stina would give him a verbal jab to parry, but instead she pursed her lips and sucked in a lungful of air.

Jens gasped in surprise and lunged at her, his fist cocked. So quick, I barely saw all of it, Jens socked Stina in the nose with force meant to combat a large man. Her head snapped back, and she stumbled. Jens caught her, anticipating she would fall backward, and lowered her to the ground gently, as if he'd not been the one who'd just leveled her with a single blow.

I screamed with my hands over my mouth, shocked that the puppy prone to misbehaving was capable of biting. The gravity of the situation hit me afresh; I knew nothing about Jens.

Jens glanced over at me, chagrinned that he'd been a horrible person in my presence. He shrugged as if to say, "What else was I supposed to do?"

I ran to the woman, shocked and appalled that I'd let a smidgen of my guard down around him. I passed through the gate and helped her up. "Are you okay? Jens!" I thrust open the car door and fished around for some napkins, pressing them to her nose and pinching the bridge so the red globules would clot.

Stina spat blood onto the ground and sneered up at him, delivering a swift shove to my chest to scold me for helping her. I caught myself before I could fall backward on my rear, surprised that she lashed out at me when I'd had nothing to do with her bloody nose. When she spoke, everything was gulpy and nasal. "I can do whatever I want out here. You forget we have free reign of the Other Side. When you need to get out of a tough spot, I'm the one you want, but now you're all high and mighty when I try to use my whistle just to calm you down?" She spat more blood on his black boots, but Jens didn't even flinch.

Instead, he stared down at her imperiously. "Don't you ever try anything like that on me again." He yanked on my arm, and I had no choice but to bob along behind him like a rag doll.

Finally I regained my footing and jerked myself out of his grip. "Get your hands off me!" I shouted, stomping in the opposite direction.

"Lucy, we have to go! You have no idea how dangerous Stina is."

"Stina hasn't punched anyone in the face!" I countered, stomping past the woman who still had blood trickling out of her nose. Her lips pursed together again, and I could tell she was trying to whistle, but couldn't manage it with her face in such disarray.

In only a few steps, Jens cleared the distance between us. His hand banded around my waist, but he surprised me by jerking my head to the side. His lips suctioned to the space between my shoulder and my neck, confusing me more than anything. I felt a slight pinch when he bit me, and felt my chest constrict after I choked out a scream. Jens was talking to me in that irritated tone he gets when I piss him off, but I couldn't make sense of the words that tumbled out of him too fast.

He steered me back toward Matilda, and I walked with leaden feet as I tried fruitlessly to protest.

"Jens! She's positively white as a sheet. Be careful!" Matilda called, pushing a button to let us through the turnstile.

"It's only a half dose," he said, as if whatever he'd done to me had a good excuse. I tried to dig my heels in, but I only managed to trip myself and ram my hip into the metal bar.

This was it. Somehow I'd just been roofied by a vampire who thought he was a garden gnome. It was the only explanation.

Jens righted me, but my knees were shaking. I could smell hot dogs and a stomach-churning mix of amusement park foods. The hot dog made me think of Tonya and her creative, yet appalling hot dog casserole. I wondered if she made it with cabbage, like she did last time she concocted the creation. It smelled the same going down as it had coming back up. What I wouldn't give for her casserole now. I'd muscle my way through the whole thing if it meant I got to see her again.

Apparently, I'm dead now, since Jens had my apartment

burned down and me declared deceased. My last meal had been that tasteless granola bar I'd stolen from Danny. He was probably just getting home now to find his belongings burned. Tonya would cry on his shoulder. They'd get closer. He'd probably count it as a gain when it was all said and done. He'd do the obligatory "feeling sad" dance concerning my death for Tonya's sake, but there would be no funeral. Who would come? Everywhere I went I was erased shortly thereafter.

Jens was yammering at me, but I didn't hear anything. He wanted me to walk faster.

I clutched at my chest in what felt like slow motion. My limbs were stalled as if moving through Jell-O, each gesture an effort.

Then I couldn't move at all.

The air was too thick to breathe. I looked around for anyone who could help me, but Jens was the only face I could focus on. Then I lost even that. My anxiety peaked when I realized we were the only people in the entire park. Even if I could scream, no one would hear it.

My vision blurred as I tried to resist his iron grip. "Lucy, it's okay. I've got you," he insisted, as if that was supposed to be a comfort. I whimpered in his arms, and then, just like the Gravitron carnival ride we were standing next to, the bottom dropped out from under me.

BRITTA AND JAMIE

*U*nconsciousness had been a blessing that couldn't have come at a better time. I slowly came back to myself, but kept that little fact a secret, so I didn't have to deal with Jens's unpredictable violent tendencies. People were moving around me, but I didn't open my eyes. My throat was so dry; I couldn't recall the last glass of water I'd had. I did my best to listen to my surroundings and gather information before I was forced to participate in whatever this new life was. I kept hearing a swish and then a bang. Sort of like darts, but harder.

"So then what?" asked a female voice that sounded just a couple years more mature than mine.

Jens answered, "Then I brought her here."

Another swish sounded. "Mine got closer than yours," the woman bragged in an impish manner.

"You've had more time to practice. This one keeps me on my toes. She's a pistol, that's for sure."

"Pretty, just like you described her. Doesn't look like

she's seen the sun. And so short. Is she well off where she comes from?"

"Nah. Humans are different, Britta. Most of them aren't farmers. I told you that. Her skin's normal for her kind." Another swish. "Ho! I win."

"No! I was so close."

Jens stood and walked across the room. I heard his black boots heavy on the wood floor. I peeked with one eye as he jerked the knives they were using as darts out of the wall. My eye shut quickly before I gave myself away.

"You think she'll like me?" The girl's voice wavered with insecurity. She sat on the edge of the... bed? I touched the sheet beneath me. Yup. I guessed correctly that I was laid out on a bed.

Jens's tone softened. "Of course she will. Who wouldn't like you?" Their easy and tender back and forth threatened to melt my heart, so I put up a mental fight to recall the reasons I despised Jens.

Britta scoffed. "You're a sweet big brother. But you know I'm the leper around here."

"Maybe it's because you play with knives," he teased. "Nah, I'm kidding. Toms are backward. There's nothing wrong with you." He sat back down on the chair next to his sister, and I peeked and saw him rocking it back to balance on the rear two legs. "How's work going? Anyone giving you any trouble?"

Britta's answer sounded carefully selected. "It's fine. Not many've been hanged lately. I'm glad you talked the palace into paying me annually, instead of by the hanging. The less I have to actually do my job, the more people start to forget about it. Much more time for gardening."

"I want you to be honest with me, Britt. If anyone's giving you a hard time, tell me who. I'll take care of it."

"Yes, well the last time you 'took care of it', I had to clean up after yet another hanging. I'm fine, as I always am." There was a precious note of silence between them before Britta spoke in a quiet way that seemed to calm Jens's arrogance. "You've never brought a girl home before."

Jens chuckled bitterly. "Well, this sure doesn't count. She's a job, not a girl. Don't get attached to this one. And if I ever do bring a girl home, she'll be conscious."

"And thanking her lucky stars, no doubt." The third voice was new to the mix. The man was a few meters away. "When'd you get back, Tom?"

Tom?

Jens rose from his chair and slapped the newcomer in what sounded like a bear hug. "Not too long ago, Tom." I peeked to see their prolonged embrace that went several seconds past the obligatory guy hug. They gripped each other in an unshakable way, as if breath was easier now that the other was around. It was a beautiful thing. A brothers by choice moment not often seen in nature.

The man's voice took on a reverence when he turned toward the girl. "Britta."

"Hello, Jamie." I didn't need my eyes open to sense the sexual tension between those two. Yikes.

Jens paid it no mind and collapsed back into his chair. "Did I miss anything interesting?"

"My father still hates you, so nothing new here." His voice turned toward me, his excitement that of a boy on the eve of Christmas. "Oh! Is that her? The famous Lucy Kincaid?"

"Shut up." Jens sounded embarrassed.

"I half-expected her to float or have sunbeams shooting out of her fingertips."

Jens shushed his friend. "I brought you something, but I'll only show you if you shut up."

I heard Jamie strolling toward me for a better look. I fought to remain motionless. "Can I say I'm not terribly shocked you had to knock her out? What? Did she want an actual conversation?"

"Oh, Jens." Britta sounded disappointed.

Jamie's voice was almost giddy as Jens fished through his red bag. "Please tell me... Oh, amazing! This phone's even better than the last one! How much battery does it have left?"

Jens's tone was light and familiar with the man. "Not much. Put it on the solar charging pad I got you. I'll show you how to work it when I come over next. She's got a few games on there you've never tried."

I peeked and saw that they were fondling my cell. My eyes flew open and I tried to sit up, clumsy fingers gripping the rough bedding I was laid atop of. "Hey! That's mine!" Then I started coughing, making my anger less intimidating. When I brought my hand to my mouth, I saw that my sleeve belonged to nothing in my wardrobe. I glanced down and observed with horror that my jeans, green long-sleeved T and purple tank top had been replaced by... a dress.

I could not recall the last time I'd worn a dress. I didn't go to my prom, which would've been the last logical reason for me to don a girly frock. This one was beige, cut just below my bust, and flowed well past my bare feet. At least I still had purple nail polish on my toes. That was an indicator I'd not been unconscious for days. Tonya and I had given ourselves pedicures the morning before last.

My hacking cough stayed my cavalcade of questions. Britt or Britta or Brittney or whoever was at my side in an instant, tipping a glass of water to my lips, lending her arm around my back for me to lean against in a sort of cuddle. It was three swallows before it dawned on me that I was drinking out of a cup of liquid I had not poured in a captor situation. My clothes were missing, and I was in a foreign place. I spat the water at Jens, who was on my other side, helping Britta hold me up in a sitting position.

Jamie laughed at the water dripping down Jens's face. I scrambled off the bed and bolted clumsily toward the exit, but Jens beat me to it, keeping the front door shut. I evaluated my rural surroundings. I appeared to be in some kind of quaint wood cabin with a roughly hewn floor. It was all one room, save for what I assumed was a bathroom off to the side. Panicked, I snatched an iron poker from the hearth and held it cocked, as if I knew what I was doing with it.

Britt shouted her alarm, and Jamie gallantly moved in front of her, acting as a human shield.

"It's fine, Britta," Jens assured her with a cocky smile. Oh, how I wanted to knock it off his face. "She won't do anything. She doesn't believe in violence. She's just trying to scare me."

Jamie cocked his head to the side, observing my juvenile grip and the stance of a non-fighter. I was trying to copy the swordfighters in *The Princess Bride*, but knew I was doing a horrible job. I wondered if a deadly "Prepare to die," might help sell the act. Jamie's nose scrunched as he watched my every move. "Doesn't believe in violence? That's not a thing."

"It is in the human world. Not often, but it's there. She's never had to hunt for her food, though. Humans can afford that kind of ideal." Jens addressed me as if I was a kid joking around with a toy knife. "Put it down, Loos. You'll hurt yourself." When I didn't budge, he shook his wet head at me. "What would Martin Luther King Jr. say if he saw you like this?"

Ouch. Well played, jerk who apparently knows me pretty well. Really should've chosen Genghis Khan as my role model. I lowered the weapon, ignoring Jens's sniggering.

Britta was holding onto Jamie's waist, which is why I assume he did not lower his guard right away. Her emerald eyes blinked at me with equal amounts of curiosity and wariness. She had two long dark braids coming out from under her white Amish bonnet.

"Where are my clothes?" I demanded. "You didn't… you didn't dress me in this, did you?" My cheeks were hot, and I couldn't manage to look at him.

Jens's smirk died on his lips. "Of course not. My sister did. Britta washed your clothes for you." He turned his head to the side. "Britt, are her things dry yet?"

"Probably not. Just a little longer. They're in the sun and it's a breezy day, so they'll dry fast." She addressed me as if I was a wild animal. "It's okay, Miss Lucy. No one's going to hurt you."

Jens cleared the distance between us and covered his hand over mine that was still clutching the poker. The warning in his eyes could not be ignored. "*I* know you're harmless, but you won't threaten anyone in the presence of my sister again."

"Who knew you had a heart?" I hissed, glaring up at him to show I wasn't afraid.

"Whatever. You'll get your precious jeans back soon enough, Moxie."

Crap. That was a great nickname. I kind of loved it.

Jens placed the poker back in the sheath on the hearth. "Would it kill you to dress like a girl for once?"

"Yes. Yes, it would. Just as much as it would kill you to give me a straight answer." I sniffed the stale air that smelled of sweat and a little like cookies. "Or bathe. Honestly, is it a rule that guys have to smell like a sweaty gym wherever they go?"

His arms flailed out in exasperation. "I killed a Were so you would be safe! Then three Weredogs!"

Oh, yeah. He got me there. Change the subject. "Where am I?"

He spoke slowly, as if I were mentally handicapped. "This is a house. My house." He stomped his foot to the wood surface. "This is a floor. It's what you use to pass out on."

My fists clenched at my sides as I glowered. "Why am I here, smartass?"

"When you're done being a pain, I'm going to take you to your Uncle Rick. He can answer all your questions."

"And you can't?"

"Can, but won't. Your questions just multiply. Answer

one, and fifteen more appear. My job was to keep your family safe and move you if Pesta tried to take you."

"Pesta?" A faint ping sounded in my brain, alerting me that the name sounded familiar.

His smile was infuriating. "That sounds like another question for Alrik."

I let out a noise of frustration. "It's like you get off on being annoying. Do you have to be so difficult?"

He scoffed. "Whatever. I'm a joy."

I had no words for this. No ladylike ones, anyway. "What about my phone? You're just giving away my stuff now? Kill me off on paper, so my belongings are up for grabs? That phone is precious to me!" It had my brother's voice on it, voicemails saved that were the last remnants of my other half. I think threatening with a knife was a reasonable path. I touched the heart on my necklace to remind myself that Linus was still mine.

Jamie handed over my phone with a guilty expression weighing down his brown eyes and too-tall build. He touched his curly brown hair and stood straighter. "I'm sorry, Miss Lucy. I meant no disrespect."

I clutched the phone as if it was my lifeline, my ticket out of here. I took my anger at Jens and directed it at Jamie. "Don't touch me or my stuff."

Jens sobered marginally. "It had to be done, Loos. We can't have Pesta looking for you."

Anger I'd not properly suppressed made my voice rise to a shaky shout. I grabbed the glass of water next to the straw mattress and flung the rest of it in his face. "You erased me! Now no one will ever look for me!"

Jens took a step toward me, but I held the empty glass

up as if it was a menacing weapon. He respected the charade and held his hands up in surrender to my pain. "Alrik will make you understand. It was necessary to keep you alive."

"Dead on paper, alive in a smelly man cave. No, thanks. I'll go on my own where people don't fake kill me and steal my things." I moved past him in my too-long dress and flung open the door.

The sight that stung my eyes in the bright daylight shocked me more than I was prepared for. The noonday sun was brighter and bigger than any I'd ever seen. I stumbled backward, shielding my eyes from the blinding otherworldly light. Squinting didn't help at all, and I sorely wished for sunglasses. I peeked, but could barely make out shapes. Farmland as far as I could see produced a wide array of crops. There were men in overalls and women in dresses hoeing the dirt. The sun took up half of the sky. Like, literally half. My eyes watered and shut, unable to take any more light. I inched further back until I bumped into Jens, willing my brain to make sense of the odd scenery.

"Shh," Jens cooed as his arm went around my waist.

"Don't touch me or talk to me!" I protested, whirling around to face him as I wriggled out of his grip like an eel.

Britta's dainty pitch reached me, but did not soften my anger. "Jens, don't! Give her some time to adjust. You're scaring her!"

He did not back away, but grabbed me with rough hands that scared the irritation right out of me as he breathed in my face. "She's had enough time. Alrik needs us now."

I screamed, but it made no difference. He spun me around and pressed my back to his chest, jerking my head to the side as tears I'd been fighting off finally surfaced. "No! Please don't!" I whimpered through my fruitless struggle.

"Shh," he whispered in my ear. "I won't hurt you."

The last thing I felt was his mouth on the space between my neck and my shoulder, and that same sharp pinch when he bit me. A sensation that was both cold and warm flooded through me before I lost consciousness. It was the same gelatinous paralysis I experienced in the amusement park, but in warp speed.

Then I felt nothing, and it was bliss.

8

UNDRALAND 101

I awoke in a different bed and a new house that was far grander than Jens's hut. Cream-colored curtains framed the windows and painted the walls, giving the whole room a heavenly glow.

My body was weak, though that could have been from passing out or not eating or the whole being kidnapped thing. The sun coming in through the window was still far too bright, but I looked sideways out the glass anyway through my fingers, trying to put this new world into an order I could accept. When my eyes finally began to adjust to the slice I could sort of see, I found that I was on the third floor of a home, and there would be no popping out the window and jumping down to safety.

I touched the space between my neck and my shoulder, wondering if I'd ever feel safe again. A bandage covered the spot where Jens bit me, so naturally I peeled it back to get a look at the wound. Two puncture marks stared at me like snake eyes, and I covered it back up with a shiver. I was still wearing the stupid dress and no shoes, which did not bode well for any sort of escape plan. From the third floor. Of who knows where.

A gentle knock shook my heart in my chest. "Who is it?" I demanded.

"It's Sir Jamie, Miss Lucy. May I come in?"

Such a pretentious title for someone I did not peg as arrogant. Though, he's helping drug me and hold me hostage, so what did I know?

I opened the door, taking notice of the four locks that hitched on the inside and the rabid-looking scratches all up and down the door. I backed against the furthest wall when he entered. A little shorter than Jens, but still a respectable six feet and handful of inches, Jamie's proper stance and genteel brown eyes took in my distrust with sorrow. He opened his mouth to begin a sentence several times before the correct words actually came out. "Are you well, Miss Lucy?"

I blinked at him, wondering if he wanted an answer to such a stupid question. "Um, no. Where am I?"

"You're in my home."

I slumped down against the wall in the corner, not caring that I was making a mess of my dress. "I suppose you're going to tell me something like I'm being held here for my own safety or something." I hugged myself to keep my body away from him.

The pity in Jamie's voice kept my mind from going to the bad place. "Miss Lucy. I mean you no harm. Don't worry. I can take you to Jens, if you'd feel safer."

I scoffed. Yes, please send me to the man who punches women in the face.

It was then that the only source of comfort left in my world entered in behind Jamie. "Who's been hiding my favorite niece from me so cruelly?"

"Uncle Rick!" I scrambled clumsily to my feet and stumbled into his long, outstretched arms. He had always been crazy tall, though it seemed everyone I was meeting in this strange place was uncommonly stretched. His hug was familiar, which was all I wanted out of life in that moment. Something, anything that felt real. And here he was, holding me with great affection, as he always had. "Uncle Rick, what's going on? Why am I here? There was a bear, and then Jens, and now everything's a wreck!" Before I could stop myself or listen to his explanation in that beautiful deep voice I'd missed so much, I was recounting everything that happened to me since Jens abducted me from my apartment.

Uncle Rick listened patiently until I finished. Then he turned to Jamie and waved his hand toward the door. "Go fetch her the clothes she came here in, James. Britta should never have taken them without her consent."

I could tell Jamie wanted to defend Britta, but he nodded and left. Uncle Rick patted the top of my head, making me feel like I was a child again. Like I was safe because he was there. "I need answers, Uncle Rick. I don't understand a thing." I shook my head at his gray wizard costume. "And why are we both wearing dresses?"

"When in Rome, dear." His ebony skin had acquired a few more wrinkles, but the life in his eyes was as youthful as it ever was. Really, he's my mom's friend, but we always called him Uncle Rick. It's a little obvious we're not blood relations. I mean, I'm fair-skinned and blonde, and he's a towering black man with the kindest smile in the world. He was the only family I had left, and I clung to him as such. He smoothed my blonde hair away from my face and smiled as if I was something that brought him joy. Man, did I miss that fatherly affection. "Lucy, Lucy. You already know everything about my world. Don't you remember the bedtime stories I used to tell to you and Linus?"

I let out a gusty laugh I had not accessed since I left home. "Sure. The ones about elves and garden gnomes, dwarves, Fosse-what's-its and stuff like that? We loved those." The adventures he spun always featured Linus and me with Uncle Rick, fighting bravely and saving the day against an evil siren queen.

That nagging unsolved puzzle clicked into place.

Pesta. The Siren Queen.

Linus and I used to act out the battles, fighting over who had to be the bad guy that was vanquished and who got to be the hero.

Linus. He'd needed a hero, and I hadn't been able to save him.

"Sit down, Goose." Yup, my nickname as a kid was Goose. Lucy Goosy. Super clever.

I obeyed, sitting on the side of the bed and tucking my hands under myself. He sat at the foot of the bed, his large frame sinking down so much, it tilted me slightly. He scratched his half-inch long thick gray beard that had not changed my whole life. "Tell me what you remember about elves."

I shrugged. "They do magic, usually connected with the elements. They study different charms they can use to heal people, fight battles and help out. Stuff like that."

"We don't age properly, either."

"We?" I raised my eyebrow at his admission.

Uncle Rick nodded, his smile still in place as he watched my facial cues for freak-outs. "I'm an elf, Lucy. I'm three hundred four years young. The wise mage in my stories? Those were about my mentor, King Hallamar of Elvage."

Understand, I'm not gullible. But Uncle Rick and I have a deal. We never lie to each other. Never. When I asked him as a kid where babies came from, he told me, and then made sure my mother did a proper woman's version on the birds and the bees that very night. When I was five and Linus's leukemia came back and put him in the hospital, everyone around said with terrified expressions that Linus was going to be just fine. When I asked Uncle Rick, he told me the truth. That there was a good chance Linus might not be okay, but there was always hope.

If only I could blame his confession on a growing senility in him, but that was not probable, either. So I relied on a tactic I employed in my angst-filled days as the new kid. It was Rule #1: *When in doubt, shut your mouth.* I looked up at my uncle and nodded to at least let him know I was listening.

Uncle Rick continued on with his education of Lucy Kincaid. "I've mentioned the nation that resides in the Warf, correct? I believe Linus was particularly fascinated with that race."

I nodded, recalling many an excavating venture Linus took me out on with his shovel in hand when we were little. "The Warf? Yeah. Dwarves, right? They're shorter, hairier and mine for treasure."

A polite knock interrupted his flow, and Uncle Rick beckoned the caller inside. The door swung open, revealing Jamie with a folded pile of familiarity in his arms.

"My clothes!" The wave of relief that washed over me shone on my face as I took the pile from Jamie, who seemed uncomfortable to be holding such mannish women's clothing. I hadn't noticed before, but he had on a red sort of hat atop his wavy brown hair. It was the size of a yarmulke, but was pointed at the center like a miniature gnome cap.

And he thought my clothes were embarrassing.

Uncle Rick motioned to the partition in the corner of the room, so I ducked behind it and found a water basin and soap to wash myself with. "Space, guys," I ordered, jerking my thumb toward the door. The men bowed politely and gave me the ten minutes it took to sponge off and get dressed. The simple gown was flung over the partition, and I emerged in my jeans, green long-sleeved T, purple tank and mismatched Chucks. Oh, the difference being in your own clothes makes. I almost felt like I had a right to ask questions again.

Alrik smiled indulgently at me when I let him back in. Jamie studied me with curiosity, as if I'd come out with a bird's nest on my head.

Yes, it's my nest, and I'll wear it proudly. I dare you to criticize my shoes.

"Are you well, Miss Lucy?" Jamie asked; his erect stance bent slightly whenever he spoke to me. It was like he wasn't sure I could understand him from my shorter stature. I'm 5'7", so I wasn't used to being the shortest one everywhere I went, but that seemed to be the case in Jens's land. Or Uncle Rick's. I really wasn't sure where I was anymore.

"I'm getting better." It was at that moment that Jens let himself into the room, not bothering to greet anyone. "I spoke too soon." I backed up, giving the larger men the floor to converse without me.

Jens was all business, accessing none of the biting humor we exchanged in the car. "It's past the midpoint of the day. If we're going to meet with your friends and talk to the king, now's the time. Tor's already at my place, stinking it up."

Jamie shook his head at his friend. "You know you shouldn't be here. If my father finds you've been in my house, he'll have you thrown out for sure. I told you I'd bring her out for you."

A cold look settled over Jens, his upper lip sneering. "I couldn't care less if your father finds me. He's already tried offing me three times. Four would just be amusing at this point."

Arrogant prick. I didn't know totally what they were talking about, but I recognized haughtiness when I saw it.

Uncle Rick's disappointed expression was directed at Jens. "Patience was never your strong suit. It won't do to provoke King Johannes before we meet. Sneak back out, Tom."

Jens glanced at me with a hard look in his emerald eyes. "You couldn't wear a dress to make things easier for us, could you?"

I kept my voice deadly quiet as I glared at him, fists clenched at my sides. "Look, Jimmy, I don't have to lift a finger to make your life easier. And you can get your rocks off looking at women in dresses all the livelong day. I won't stop you. Just look elsewhere."

"Jens," he corrected, steaming already. His posture stiffened as he spoke. "My name is Jens, and if the others don't respect you, they won't listen to Alrik and come with us. It's more important than your precious feelings, what we're dealing with here."

"What who's dealing with? You want me off your team? Fine by me. Drop me at the nearest Y." My stomach was upset, and it was making me more irritable than usual.

"You still don't know? Come on, you can't be this slow." He pointed to Uncle Rick. "Alrik, elf. Jamie and Jens, Tomten. You, human brat."

I bristled, shaking my shoulders as if that might rid me of him. "Lay off, Jens. I'm warning you. You burned my apartment down, let them take my clothes, poisoned me with your vampire fangs, bossed me around and pissed me off." I touched the bandage on my neck. I could still feel the faint sting where he'd bit me. "Get out, Lestat!"

Uncle Rick waved Jens off. "We'll meet you back at your house within the hour. I trust by then you two will learn how to get along?"

I wanted to stick out my tongue, but didn't think that'd be as intimidating as I wanted to appear.

Jens looked like he wanted to shout at me, but held his tongue out of respect for Uncle Rick. He stepped to the door that had far too many locks and bolts on it and tugged on his ear, tossing me an unfathomable look before disappearing.

Like, literally vanishing into thin air.

9

THE KINDNESS OF STRANGERS

Though the sun was unbearably bright, I followed Uncle Rick's robes that flowed ahead of me. That was about all I could see, and even that much was overwhelming and made my eyes water. My eyes were only slits with my hands shielding them, and I wondered if the sun was actually that bright, or if Edward Cullen's venom was making me light sensitive. Either way, I had about a foot of vision. Beyond that, I was left guessing and fumbling.

And falling. I tripped over... something and pitched forward. My embarrassing squeak was interrupted by Jamie, who had been walking beside me.

"Are you alright, Miss?" He reached out and grabbed my arm, righting me before I face-planted on the grass.

"Yeah. Um, I can't see anything. Did Jens do this to me? Why is it so bright here?" I could hear people a few meters out whispering in my direction, but I held my head high. Let them get a good look at the weirdo. Fine by me. It was similar to the time Linus and I briefly attended a middle school where most of the population was Latino and spoke Spanish. They all called me "rubia con chichis grandes", which I tried to ignore. Linus cringed or bit back every time that nickname was used. He got in a lot of fights at that school.

"Allow me." Jamie offered his arm to me, helping me by lacing my arm through his. "Jens mentioned our sun is a bit brighter than yours. It might take some getting used to." When I did not respond (I mean, what was he expecting me to say after that?), he continued in the kind cadence of a tour guide. "Our lands have no set season of death, so the sun beats bright on our crops. Our kingdom has no shortage of bounty. Every year, it grows."

"Would it be cool if I closed my eyes? Can you make sure I don't fall? I really can't see anything, and the sun's giving me a headache."

Jamie consented, and I gripped his arm tighter with both hands. "I confess, I've never met a human before. You're a rarity, to say the least."

"Excellent." Once again, I was the new freak in school. Rule #3: *Don't let them smell your fear.* "And if I remember Uncle Rick's bedtime stories correctly, you're Tomten. Or at least that's what I'm supposed to believe." I was not sure how elaborate a stunt had to be for them to manipulate the sun, so I gave into the inevitable – playing along in my uncle's games.

Jamie chuckled. It was a gentle sound that let me in on the fact that he was a kinder soul. Can't imagine why he kept company with the likes of Jens. "You're supposed to believe it because it's true. I'm Tomten. So are Jens and Britta."

Uncle Rick chimed in from his place in the lead. "Tell me what you remember about the Tomten, Lucy."

I heard a few people passing nearby whispering about the "girl with the yellow hair". I can only assume they meant me, who was stumbling along like the village idiot. Uncle Rick cleared his throat to regain my attention, and I rifled through my mental Rolodex for obscure bedtime stories we'd begged him for years ago. "Tomtens are garden gnomes. Jens gave me the refresher course on his people."

"Good, good." Uncle Rick paused his lesson to scold a particularly emphatic gossiper. Apparently, I was too short to be human. I must be a dwarf.

"So dwarves are real, too?"

"Too real," Jamie answered. "One's already holed up in Jens's place waiting for us."

"Oh, good. I was hoping this would get weirder." I knew Uncle Rick would ask, so I went ahead as if he was my teacher, and I, the student. "Dwarves are shorter, hairy, and they mine for treasure." I probably sounded racist, boiling an entire fake species down to the stereotypes Uncle Rick told me about, but I was past caring about social faux pas.

"Excellent! And do you recall the Fossegrimens?" I could hear the smile in Uncle Rick's voice. I half expected a candy treat, like he used to give us the couple times he helped to homeschool us while we were transitioning schools. I always earned at least double what Linus did, so I ended up sharing some of mine with him at the end of the day. I hated it when Linus was bummed.

I clutched tighter to Jamie, aware that I did not know

him, but also very aware of the other Tomtens watching me and talking about my every move as we passed. "Fossegrimens. Uh, are those the guys that're under some kind of curse from the Siren Queen? They play music that controls people. Fiddles, I'm thinking."

Uncle Rick had a smile in his voice. I could tell he was happy to finally share his real life fairy tales with me. "Not controls. Persuades. There's a big distinction there."

"Right. And they've got a gang war against the Nøkken, who use their singing voices to try and persuade people and nature and whatnot with their songs." I heard a group of people nearby whispering about the girl with Prince James. Apparently, junior high was transferrable to Undraland.

"You are every bit as brilliant as you've always been. If I had a green Skittle, I'd give it to you straightaway."

He remembered.

"Well, they changed the flavor since I was a kid. It's some shade of disgusting now."

Uncle Rick chuckled. His laugh was the best. It was easy to access, and always joyful, never biting. "Now, that is a shame. I suppose I shall just give you a gold star, then." We stopped and he turned, pressing his thumb to my forehead, sticking what I assumed was a gold sticker there.

"Do you just carry a stash of those around with you?"

"This one's a bit more special, if you'll allow me to be impertinent. It's an *arv*."

"*Arv?*" I inquired.

Jamie made some noise of appreciation for what was apparently a grand gift. I felt my forehead, but did not find a sticker. There was a warm, tacky to the touch spot there instead. It began to dissipate into my skin. "What is it?"

"It's my mark. I have a limited number of heirs, so I've marked you as mine. Wherever you go, we'll be able to find each other now. Does that reassure you, even though I had you brought to this foreign place?"

I reached around with my eyes closed for his robes. "If I could see you, I'd give you a giant hug, Uncle Rick. Thank you. Your heir? Like, I'm your daughter sort of?"

"More than sort of. You have family in Undra now."

I paused. "Can I still call you Uncle Rick? I kind of want to leave my dad as my dad, if that's okay."

"Of course." My uncle chortled, deep and velvety, and I could feel the love in his eyes. "You're causing quite a stir, holding onto Prince James like you are. He's betrothed, you know."

Rule #2: Learn the law of the land quick and abide by it, no matter how stupid.

My face heated, and I dropped Jamie's arm. "Jeez, I should've guessed with the whole woman in jeans scandal that it'd be weird for me to be near you. I'm sorry. Wasn't thinking. Do you want me to talk to your fiancée? Let Britta know I'm not stealing her man?" I felt so stupid and turned around. I could sort of make out Jamie's form, but I could not see the amusement he spoke to me with.

"That's alright, Miss Lucy. And I'm not betrothed to Britta. My fiancée is Freya." He spoke her name like it was a species of insect that had yet to be determined as useful to the world.

"Oh. My bad." I held up my hand for a high five to break

the tension. "But prince? Not too shabby, Jamie. That's pretty cool. Should I bow?"

He gave me a gentle high-five. I could tell he didn't totally understand the gesture. "In front of my father, sure. But I'm third-born. Not worth the curtsy." He reached for me again, tucking my arm in the crook of his elbow. "It won't do to have you falling in front of your audience. You're the first human in these parts. You'll want to leave a good impression as a representative of your people."

"Whatever. I heard that woman. They think I'm part dwarf." I kept my eyes closed, but the light was too bright for my eyelids to properly filter. I put my hand over as a blinder. "Why is it still getting brighter out? Not to be a whiner, but this is kinda painful."

Jamie fielded this one. "We just left the city, and it's mostly farms out here, so there are less buildings to block the sun from you." He patted my hand. "Plus, there's probably still a bit of Jens's venom in you. Do you have a terrible stomachache?"

"Yup."

"It will wear off," Uncle Rick assured me. "The after-effects are a bit like a hangover. Let this be a life lesson to you that you never want a real one."

"No, sir."

Uncle Rick called out to someone in the distance, beckoning them to us. Jens answered, and I heard him running closer. Now the whispers around me included Jens's name, too. They spoke of him in the same awestruck and excited way Tonya would have gushed if Vin Diesel walked into the room.

I sighed. "Oh, good. I was wondering if there was a way

to make this whole experience worse."

Jamie's smile could be heard in his tone. "Now, now. He's my best friend. A real solid Tom. He's the best protector we've got to offer."

I had several disparaging remarks to this, but I kept my mouth shut. Jamie was just too sweet for me to burst his bubble about what a jerk his friend was. "That's nice," I lied.

When Jens reached us, he sounded concerned. "Why are you guys taking so long?" He smacked his forehead as it dawned on him. "My venom. Sorry about that. I didn't think about your whole being human handicap." He turned to Uncle Rick. "Foss is on his way. Tor and Nik are here, but they're already starting in on each other. I hope you know what you're doing, Alrik."

"Yes. If you'll excuse me. I'll go on ahead and see to quelling their fight. I fear if I wait for Lucy, your hut will be in cinders by the time we reach it. Excuse me, Goose."

"Huh?" My foot snagged on a root, so I clung tighter to Jamie.

Jens touched my shoulder. "I gotcha."

"Get your paws off me," I warned. "I'm getting along just fine."

I could hear Jens's disapproval. "I can see that. Look, this isn't Ohio. You can't hang onto an engaged man like that, Loos. People are already talking."

I harrumphed, dropping Jamie's arm with chagrin. "Fine! How do you expect me to get anywhere if I can't see where I'm going?"

"Hold onto me instead."

I stopped walking and crossed my arms over my chest,

miffed that Alrik left me with the jerk who attacked me twice and punched out another woman. "Dude, that's not gonna happen."

He let out a noise of irritation. "Fine. Go on to my place, Jamie. Help Alrik get them all cooperating with your diplomat-speak. Tor's out in my orchard, but he'll be back. I'll make sure Lucy doesn't kill herself tripping over her own two feet. Oh, the glory of guard duty."

Jamie trotted off, leaving me to Jens's devices. Apparently I was headed in the wrong direction, because he kept telling me to walk a little more to the right.

"You seem pissed," he observed.

"Well spotted." I huffed when my stomachache started to get to me. "You know, if I had a fiancé, I'd want him to help someone who needed it, even if it was another woman. Your culture is weird."

"You won't get any arguments from me. I'm barely here anymore."

"Because the king wants you dead?"

He scoffed. "If anything, that's a reason to stay. The more King Johannes tries to off me, the weaker he looks. He's an idiot."

"Whatever. Could you rage against the machine a little quieter? Your voice is like a foghorn." Plus, there were people yelling their greetings to Jens, as if he was a celebrity.

"Keep going right. Follow my voice, Loos. Go to your right."

I could hear a group of women nearby gossiping about Jens the Brave and "the human female". Apparently, him being out in the open was almost as much of a scandal as me being here. I could feel people watching me as I walked where Jens led, and I hated it. I felt so foolish, plodding along with my eyes shut, stomach churning and flesh baking in the too-hot sun. "So what's this meeting about?"

"Not really something to talk about in the open." He turned to the side. "Hey, Helsa. Did I miss anything important around here?"

Helsa seemed enthralled that the great Jens was speaking to them, her voice all high-pitched and giggly. *Oh, brother.* "Yes! Farmer Amund's goats got into Davin's potatoes and nearly caused a riot between their families."

The other female piped in eagerly. "And Prince Jamie's betrothed is coming in three days to inspect the land. If she likes it, she'll stay, instead of taking Prince Jamie to her father's kingdom."

"Great," he answered, though I could tell he had opinions about this.

Not to be outdone by her friend, Helsa added, "There's a wolf about, Jens. Do you think you could see to it while you're back? How long do you think you might stay this visit?"

"No idea," he answered, and I could tell he wasn't even looking at her. "To your right, Loos."

"Okay." I took another step, and then stopped. "Are you leading me in a circle?" I cracked open one eye at his laughter, but it was a mistake. The light was so bright, I stumbled back, landing on my rear and making a fool of myself, which only made him laugh more. Helsa and a dozen more people nearby giggled at the stupid, clumsy human. Their exact words.

His voice turned sharp. "Hey! Knock it off, Helsa. She's

not stupid. She knows how to drive a real car."

This inane factoid about me earned deferential gasps. What a culture. I wonder what they would've done if I mentioned my mad parallel parking skills?

I allowed Jens to help me up, and did not even protest when he held my hand and wrapped his arm around my shoulders in what felt like a protective hold. "Please stop making me look like an idiot and get me out of here. My stomach seriously hurts, and you're just parading me around, showing them how dumb I am."

"I'll take you now. I'm sorry. I just wanted to waste a little time out here. Once we get to my place, it'll be chaos. Thought we could have a little fun first."

"Fun? You think any of this is fun for me? People laughing at me? You making me look like a fool in front of your snobby groupies?" I hated that his apology actually sounded sincere.

"Your stomach's really hurting that bad?"

"I just want to lie down somewhere that doesn't burn through my retinas. Can you be a grownup and make that happen?"

"Yeah." He clutched me tighter to keep me from falling when I tripped yet again. "Here, hop on my back."

"Come again?"

"Sure. Hop on. I was being a jerk. Let me make it up to you by being your pack mule."

I rather liked the sound of that. Pretty much any option to get me out of the blinding sun and open ridicule was nothing to turn my nose up at. "Anything that makes you look like the horse's backside you are. Alright." I sized up his back with my hands as he laughed. "Um, you may have to help me. You're like, a foot taller than me." He bent down and reached for my hand, helping me up with a swift yank. I held on for dear life, not used to being this high up off the ground. He set off in the direction I assumed his house was in. "I'm not... um, I'm not too heavy?" I weighed the cons of the five-egg omelet I had two mornings ago.

"How much would you hate me if I pretended to fall over from the extra weight right now?"

"Seven."

"Seven?"

"That's how much I'd hate you. Seven."

"Out of how many?"

"Irrelevant. You don't want me to hate you seven. It's painful."

"Yikes." I could hear the smile in his voice. I hate that it made him seem less of a monster. "Hey, how are you doing?"

Another nicety. I was going to have to work harder to despise him at this rate. I pushed my face to the back of his neck, relaxing when I could no longer see too much light through my shut eyelids. "Oh, you know. New town. New rules. No home. Just another day."

"Homes are overrated."

"You're overrated."

"Ouch." He turned his head in my direction. "You know how when you'd move to a new place, you'd keep quiet for a while until you got the lay of the land?"

"Apparently *you* do," I grumbled. "Thanks for stalking me for so long. Really. Feels great."

"You're welcome. Your family paid me a lot of money to 'stalk' you all."

I thought this over for a minute as he hauled us both up the hill. "So after they died, why'd you stick around? Paychecks had to have stopped then. I know I'm not shelling it out for your stellar services."

"Alrik pays me. I've been working for him for ages. There aren't many of us still on active duty. Most retired." He hefted me higher on his hips. "You know those lawn ornament garden gnomes you see in people's yards? Those get left behind at our last charge's home when we retire."

"You already told me that," I reminded him.

"Well, smarty-pants, it holds a permanent protection charm on the house to keep it safe. Mine'll stay with you, since I'm bound to your family for the length of my career." When I did not speak (I mean, honestly, what could I say to that? I've probably seen a couple hundred of those creepy things on people's front lawns and never thought twice about it), Jens pinched my calf. "I know you've got a million questions. Hit me."

"So, there's lots of you, then?"

"Not anymore. There used to be, but more and more are taking their retirement early. There are only a handful of guardian gnomes in Johannes's kingdom, which is where we are. Most are the gardening kind."

I kept my face buried in the crook of his neck. "Why do humans need protection? Can't all be from bears."

"Pesta. She's the last siren."

"A siren? Like…"

"Like in your English Lit classes you hated so much and should've paid better attention in? Yeah. Pesta's the last siren in existence, and she's chained to the Land of Be."

I sighed. "I love that you think any of those words make

sense to me."

"The Land of Be is a place we can go where there's no pain. There's nothing sad, nothing violent, nothing at all, in fact. You go there to check out. Apparently, it's bliss. You go there to just be."

"Alright. That sounds nice. Why are you guarding me from her?"

His voice took on a serious note, which I did my best to respect. "Because it's not as simple as nirvana. To get in, you have to give her your dominant arm and the use of your soul."

"Come again?"

"That's why when you go there, you don't feel anything bad, or anything at all. She animates the arms and uses them to keep the people there locked inside. Not that they would try to escape." He stomped through a bunch of chickens, ignoring their clucking as they scattered.

"Jens! Slay any trolls while you were away?" a passerby called out.

"Not today. Maybe next time."

"Good to have you back. How long do we get you for this time?"

"Not long. Say hi to your father for me." We kept moving, and Jens was greeted by a few more farmers in a similar fashion.

"Is that the human female, Jens? Well, I'll be. Why've you dressed her as a man?"

The smirk in Jens's tone seemed to be a fairly common thing. "That's her, alright. She's a dangerous one. Caught her with my bare hands." He pinched my calf again, this time with a hint of flirtation.

The audience was floored. "Wow!"

I chuckled into his neck at the sincerity of the stranger's exclamation. "They've really never seen a human before? I don't look that different from them." When I breathed in, I could smell his skin. A caress of sugar cookie dough seemed to waft off of him no matter where I pressed my nose. It was the same smell our house always had, and even after my mom died and there was no one to make cookies, the scent followed me. Even Tonya would comment occasionally and ask if I'd been making cookies.

Now I knew. It was Jens. Sweet as sugar, mean as a bull.

Jens suppressed a slight shiver any man gets when a woman sniffs the back of his neck. Goose bumps broke out on his skin, which we both tried to ignore. I cringed, hoping he wouldn't call me out on my nasal indiscretion.

Jens continued the conversation as if I had not just been a freak who smells strangers. "You're shorter, paler. You wear street clothes. The women here wear only dresses. You have access to all sorts of magical gadgets like phones, cars and things like that. Now, where were we?"

"Um, all the things I hate about you?"

"No, we covered that already."

"Trolls, then."

He hitched me further up again. "Right. Eighteen to twenty feet tall usually, pure muscle and not given to diplomacy."

"Are there actual real live giants around here? I'm trying to be cool, but that'd test my ability to compartmentalize big time." I let out a short laugh. "Big time? Giants? I'm funny."

I could tell he was half-smiling. "You are. Kept me

entertained on many a boring stakeout." He shifted me on his back. "There aren't any trolls in these parts anymore. Used to be, but you don't have to worry about that."

"You slayed them all with your massive gnome muscles?" I teased.

"Shut up." He sniffed. "And, yes, I did. You gonna take back that 'horse's backside' comment?"

"Nope. Giddy up, horsy."

He neighed, which, I admit did entertain me. "But that's not what we were talking about. Pesta."

I nodded into his neck. "Right. The siren who lobotomizes your magical fairy people."

"That's a good summary, actually. So she claims to set the truly pure souls free by giving them a new home inside of bears. Sort of like reincarnation. A second chance at life. It's been in the past few years that she started weaponizing some of the less desirable souls in her possession by using the not-so-pure ones. Breach of her agreement with all us 'magical fairy people'. The bears aren't tame when the souls go inside anymore. They're the Weres you saw when we first met."

"Do they turn at the full moon, like werewolves?"

"Werewolves don't exist," he chided me, as if I were being impertinent on purpose.

But vampires do? You bit me, jackwagon. You injected me with your Edward Cullen poison. "Silly me," I grumbled.

Jens continued on, motioning with his hand. "Pesta only has dominion over bears, and they don't turn at the full moon. The moon's got nothing to do with it."

"What about the Weredogs we saw in the parking lot?"

"Exactly. That's part of the problem. She's only allowed

to put souls inside of bears. That's a big step out of bounds."

There were a few beats of silence before I spoke the non sequitur that had been on my mind. "I don't like that you punched that Stina girl. You shouldn't solve your problems with violence, least of all violence against women. Kind of makes you a giant tool."

He sighed. "I can't believe it took this long for you to bring that up. Stina's a Huldra. She can control people with her whistle. It's not just suggesting things like the Nøkken and Fossegrimens can do. Huldras are women that can actually control us. Part of Pesta's agreement to allow herself to be confined to the Land of Be was that she wanted the Huldras banished from Undraland." He cleared his throat. "Stina was about to whistle me into doing something, and I won't be controlled like that. It's dangerous, Loos. She could whistle me off a cliff, if she wanted. One guy who got tired of her was whistled into the middle of the freeway. I won't go out like that."

I leaned my chin against the thin rope around his neck that dipped in the front under his shirt. "Oh. I guess that's pretty bad. Still, it scared me. If you want me to trust you at all in this, you can't go punching women in the face. Pretty much common sense 101."

"Since there aren't any Huldras in Undra since they got driven from the land, I can agree to that."

"What are we doing now?"

Jens paused, probably debating if I would screw up the master plan. "Alrik cherry-picked a handful of us for a mission involving standing up to Pesta. He's pitching the plan to everyone as soon as they all get to my place."

I let the flood of questions I still had lap at my insides until they quelled. There were too many things I didn't know, and each thing he answered only presented me with more questions. I clung to my gnome in silence as he wore me like a backpack up the grassy hill.

"You're all quiet now. That usually means you're freaking out."

I frowned when I tried again to open my eyes, but was met with the same blinding sun I was not even close to getting used to. "I don't think it's fair that you know things about me a stranger shouldn't. I don't like it." I hugged his waist tighter with my thighs when he reached the plateau at the top of the hill. "You don't have any pictures in your house."

"That doesn't sound like a question. How unlike you."

"You don't have anything there that marks it as yours."

"Still not a question. Stop psychoanalyzing me."

Nice try, jerk. You poked the wrong bear. "It's like everyone knows you, and no one knows you. Kinda sad."

"Do you want me to drop you? Because I will."

I held on tighter, in case he wasn't bluffing. "How much time do you spend here? I mean, you're off my case probably, and you're already signing up for some secret mission with Uncle Rick? What's got you running?"

"I swear, Lucy." His threat went nowhere, but I could tell there was more to that sentiment. "Don't go asking questions you don't need the answers to." With that, Jens ran down the other side of the hill, as if he could outrun being seen by the girl with her eyes still clenched tight.

10

A GIFT FROM HELSA

I thought I was good with weird. I'd seen enough in my travels, but this was a new thing entirely. "You're a Nøkken, and your name is Nik? Nik the Nøkken? That's cute."

Jens rolled his eyes as he drank the homebrewed "Gar" Nik brought. "Actually, it's as common as Nick is in your world."

"Oh." Why did Jens have to make me sound like an idiot in front of the model from the Swedish Alps? Nik was tall, like the rest of them, young thirties with a charming smile I am not ashamed to admit I found attractive. It's like once I got my eyesight back in the comfort of the cabin, my eyes only wanted candy. Yum. The only thing weird about Nik that I couldn't reconcile was his hair. It was a bluish white, styled like a Disney prince, and had a brush of iridescent sparkles throughout. He stood with perfect posture and his chest puffed out, his movements slow and graceful. A young Baryshnikov with a roguish smile.

"And you're a human?" Nik asked, stirring the tea Britta brought him that he poured a little Gar into.

"Yup. Since I was born."

He eyed my hair with admiration as he sipped his beverage. "Wow. Blonde hair. So pretty. Are you all guldies?"

"Come again?"

Jens was not thrilled with Nik being nice to me. "It's slang for golden hair. You'll be the only blonde in Undra-land, so get used to people staring."

Nik's eyes were dancing with excitement at being able to interview the odd creature that apparently I was. "So, you have a typewriter?"

"Um, I have a computer. Had." I jerked my thumb in Jens's direction. "He torched it."

"You're welcome," Jens grumbled, toasting me with a sour expression.

"I don't remember thanking you for that."

"And I forgive you." Jens took another drink. "It's getting crowded in here. Pets outside." He shoved me toward the door, passed Uncle Rick and Britta, who were in quiet cahoots over a jagged knife I recoiled from.

Oh, I wanted to smack Jens. Martin Luther King, Jr. would've been very disappointed in the mental images I was entertaining. His personality went hot and cold in an instant. I couldn't even have a conversation without it turning bitter because of him. I was grateful he'd been invisible all those years he was protecting us. *Jerk.* "I'll miss you and your hospitality so much. Really. Thanks for bringing me here only to throw me out." I blew him a spiteful kiss he blanched at, and turned to exit the hut.

I ran smack into the most enormous and terrifying man I'd ever seen. Easily seven feet tall, Mediterranean tint to his skin, horizontal lines tattooed up his forearms like rungs of angry ladders and an expression that tolerated zero irritations, which I quickly sensed I might be to him. He looked kind of like The Rock to me, but without that adorable charm that makes you want to just pinch his cheeks. The charm was replaced with an unhealthy dose of loathing.

In response to me running into him, he shoved me.

Jamie postured, but no one said anything.

Nik stood. "Foss was brought in on this? Really? I don't know how I feel about this, Jens."

The angry newcomer slid his quiver full of arrows off his shoulders and dumped it in my hands without so much as a second look. "Sharpen these, rat." He had a gold ring on his finger with a ruby so giant, I had to look twice.

I raised my eyebrow to Jens, who took the quiver from me and sent me out the door before I could address his rudeness.

The sun was growing less painful as it neared early evening, so I could make out almost two feet in front of me if I squinted. I sat in the dirt and leaned against the hut, irritated I'd been cast out from the grownup table like a child.

About half an hour later, a gaggle of girls around my age or a year or two younger came giggling up to the house. When they saw me, they stopped short, ending their feud over which feature of Jens was their favorite.

"That's her!" One of them said, pointing at me. "You're the human female that belongs to Jens, right?"

Great. Now that's my title. "Lucy," I said, standing to offer my hand to them.

My limited field of vision kept me in the dark as to their predetermined disdain for me. While the farmer guys seemed awed by the sight of a human, all these girls saw was competition. I would recognize that look anywhere, no matter what world I was in. It was the universal hatred for anyone with bigger boobs that's standing in the vicinity of the man you want.

Super.

"Lucy? I'm Helsa, and this is Kerena, Inga and Siri."

"Hey."

Helsa did not look too pleased with me. They were holding baskets of homemade food and a pitcher of water for their returning hero. "Well, I don't know if you heard, but Jens is already spoken for."

I shrugged. "Have at him. He was only assigned to my family. I have a boyfriend back home." This seemed to mollify a couple of them. I fished around for a name. "His name is... Vin. Vin Diesel."

Darn you, Tonya.

Their leader was a foot taller than me, easy. Everyone in this world was far taller than me. "Jens and the princess are together, so don't get any ideas, human."

Their princess is slumming it with that jerk? What is this kingdom coming to?

The redhead piped in, "Yeah. Everyone saw the way you were hanging on him."

Come on. No matter where I go, into my life, a little Helsa always falls. "You mean when I was literally hanging on him because I can't deal with your sun? He was just getting me out of everyone's hair."

"Are you a dwarf? I swear, I've never seen a full-grown woman so short. Unless the rumors are wrong. You're marrying age, right?"

Red light! "Um, no. I'm twenty. And where I come from, I fit in just fine at this height." So long as there aren't any supermodels around.

Helsa looked up at the pinkening sky curiously. "Oh, my. It looks like it's going to rain soon." Then she took the pitcher and dumped its contents over my head.

Martin Luther King. Martin Luther King.

I stood there, soaking wet, searching for the remnants of my kindness, which had gone missing at their arrival. "You know, if you wanted a crack at Jens, he's wide open. Trust me, I'm not the reason he won't look your way."

Yeah, I provoked them that time. Helsa pushed me square in the chest, knocking me down.

"Now, ladies," a gravelly accented voice of a man interrupted the mean girls' showdown. "Ya don't have ta fight over me. There's plenty of me ta go around. Plenty. I don't care what ya've heard. Dwarves got plenty."

The girls placed their gifts for Jens in front of the door and scattered at the presence of an actual adult.

"What're ya doing there on the ground, female?" A hand with thick red hair on the back extended itself to me, and I found myself being lifted off the ground by a very short man. He looked me up and down, as if appraising me as an ally. I was about six inches taller than him, but his wild red hair was so wiry, it stuck up almost to my height. "You're Alrik's human female, aye?"

"I guess I am." I extended my hand to greet him, but he continued sizing me up with a squinty eye. "And you are..."

"Tor. I hear humans are lazy, and here I find ya sitting on the ground outside the most important meeting of century."

I frowned, not liking his tone. "I've been banished. Circus freaks outside, VIPs inside." I nodded to the door. "Knock yourself out."

A melodic laugh flowed toward us from inside. The dwarf cringed. "Nøkkens. I can't believe it's come ta this." He shook his head at me, as if I should be just as upset at the Nøkken coming as he was.

"Humans, Nøkkens and dwarves. Oh, my!" I pulled my humor from *The Wizard of Oz*, but upon the dwarf's distrustful evaluation of my intelligence, I shut my mouth. I was dripping where I stood and wished for a towel. Actually, if I was wishing for things, I'd genie myself out of here.

I would also like a puppy.

"Get inside, female. Ya've got every right ta be here. Humans should be just as outraged as we are about Pesta." He made his opinion of her perfectly clear by spitting on the grass a thick, green globule. "Represent yer race with honor."

"Alright." Sure. Kick me out. Scold me for obeying. Dump water on me. I don't care. Whatever gets me out of here fastest. Maybe my new place can have a dishwasher. Wherever I land, I'll be sure to get it sprayed for garden gnomes after this.

When I entered with Tor, Uncle Rick quieted the men in the cramped space. Boy, did the cabin smell like man feet. Gross. "Lucy, have you been playing in the water, dear?" my uncle asked me.

"No," I grumbled, shooting Jens the evil eye as the room quieted at the sight of a sopping wet woman. "Just the welcome wagon for Jens. Might want to spread it around that I'm leaving soon, and I won't be sticking around to win whatever lump of coal passes for your heart."

Jens grimaced. "Sorry about that. Was it Olina?"

"No."

"Saga?"

"No. Sheesh! How many delusional women do you know? It was Helsa and her cronies. The sooner you send me back, the better."

Jens softened, handing me my green backpack. "Change of clothes in here. But Lucy," he began, and then stopped. The look in his eyes made me pause.

"What?"

Uncle Rick stepped in and delivered the blow for him. "You're not going back just yet."

"Fine. I can wait until tomorrow. You're having your meeting. I'll go back outside." Seven sets of eyes stared at me, observing the human in her new habitat. Nik, who was sitting down, had risen to acknowledge my presence.

"Go change," Uncle Rick ordered. "I'd like you to join us when you're ready."

11

THE FELLOWSHIP OF THE RAKE

I locked myself in Jens's cramped bathroom and fished through the pack for something dry that felt like home. *Ah, my lucky red Partridge Family t-shirt.* It was the good kind of T that was so washed, it was soft as a blanket. It was my nice people barometer. The Partridge Family has hardly any following by my generation, so when someone does comment on it, it's usually the nice ones. The beatnik flower children who don't cause many problems. Crucial weeding tool for starting over in a new place. Plus, the Partridge Family is awesome. You try being in a bad mood when David Cassidy's telling you to "Come on, Get Happy" with that cutie pie smile of his.

I changed in record time, hanging my wet stuff up on Jens's rustic shower curtain rod. I took a moment to put my hair in clips so it didn't drip in my face. When I emerged, everyone stared at me, as if they had not moved since I left them. "Um, hi. Carry on, guys. Don't mind me."

"Actually, we were just about to start. Everyone's here, and this concerns you, too." Uncle Rick motioned for me to join them.

The cabin was small, built for one large jaggoff. Filling it with five oversized men, one tall woman and a dwarf made comfort impossible. I decided to sit on Jens's straw mattress, since that was the only space not occupied.

Uncle Rick called the meeting to order, stopping a few brewing arguments over which of their war heroes was great, and which were blights to their kind. I was just glad to be out of that blinding sun. I could actually see in here.

My uncle stood in the center of the room with his bearded chin raised. "Most of you know why I've called you all here. Thank you for making the journey. There are some who were invited that chose to ignore my summons." This brought about a grumble in the ranks. Uncle Rick continued, "There's no other way to say this, so please hold your questions until the end. Pesta is on the move." Despite his request, questions broke out, and were promptly ignored.

Jens whistled to rein everyone back in.

Uncle Rick continued. "Thank you. As I said, Pesta has become unsatisfied with her number of souls, so she's petitioning to recruit more. I have it on good authority that she's constructing a portal for humans to add their souls to her collection."

Then there was chaos. So many robust personalities in one room collided and made for a noisy audience. Uncle Rick clapped his hands. "Some of you are aware of her recipe for constructing a portal using the broom of the first siren. She uses a myriad of spells to enchant the entrance, which is built out of the bones of the race she wishes to capture. She has stolen almost enough bones to make a new portal. Humans are the only race she has not yet conquered." His use of the word "conquered" cause many disparaging comments. Poor Uncle Rick. I was beginning to understand the plight of the average substitute teacher trying to maintain control over a new classroom.

Nik spoke up, his blue-white sparkle hair perfectly in place, setting off his glowing white teeth nicely. "Maybe she's just repairing one of her existing portals. What race were the bones from?"

Uncle Rick's answer brought about silence to the arguers. "They were from a human family who were also Undran." He turned to me, now that the room was deadly quiet.

"Huh," I offered lamely. This was all very interesting, but I could not imagine why I needed to know any of it. I was light years behind everyone else in the room, as far as magical world knowledge went. Uncle Rick was sweet to slow things down for me.

"The portals are taking in too many. Soon it will be that the number inside exceeds those of us in Undra. I believe Pesta's on the verge of waging war against us. Targeting humans is her last move. After she depletes their population, we will be helpless to stop her from overpowering us all."

There was silence still, a few wary glances exchanged to imply uncertainty of Uncle Rick's accusations. "That's a bit of a leap, don't you think?" chimed in Nik.

"Not at all. The souls she welcomes into her Land of Be are not prone to aging or death. They keep adding to her numbers daily."

"Sure, but they're stuck in Be, so there's nothing to worry about," Nik argued.

Uncle Rick was patient. Linus and I had trained him well after years of "Are we there yet" and "I don't understand". My uncle's voice only grew quieter, forcing even the noise from shifting feet to die down. "Pesta's already breeched the contract she made with the kings when she was originally sequestered to the Land of Be." Then, with an air of awesome finality, Uncle Rick dug in his satchel and pulled out a dead bunny.

Well, it was sort of a bunny. It had a squirrel's tail, brown bunny face and ears, and its body was striped brown and black, like a raccoon's tail. For the sake of argument, we'll call it a bunny.

Uncle Rick smacked it on the floor in the center of the room. "This is what she's done. This kanin had a soul in it. The treaty stated she could have dominion over the bears, and she promised to give the peaceful souls free reign inside the bears. A second glimpse of life for the worthy. The Other Side now has all manner of Were animal, inhabited by souls that are anything but peaceful." Then he turned to me. "Jens, can you attest to there being Weredogs on your side?"

Jens nodded, his arms crossed over his chest to fend off any disbelief that might come from the others. "Three Weredogs were tracking us on the Other Side. Pesta's gone way past her boundaries. The souls she put inside them weren't the peaceful kind, either. Hunt to kill."

Uncle Rick continued, motioning to Peter Rabbit on the floor. "This is a Werekanin. Jens found it in Undraland and brought it to my attention."

Questions and comments broke out once again, shattering the hold Uncle Rick had on the conversation. The bunny carcass was poked and prodded until each member confirmed it was a Were animal. I was grateful no one passed the poor thing to me.

"It's impossible, Alrik!" Foss protested. His voice was deep and made me want to look away, lest he get angry with me. I kept my body tight to the corner of the cabin atop Jens's bed with my knees hugged to my chest.

Uncle Rick slid open the bunny's furry eyelids, revealing pale yellow irises like the Werebear and the Weredogs that attacked Jens and me.

Foss's voice was stern, his face etched in a scowl that appeared permanent. "This thing you're telling us, it's not an option. She's tried making a portal from human bones before, but they never worked."

"Ah, but these bones came from two Undrans who married and reproduced. A Huldra woman and a half-human, half-elfin man." Uncle Rick turned to me. "The half-breed was a friend of mine who grew up near me in Elvage."

Jamie spoke up, his finger in the air as if raising his hand in class. "I know elves are progressive as far as their stance on intermingling with other species, but a half-human? I'm certain I would've heard of it."

Uncle Rick nodded. "Which is why this forward thinker left Undraland for the Other Side over two decades ago when the Huldras were forced out. He went over with his newly married Huldra wife when she was banished." Uncle Rick turned to me. "Part of Pesta's treaty with the rulers of Undraland was that she would only leave for Be if the Huldras were banished. She reasoned that if sirens were dangerous, Huldras were just as much." Then to me, he explained, "Huldras control people with their whistle, and sirens use their voice." He scratched his beard as he spoke to the group. "We agreed, to our great shame, and Huldra refugees were set loose on the Other Side, which is your world, Lucy. A peaceful race turned bitter overnight."

Britta was playing with her knife as if it was a pencil, twiddling it on her opposite hand mindlessly. "So the half-human half-elfin man married a Huldra, and then they were sent to the Other Side?"

"Britta, you're right on the nose, dear." Uncle Rick smiled. "The half-breed man's mother was an elfish nurse-maid before she got pregnant. She confided in me she had crossed over to the Other Side so she could find a man to impregnate her, since it appeared her husband was sterile. Not even her husband knew he was not the father. They raised their son, the man who grew up to marry the Huldra woman, and retired to Be. No one knew, save for me. I was quite close with the half-breed's mother." He stroked his beard, his eyes far off as if a memory of warmth rose up in him, but he had to put the fantasy away. "Thus, the man in question Pesta found for her human portal is half-elfish, half-human."

"The one that's married to the Huldra," Nik clarified.

Uncle Rick nodded. "Exactly."

Tor's astonishment matched the others', except for Jens, who moved over and sat atop the foot of the bed I was huddled on. Tor threw his hands up, flummoxed. "I didn't know that was an option. Humans inter-doing with Undrans. What's next? A bird with a fish? Pesta must've been looking long and hard ta find that sorry lad."

Jamie shifted his weight from one foot to the other as he leaned against the wall. "But the bones of one man. That's not enough. She'll need more."

Uncle Rick nodded. "And so she hunts for more."

Nik spoke up, his arms crossed over his chest as he leaned on the door. "With all due respect to you, Rick, I don't see what we can do to stop Pesta from creating a new portal for humans. The most we can do is tell our kings and let them deal with it."

"Oh, I plan on doing exactly that," Uncle Rick assured the group. "But I cannot imagine anyone closing their portals voluntarily."

Tor shouted above the arguing this brought about. "But if ya close the portals, the souls're stuck in the Land of Be forever! No one can get in or out, Alrik. That's no solution. Ya close off people's retirement plan, ya'll find yerself dead by morning."

"It's true." Uncle Rick's tone was even. He was always unshakable. I loved him for that. "People go to the Land of Be for many reasons. Some work their whole lives so they can one day leave this world of toil and go there to be free from it all. Others are in such pain, their only way out is either death or Pesta's land of perpetual relief. No one wants to believe she's capable of taking down humans now. No one will admit that she's grown too power-hungry and is zealous for more souls. We were promised the Were-bears would never harm a living person, but we all know she never intended to keep that promise. When that was violated, the agreement should have ended. Step by step, she's taking more ground from us because she knows we will do nothing to stop her. We covet the potential for eternal escape far too much. No one sees what she's really after."

"And ya think ya know?" Tor questioned, his wide gait and too many clanging items hanging off his belt shifted as he spoke.

"Shut up, dwarf," Foss snapped.

"Do ya want ta throw down here? It's been too long since I've strangled a Fossegrimen. Useless fiddlers."

The angry The Rock scoffed. "At your height, you'd be strangling my waist."

Uncle Rick held up his hands, but silence fell only at Jens's commanding bark, which made me jump. "Shut it, or get out. None of you has to be here for this. Alrik and I'll do what we have to, with or without your help."

Nik postured. "The day I leave fate in the hands of a lowly Tomten farmer will be a cold day in the Darklands."

Britta's knife went from toy to weapon in a flash. She postured and darted to where her brother sat on the bed, standing before him with a vicious sneer that belied her genteel language and Amish bonnet. Jamie moved in front of Jens, chest puffed out and a deadly expression directed at Nik, who held up his hands to show he didn't mean to physically attack Jens.

Jamie snarled, "Do you know who he is? Jens the Brave slayed a tribe of trolls to protect the 'lowly Tomten farmers'. You'll show proper respect to a hero in any country."

Nik shook his head. "An aged elf and a garden gnome? You have to know your mission is doomed."

I wanted to slap his arrogant face, but part of me knew Nik was fronting.

Britta drew her knife back, as if one more wrong word would send it plunging into Nik's belly. "My brother is one of the last guardian gnomes. And you'd do well to respect the rest of us."

I always thought of myself as someone who went for blood if you messed with my brother, but Britta took that to the literal interpretation.

Jens stood and crossed his arms over his wide chest. "That sounds like you're volunteering to help, Nik. Good. That's three of us, then."

Foss had enough of a woman posing any kind of threat, so he threw his two cents into the mix, towering over her with his handful of superior inches and dense musculature. His sculpted lips molded into a sneer. "Britta, Britta. I know of your profession. You're the unfortunate soul in charge of taking down and burying the dead bodies after a hanging. I can't imagine that's made you many friends."

Britta lowered her head in show of respect to the great Fossegrimen chief, but I could tell she was still seething. I tucked myself further into the corner. "I don't need friends. I have enough money to live. No one will fight me for that job, so my livelihood's secure."

Foss spoke slowly, gearing up for the punch. "You've never been a proper garden gnome. Known for your knives and your ill-chosen career, but you're certainly not known for your tomatoes." Foss looked down at her chest pointedly.

Jamie and Jens were on Foss in a second. They shouted and punched as the three wrestled on the floor in the small cabin. I could tell neither of them meant to do permanent damage, but it was clear dominance had to be established. Britta couldn't be talked to like that, and Foss would respect it. I stood next to Britta for solidarity.

Uncle Rick rolled his eyes and clicked his fingers. Water shot out of his palms like a fire hose, dowsing the men until they broke up their pit bull fight. This was the thing I shrieked at. Real magic was such a new concept to me. Uncle Rick cast me an apologetic look at introducing me to his quirks in such a manner. I nodded once with wide eyes, letting him know I was only medium freaking out.

Uncle Rick continued on as the sopping boys returned to their corners. "Back to business, children. I propose we close the portals if the nations of Undraland will not do it themselves. Souls are in more animals now. It was one thing when it was only bears. We knew not to eat them. But with this, we could eat anyone's soul without knowing. Then their trip to Be was for naught. Their soul will die inside us, and when that happens, their body will die in Be. Pesta needs fresh souls for the uprising she's planning, and I, for one, will not stand idly by so others can buy into her line of folly."

"This is all well and good," Jamie said, his regal status making the others quiet marginally, "but how do you propose we destroy the portals? That's never been done before."

Uncle Rick nodded to a dripping Jens, who yanked

open his red drawstring pack and reached his arm all the way in up to his shoulder. He fished around and pulled out... my dad's old rake?

"Holy Mary Poppins, Batman!" I exclaimed without thinking.

Jens tossed me a cocky smirk at being referred to as a superhero. "I'll answer to Batman."

I knew from experience that the handle was not collapsible, but the entire thing emerged from the average-sized pack. No one said anything to this bit of magic, but it was new to me.

Sure, my parents were sentimentally attached to the rake. They'd jumped over it at their wedding, so it hung over the entrance at every house we'd lived in. It was a nice constant in our world of change, so I respected the tradition.

However, nothing like the reverence these men stared at the rake with had ever crossed my face when I looked at the old, wood-handled garden tool. I sat back on the bed as I observed the awestruck reactions around the room.

"Is that... It can't be!" Nik exclaimed, his hand cupping his mouth.

Jamie placed two fingers on it with great deference. "This is Pesta's rake. I recognize it from the paintings. Her lost rake that keeps the souls in Be."

Um, okay. Better use than I have for a rake. I was just, you know, raking leaves with it or letting it collect dust in the closet. I hadn't even noticed when Jens ganked it from the apartment.

Foss and Nik stepped back, not ready to touch it. Uncle Rick stood straighter, now that he had their attention. "She uses her broom to build the portals, but the rake destroys them, among its other uses. This is how we'll save future souls from Pesta's use." He motioned to the dead bunny creature on the floor. "Then we'll have to simply face our lives and accept them for what they are – the good and the bad."

"Where did you get this?" Jamie asked with wide eyes. "It's rumored to've been stolen from Pesta, but no one's seen it in years! Do you know it's treason to have this in your possession? It belongs to the last siren, evil though she may be."

Uncle Rick's voice turned sharp, and I instantly shrunk. "I'm aware of the grand tradition of people stupidly turning on their own to protect a false promise of happiness. That's why you are the only ones who know about the mission. About the rake."

"Where did you find it?" Jamie asked, mesmerized by the important piece of history. He didn't look greedy, just flabbergasted at the awesomeness that was my family's old rake.

Uncle Rick stroked his beard, purposefully avoiding my eyes. "When Pesta demanded the Huldras either be banished to Be or to the Other Side, the young Huldra girl married to the half-breed was enraged. She signed up for Be, pretending to submit to an eternity separated from her soul. She marched through the portal and attacked Pesta, hoping to kill the last siren who would scatter her people so." A fond look of fatherly pride sparkled in his gray eyes. "Though every Huldra was incensed, she was the only one with the courage to do something about it."

Foss clenched his fists. Then he grabbed the only chair

that was not being used and smashed it against the wall. "I've never heard tell of this!"

I covered my squeak of fear with my hand, but suddenly really wished I wasn't in the furthest corner from the door. I wasn't used to such violent mood swings.

Instead of fighting back, Jens rolled his eyes. "Really? Do you have to keep the Fossegrimen stereotype alive? You have to Hulk out and smash my furniture? Be cool, Foss."

Foss fumed as if he wanted to obliterate Jens's face next, but Jens did not dial back his cocky stance.

Uncle Rick kept speaking as if there had been no interruption. "It was foolish. The girl had no help, only a strong will and a plan." Another small smile touched his face. "But she was never afraid of anything. She knew what needed to be done and never backed down from a fight. She didn't know she could trust me with her intent back then. I would have helped her finish the last siren."

This brought about more shouts of confusion and strong opinions.

Uncle Rick continued. "The young woman did not succeed in killing Pesta, but she did wound the siren, stole her rake and escaped with her soul intact. One can only come out of the portal with Pesta's rake in hand. This young woman is the only soul to have gone into Be and come out still in her body, unharmed."

Jamie whimpered slightly at the thought of the precious weapon falling into the hands of a manipulative Huldra.

Our rake. A fearless woman. Please don't be my mom. Please don't be my mom. My mom's a human. I'm a human.

Tor's fist in the air demanded answers. "Who? Who's

this Huldra, and why haven't I heard of her before? Ya've got her rake, but not her?"

Please don't say my mom.

Uncle Rick turned to me with the same determined face he'd come to me with when he had to explain that Linus's chemo stopped working. "Upon her recent death, it was given to her daughter, born of the half-elf, half-human man. He served as Hilda the Powerful's guard when she fled to the Other Side after her assassination attempt failed."

"Hilda the Powerful?" Foss questioned. "I remember stories about her. She was the strongest Huldra of her generation."

"Indeed," Nik agreed. "I believe there's a song about her from my childhood."

My heart began to pound and my arm hair stood as Uncle Rick's hand swept toward me as if in slow motion. *No. Please don't say my mom. My dad was a normal dad! Please don't say my parents.*

"Gentlemen, may I introduce to you Lucy Kincaid, human daughter of Hilda the Powerful and Rolf. Sister of Linus. Rolf had enough magic in his bones to be of use to Pesta, but also enough humanity in them to open up the doors to add humans to her catalog of souls. The portal is incomplete, but Pesta's searching for any trace of Hilda's human family to complete her portal on the Other Side." He turned to me and mouthed, "I'm sorry."

My mouth tasted like cotton. I had no idea how long it had been hanging open.

There was more information to grasp, but I was overflowing with confusion and white noise.

I was cold on the inside and felt freezing on the outside, despite the Florida-like temperature in the air.

My mom had this whole other life before me. My mom lied to me.

My eyes slid out of focus, and then my mind went blank.

SOMETHING TO FIGHT FOR

I suppose they were talking to me, but I heard none of it. It's possible I was asked important things, but nothing after that blow mattered.

I mean, come on. If what they were saying was true, the magical world of Narnia had been around me my entire life without my knowledge. It was… everything was…

I guess there's just no finishing that sentence.

Uncle Rick was saying something probably important, judging by the look on his face. Someone was patting my back.

Jamie.

Okay. I don't mind Jamie being nice to me. His harem might stone me for being in arm's length of him, but whatever. At this rate, I doubt I'd feel anything short of a bullet through the gut.

My mom and dad had lied to us. Our whole lives, there was a world we drew blood from that we knew nothing about. There was no Witness Protection Program or whatever that kept us moving. It was my parents running from Pesta, hiding the rake.

Did we have relatives here? Would their bone marrow have worked when mine wasn't enough?

Nope. Not going there. That memory gets tucked away for a time when I can afford a proper mental breakdown. I don't have time for that right now.

I stuffed all sorts of things away so I didn't vomit all over Jens, who was in my face saying... something. Not that Jens didn't deserve a faceful of chunks, but being that I was the first human most of these guys had met, I guessed some measure of decorum was a good idea.

So I sat, unblinking as Uncle Rick and Jamie talked at me. At one point, Uncle Rick picked up a wrist that looked like mine and slapped my face with the hand. I suppose that should make me mad.

But I felt nothing.

Nothing, that is, until Tor hefted me up, pulled me to his level by the front of my shirt and growled in my face. "Pull yerself together, female! Ya've got a choice ta make now, so either get up and fight with me, or go home and bury yer dead. But anyone who sits there and does nothing *is* nothing."

Finally my lips moved to speak to the abrasive dwarf. "I already buried my whole family."

Tor looked me dead in the eye with so much resolve, it must have been transferred to me through osmosis. "Then it's time fer ya ta stand up and fight with me."

I nodded, righting myself when he released me. I took in the room around me and nodded. "So, what's the plan?"

"That's my girl." Uncle Rick smiled through the pain

of mine that somehow attached itself to him whenever I was too sad. "We have the rake, which is the tool to destroy the portal. We'll go to each kingdom and petition peacefully the king to see if he'll help us. If he won't, we'll do it ourselves." He nodded to everyone around the room. "We'll need someone from each race to use the rake to break the portal. That's the only way it can be done."

"I'm in," Nik offered, spitting on his palm and shaking Uncle Rick's.

"Ya know I love a good fight," Tor chimed in, spitting in his palm and doing the same.

Jens and Jamie also did their gross man handshake with my uncle.

Foss hesitated. "The Tomten prince is going?"

"Yeah. What of it?" Jens challenged, puffing out his chest.

Foss's terrifying, yet handsome face seemed to be permanently stuck on "murderous glare" mode. "Don't play stupid. I know of his curse."

Jamie's cheeks turned pink, and he looked up at the ceiling as he growled out his frustration. "Wonderful. How many others have you told, Jens?"

Jens pounded his fist to his chest, his expression wounded. "That was a quick stab, brother. I never said a word."

Foss's body language was tense, always leaning forward as if readying himself to go into the ring. "I'm one of the four chiefs, prince. Information pays if you know what to do with it." He spoke Jamie's title like it was a jab. "Or do you forget I'm more powerful than you?"

I didn't need to catch all the lingo to know I was witnessing their version of a cockfight.

Jamie sighed. "Yes, the curse is real, and yes, it still affects me. But Jens knows how to handle me when I need handling, so there's no need for worry. My bow and axe are as good as anyone else's. Take them or don't." He leveled his gaze at Foss and sniffed. "Unless one of the great Fossegrimen chiefs is afraid of the dark."

Foss growled, low and dangerous. His too-large muscles were tensed.

Jens moved to stand in front of me as we all watched with bated breath the verdict unraveling before us. "Easy, Foss. Jamie's curse is manageable. Alrik and I'll be there to watch him the whole time. Plus, it's not like the Fossegrimens got away from Pesta without winning a curse of their own. You don't see Jamie batting an eye at working with you."

"My curse is nothing compared to Prince Jamie's," argued Foss, fists clenched. "And you and I've worked together before just fine," he said to Jens, as if that alone should have nullified his apparent curse.

Jens nodded. "We work well together, Foss. You trusted me then. Trust me now in this. Where Jamie goes, I go."

Guys are weird. They'd just been insulting each other and wrestling on the floor, but now it's all oaths and loyalty.

Foss looked between the men warily, his mouth drawn in a tight line. Finally, Foss spat in his hand and shook Uncle Rick's. "I don't trust the prince, but I trust you and Jens."

"Splendid. We're becoming a team already." Uncle Rick

was unperturbed by the tension in the tiny cabin. He moved to me and placed his hand on my shoulder. "Lucy, dear? What say you? Will you help us?"

Why was I here? I wasn't magical. Then it clicked. "Oh, you need me when it's time to destroy the new human portal that's not up and running yet. Gotcha. But why me?"

"Because you're in a unique position to help us. Plus you're sufficiently motivated, given what Pesta did to your family."

I stared at my uncle and voiced the thing he would not say aloud. "And no one will miss me while I'm gone. If I die in all this, no one'll ask any questions."

Uncle Rick shook his head sadly. "I hope it doesn't come to that. I would miss you terribly if you were gone. I am not 'no one', and neither are you."

When Uncle Rick looked on me with that poor little orphan Annie expression I'd grown to hate from people, I postured, sticking my hand out to Uncle Rick's clean palm. "I'm in."

13

PEARS AND PARTINGS

I was getting a crash course in magical creatures, and I was determined not to drown in the tidal waves of new information. So far, the fact that stood out the most was that the different races did not get along. Nøkkens and Fossegrimens actually despised each other. Nik and Foss were so antagonistic, Uncle Rick sat in between them as if they were children needing a timeout. I recognized this because he'd done it quite a few times when he babysat Linus and me. Though, to be fair, we were actual children, not grownups behaving so.

"You should be hanged by your fiddle's strings for drinking out of our river!" Nik shouted. Actually shouted.

"That river belongs to the Fossegrimens, and you know it! Flanders the Terrible won it when he conquered your mountains to the east."

"It wasn't his to gamble! It'd be like you betting a rainbow on a poker game. You can't promise a river you don't own to someone. Typical Grimen society. Pretend there's a rule to follow when it suits you, ignore it when it doesn't. Plunder and pillage."

"At least my king doesn't allow the Nøkkendalig to fester in our waters!" Foss said with his nose and fist in the air.

Then the fighting really picked up.

This stupid river was a huge source of contention between these two peoples that sounded pretty similar. Nøkkens apparently could persuade people with songs, while Fossegrimens used their fiddles. I didn't see the difference, but boy, did they ever. The two could've been cousins. Fighting like brothers. Over a river and a bet placed half a century ago.

Jens eventually threw them out to go fistfight in the backyard to give the rest of us some peace.

Good luck, Nik. Foss is friggin' huge.

Jens brought in the baskets the mean girls left for him and put them on the counter for everyone to indulge in before night fell, and we set out on our journey. Jamie had gone to speak to his father about destroying the portal, and Uncle Rick left to check on his progress, mentioning something about King Johannes of the Tonttu being a slight bit temperamental.

I lay back on Jens's straw mattress and stared up at the roof. I tried to push out thoughts of my family by focusing on the details of the cabin. Wood roof, black pitch to seal it, no furniture other than one workable chair and one in shambles, and no personal touches.

Jens and Tor began making travel plans and stuffing my green pack and other provisions into Jens's Mary Poppins bag while I tried to stay out of the way of the warriors.

Every now and then, I felt Jens staring at me, but I ignored him. Britta began speaking in a quiet voice to him, so I decided to give him some privacy to say goodbye to his sister.

Tor went to go break up Nik and Foss, who were still fighting near the elderberry bushes lining the back of the house. The giant sun was just low enough in the sky that I could see on my own and get around without assistance.

I decided to walk the property in the midday light (that was actually their dusk, bright as it was). It was kind of peaceful. I never spent much time on farms. We mostly migrated to apartments and low-rent motels.

There were rows and rows of pea plants and gourds. Then there were a few lines of cornstalks, which led to a miniature orchard. The tallest non-fruit tree with the thickest trunk had a Frisbee-sized circle carved into the bark, and I wondered what significance that held.

I strolled through apple, peach, cherry, mulberry and pear trees, breathing in the crisp scent of nature that was so pure, you could almost taste the green. I couldn't imagine why Jens would take a gig watching my family pick up and move all over the nation when he could be out in this beauty, but whatever. He was running from something here; that much was clear.

My stomach lurched, reminding me of how little food was in it. I studied the bounty around me, deciding which piece of perfect fruit would hit the spot. I landed on the largest pear I'd ever seen and made quick work of polishing it off.

I sat down under the pear tree and closed my eyes. The day was too much to compartmentalize without something spilling over. Emotion caught in my throat, but thankfully stayed away from my tear ducts when I thought of my dad's body being desecrated by this Pesta character. I mean, what kind of sicko uses dead people's bones for making a door? Granted, a magical one, but still. I was grateful I'd had the option to get Linus cremated. My fist clenched around the heart-shaped vial that hung at my collarbone containing my brother's ashes.

Moisture welled in my eyes and finally spilled over. I gritted my teeth in anger at myself for giving in to this crushing feeling of being so overwhelmed with lies.

I'd pictured my family as rotting skeletons before. It's inevitable with that much death hitting you at once. But now the skeletons were mangled. Probably missing femurs and arms and whatnot. I wiped my tears away, determined those would be the only ones for now. I was glad I was alone.

And then I wasn't. That familiar creeping tingle in my spine that I was being watched hit me, so I straightened and destroyed all evidence of the childish crying. I stood and took a few steps, the grass keeping my movements from being heard.

Whatever was there was following me.

My pulse spiked, and I felt like a wild animal caught in the crosshairs.

Then I ran, not caring that I looked like a clumsy idiot when I did so. If it was Helsa and those girls, they'd have to catch me first. I looked over my shoulder once I was closer to the cabin and saw Jens running after me. I slowed to face him. "What are you doing?"

"Me?" he questioned, coming to a stop. Of course he

wasn't as winded as me. "What are *you* doing? Going off on your own without telling anyone where?"

"I didn't leave your property!"

"Yeah, but I didn't know that."

Then something clicked in my head. "Was that you back there? Were you invisible... watching me?" When Jens nodded with a note of hesitation in his eyes, I grew indignant. "You're not allowed to spy on me! Sometimes a girl needs a moment to herself. My whole world just... That wasn't for you to see!"

He shrugged at my outburst, making me angrier. "It's okay for you to be upset, Loos. It's kind of a big deal, learning about Pesta and the portal and all that."

"I'm glad I have your permission," I snarled. In the back of my mind, I knew he wasn't really being a jerk, but I carried on anyway, taking my pain out on him. "Spying on someone when they're having a private moment isn't cool. If you wanted to check on me, you didn't need to creep on me like that. You want to see me? From now on, I'll need to see you. No more stealth observation of the human."

His green eyes gave me attitude before his mouth even opened. "Fine! It's my job to keep you alive, you know. If you're going off for 'a private moment', tell me where you're going. Now that you know I'm here, keep me in the loop so I don't have to follow you."

"You're off the hook, John."

His fists clenched and his pitch rose. "Knock it off! You know my name now."

I could see it bothered him when I called him by the wrong name. That quickly made its way up my list to weapon number one to be used whenever he needed to be taken down a peg.

"Whatever. You don't have to watch me anymore. I'm not paying you to keep me alive. My parents aren't footing that bill anymore, so if I want to walk in broad daylight in a field, leave me alone about it."

"Yeah, you didn't hire me, Moxie, so you can't fire me. Stop picking a fight with me just so you don't have to feel sad."

If I were a dragon, this would be the moment I breathed fire. "You don't know me!"

He came back just as spirited. "I think what you mean is that you don't *like* that I know you. Well, too bad!" His arms flew out in exasperation. I got a waft of sugar cookie scent, and almost softened as he yelled. "I know you threw up when they made you dissect that pig intestine in Bio. I know you've had one friend in all your moves that you actually liked, and you hate me for taking her away from you. I know that you think jogging is a waste of time, and you put way too much peanut butter on your toast. How can you even eat it like that? It's disgusting!"

"What?" I was perplexed at the barrage of snooping he'd done, and the odd things he had strong opinions about.

"You think designer coffee is for posers, and you had a crush on that Jeremy guy at that school in Jersey, but you were too afraid to make a move. What a chicken! He would've said yes!"

"How did you know about Jeremy?" I demanded, my chest heaving from embarrassment and fury. I scratched an itch on my elbow. "I never told anyone that."

"I read your journal." The moment the words were out

of his mouth, I could tell he wanted to shove them back inside.

"You read my journal?" Even saying the words aloud stung. "You read my journal."

"I was bored!" Jens ran a hand through his messy black hair, and I relished his obvious discomfort at having admitted this criminal offense. "And it's my job to keep you safe. Teenage girls are secretive."

"No!" I shouted, knowing I was headed down a dangerous road. "It wasn't your job to keep me safe. It was your job to keep *us* safe! I've got nothing! No one! I don't care about me! Give me back Linus! Give me back my parents! They were your responsibility, and you let them die!"

Jens looked like I'd punched him, which was now on my bucket list. "How was I supposed to know they made a deal with Pesta?"

"What? They wouldn't be in cahoots with that witch."

Jens nodded. Despite his stoic features, his eyes gave away how much I hurt him with my outburst. "I went home for a day to grieve for Linus. I was a mess, Loos." He rubbed the back of his neck, his eyes refusing to meet mine. "Linus was real bad off right before the end."

"Don't you dare talk about Linus! Don't say his name!" I yelled, my heartbreak hurting anew.

Jens held up his hands to show me he didn't want to fight. He lowered his voice to calm the mood as best he could. "Pesta can't take anyone who doesn't give themselves to her. She can't get out of Be, Loos. Your parents snuck back into Undra the night before Linus... you know." He gulped, nervous I would lose my mind on him.

Good. He should be afraid.

"Your parents spoke with the Mouthpiece. The Mouthpiece is a guy Pesta sends her soul to inhabit so she can have a voice among us. It's how she can interact with the rulers of Undra without leaving Be. Anyway, they met with the Mouthpiece, struck a deal trading their lives for yours and Linus's. Your dad didn't know she was going to build a portal with his bones, or that she'd renege."

Too much information raced through my brain, crowding out any chance of peace. I backed away from Jens, stunned beyond tangible thought. "But... but the cops said they were killed in the car wreck. I saw the report!"

"The report, but not the bodies." Jens shrugged slowly, so as not to spook me. "It was a trade for you and Linus. It was the only way they could think of to save him. Pesta's a pretty powerful siren. Has access to all sorts of magic." His hands reached out and clutched both of my shoulders, making sure I heard him. "Lucy, I didn't know what they were up to. I should've, but I didn't. I... I... all of it. My fault. They thought they were saving Linus and keeping you safe." He rubbed my shoulders, trying to soften me through my thunderstruck demeanor. He brought me closer, his hands stretching behind me to rub my back.

Then he was hugging me.

"They didn't want that life for you. Moving around all the time, never being able to hold onto your friends. They hated it. Sure, they were alive, but Pesta won every time she got close and you guys had to pick up and move. So they surrendered, and Pesta agreed to heal Linus and leave you alone." He closed his eyes. "You know how that ended.

Pesta kept your parents in Be and didn't lift a finger to heal Linus."

After several steadying breaths, I relaxed in his arms, hating the girl in me for breaking down when I should have been running. My voice came out a scared whisper, as if I was afraid my words were powerful enough to shatter glass. "I knew something didn't line up. No bodies? I should've fought harder for answers."

"You were scared." Jens rubbed my back in a way that suggested a lifetime of knowing how to hold me, but never having been given the opportunity. He was equally strong and gentle, supporting my physical and emotional weight as important details of my life shifted and crashed over my head like so many tons of bricks. His hands spanned the breadth of my back, holding me together so I didn't break into seven uneven pieces. "Your parents loved you."

The knot in my chest I didn't realize had grown too tight began to loosen. Inch by inch, I could feel my ribs expanding and contracting, giving me a small bit of myself back in that one conversation.

Jens nestled his chin in my hair and raised his thumb to my cheek, wiping one of my tears away. "I was so turned around. Alrik's the one who put it all together. He beat it outta the Mouthpiece. Every detail. He's been on a mission ever since, putting pieces together and making plans."

There were too many things to say. Too much confusion and emotion to be rational. I was in this beautiful field, and Jens was giving a small piece of my parents back to me.

I tried hard to think of something to say to make sense of things, but I stopped short when an arrow flew through the air and landed square in the center of the large non-fruit bearing tree. The tip sunk deep in the circle that had been carved into it, evoking a girlish squeak of surprise from me. I was feeling childish for overreacting, but when my gaze fell on Jens, a lump rose in my throat.

On alert all at once, Jens released me, and then grabbed my shoulder to make sure I was looking at him. "Run! Get inside and find Foss. Stay right with him, Loos. Go!" He pushed me toward the cabin.

Tenderness over. I was too scared to argue, given the concern in his eyes. I obeyed, bolting as fast as I could.

He hoisted himself up in the branches, yanked the arrow out of the tree and pulled out a quiver and bow hidden in the limbs. I screamed as an arrow flew overhead, as if in answer to the other.

Jens slung the weaponry over his shoulder and followed behind me, passing me with his larger gait. He flung open the door and shouted, "Now! Something went wrong with Jamie and Alrik asking King Johannes for permission to destroy the portal. Journey starts now, guys." He snatched up his red pack and shoved some food from his cabinets inside. He spoke above the commotion to Nik, Foss and Tor. "King Johannes hates me. Jamie just sent a message his dad's coming for me. I have to turn invisible to get us out, which means like it or not, we're all holding hands."

Tor spoke up, hefting his pack on his back with a ready expression. "Yer not strong enough ta vanish all of us. Ya've only got two hands."

I could tell Jens was irritated at the solid logic. "Fine." He switched his backpack so it was hanging off his front.

"Lucy, get on my back. Nik and Foss, take my hands. And Tor..."

"I can vanish Tor," came a quiet voice from the doorway. Britta spoke with her chin high and a knife in her hand, though I could tell she was scared. "Don't argue, Jens. We don't have the time if you want to get to the portal before King Johannes comes for you."

Jens stared at his sister with a grave expression. "Fine, but you're to come right back after we reach the border. Understood?"

Britta nodded. "Of course. I can vanish Lucy, too." She held out her hand to me.

Jens shook his head, his eyebrows knit together. "No. She's my charge."

"Alright. Let's go, Tor the Mighty." She tucked the knife in a small sheath in her apron pocket and clutched Tor's hairy hand. In the next breath, they both vanished before my eyes.

There was no time to comment on this. Jens pulled me onto his back and grabbed onto the other two, turning all four of us invisible as we stepped out the front door. His quick decisiveness meant that no one was pursuing us just yet, and Jens made quick use of the small advantage we had.

I clung tight to him, not holding back my small noises of anxiety at danger creeping up on us so fast. An adventure with Uncle Rick sounded doable, but actually starting out and feeling the fear of the chase was a new thing entirely. While the others would surely be in trouble for pissing off the Tonttu king, I could only imagine what they would do to the human oddity if they were mad at me. I held tighter to Jens, since he was my ticket out of here. I could feel his heart beating hard as I palmed his chest, and wondered how far he would have to run us to get us all to safety. I heard footsteps ahead of us, accompanied by Tor's occasional grunts at trying to keep up with the female gazelle.

We ran toward a rectangular structure about a mile away between Jens's house and a landscape of ominous gray mountains. When we neared the rectangle, I cringed when I realized it was a door made of bones. It had a faint glow of blue wafting out of it, and when we finally reached it, Jens passed Nik and Foss off to place a hand on Britta to be vanished.

I slid off Jens's back, but he grabbed my hand and moved it to the waist of his jeans at the small of his back. "Hold onto me," he instructed, fishing through his red pack and pulling out the rake. "No matter what, don't let go."

"Okay," I answered, my voice pinched. I saw armed men charging from the castle that was miles away toward the village where Jens's house stood.

The portal was in the middle of a few clusters of trees, tall and thick, but were it not for the vanishing, we would have been seen for certain. Jens was breathing hard as he held up the rake like a hockey stick. I stayed directly behind him so I wouldn't get my head taken off by his powerful swing.

In one swoop, Jens knocked the bones of the crest of the arch to the grass. The blue light turned red like a silent alarm, and I tried to keep my fear to a mere whimper. Jens finished the job in three more whacks, and I watched the red light power down like an overused battery.

Jens stuffed the rake into his pack, hoisted me up on his back and resumed his hold on Nik and Foss. Tension was high as they all made excited comments while we ran toward the mountains.

The first portal was destroyed, and it hadn't really been all that hard.

We were half a mile away before we heard angry soldiers shouting. Despite his obvious fatigue, Jens picked up his pace. We were running toward rolling green hills and a space beyond that which was entirely rock, followed by towering mountains. I gulped and tried not to think of my fear of heights. Jens would stay with me through the whole journey. Every step would be guided and guarded by him. For reasons I was not ready to delve into, this quelled my fear.

I looked over my shoulder when we reached the top of the first large green hill to catch one last glimpse of the beautiful farming land. Jens slowed and turned, too, and we gasped as one. In the spot where his home was now stood a towering flame that was quickly catching onto the trees in his orchard. Jens allowed a noise of despair before returning to the flight out of town.

Now the scope of the journey was sinking in. There would be no peaceful encounters with these people concerning the portals. We were on a mission with grim odds, and there was no way out but forward. For me and now Jens, there was no going home.

14

TEMPERAMENTAL TOM

The moment the green vanished beneath us and was replaced by the gray solid rock, Jens slowed. Britta and Tor were a few yards away, catching their breath with wide eyes. Nik and Foss dropped their hands and instantly became visible. Jens and I were still invisible, judging by Britta's head bobbing around looking for her brother.

Jens was not ready to be seen. He covered his face with his hands and breathed heavily into his palms. His home with his scant belongings would not be waiting for him when we returned – if we returned. He was now cast out of his society, and the burden weighed heavy on his shoulders. I debated sliding off his back to give him some space, but it felt cruel to abandon him in such a devastating moment. My grip around his shoulders turned into a hug, and I pressed my cheek to his, my fingertips stroking his half a sideburn. "I'm sorry. I'm so sorry," I whispered, my mouth inches from his.

His hand moved to my messy hair and gripped the locks in solidarity. He took a few deep, steadying breaths, and then did something I did not expect.

Jens turned his head and kissed my cheek.

I like to think of myself as a fairly unshakable person. I mean, my family up and dying shook me pretty hard, but other than that I think I've handled new schools, hardly any belongings and very few friends pretty well. Judging by the way my heart fluttered, I could tell that when my first real kiss came along, it would shake me up more than I would be able to suppress with a cool joke and a smile.

My cheeks heated at the small token of affection from Jens, and I was grateful I was still invisible from the others.

I pushed down the girlish butterflies and focused on the trouble at hand. All the obligatory things people said to me about my family dying popped into my head, and I despised each one. Instead of reaching for the staple, "It'll be okay" or "I'm sorry for your loss", I whispered in his ear as my heart thudded against his, "We'll get through this together, Jens."

I rested my forehead to his temple for as long as it took for his breathing to return to normal. He nodded and relinquished his grip on my hair, and then slid me off his back, switching his pack to his back as we both reappeared to the others. I slid my hand in his and felt his grip hold mine fast.

He'd had my house burned to the ground, but no one had been there to hold my hand through it. Strangers though we were, I couldn't do that to him. It wasn't in my nature to look the other way while someone was suffering.

The four were entrenched in a discussion of how

quickly the Tomten took action, and what this would mean for our plan of getting permission from the peoples to destroy each portal. "We can talk and move," Jens stated, looking up toward the mountain we were expected to climb. "Tomten won't scale these mountains because of the rift with Elvage, but I don't want them to know for sure which way we're going in case the Mouthpiece is nearby."

My lungs felt cold and my mouth went dry. I touched Linus at my collar, hoping for a burst of camaraderie or strength. I'm not a huge fan of heights, especially the harrowing kind that stretch up to the clouds.

Britta's eyes fell on our joined hands, causing a barely noticeable intake of breath to pass her excited lips. I dropped Jens's grip, but instantly felt a traitor.

When she followed along with the others in the direction of the mountain, Jens stopped. "No, Britt. You can't come. It's too dangerous."

Britta's quiet, feminine voice had a note of resolve in it I began to appreciate. "They burned your house, Jens. How long do you think they'll let me go without questioning? How long do you imagine I'll hold up without a male in the family to speak for me?"

Huh?

I could tell Jens wanted to argue, but the logic could not be bested. He shook his head as he hugged his sister in defeat. "This is *not* what I want for you. I would never have let you take Tor if I knew this would happen." He released her. "You don't even have any provisions on you."

"She can share my stuff," I said, taking in her Amish-style dress and the seven inches she had on me. "I don't have much, but it's better than nothing."

Britta's smile showed her gratitude. "It's settled, then. You all heard Jens. Let's go."

Jens led the way for a few meters until he huffed irritably – the first sign of his personality resurfacing. "Loos, you take the lead. You shouldn't be behind me. I don't like not being able to keep an eye on you."

Oh, jeez. "I'm not going to disappear if I'm out of your vision for ten seconds. Unclench, Jens."

"No. I'm your Tom, so do as I say."

There went the glow of our truce. Even my dad knew better than to boss me around like that. I couldn't remember what possessed me to let him kiss my cheek or why I held his hand, the jerk. I blame it on temporary insanity.

My hands found their way to my hips. "I think your mission of keeping me alive doesn't matter when you're trying to keep yourself alive, as well."

"I'll decide what matters." The others passed by, leaving us to our argument. "If I say you walk ahead of me, that's what you do, with a happy little smile on your face."

"Fine!" I tromped on ahead to catch up to Britta, tossing over my shoulder, "Permission to breathe, captain?"

"Only if it pleases me!" he fired back.

Foss growled. "This is why I didn't want any females along on the journey. And now we're saddled with two? We're all going to die."

Oh, I wanted to strangle both Jens and Foss. Martin Luther King, Jr. would not approve of the number of murderous thoughts I had in the arrogant Tomten's presence.

Tor turned around to give us a well-deserved talking to.

"Look, ya two. It's goin' ta be a long hike, so make up and shape up. Yer worse than Nik and Foss!"

"Sorry, Tor," I said, reining in my anger.

"Sorry, Tor," Jens mimicked in a higher-pitched imitation of my voice. "Suck up."

The urge to retaliate was strong, but I resisted, hiking with Britta ahead of Jens, who took up the rear. "Is he always so charming?" I asked his sister bitterly.

Britta smiled and let a small giggle surface. "I've never seen him work his charm so hard before. You know, I always wondered about you and your family. He spent so much time away. Now I understand." She gave me a knowing look I tried to ignore.

"What'll happen to Jamie and Uncle Rick?" I asked the group to change the subject.

Nik answered, turning his head to look at me. "Alrik most likely disappeared as soon as things went south with King Johannes. Toms can go invisible, but Alrik's an elf. He can transport himself from one location to another without detection."

Foss had something to say to this. "Other Elves can sense if someone transports themselves. Magic like that leaves an imprint even we can see."

Nik rolled his eyes, as if I should know Foss was being impetuous. "Sure. Everyone knows that. Alrik will find us soon enough, little human. No need to worry about him."

Britta stepped over a large rock as we began our hike around and up the unsteady mountain path. "Jamie will have stayed in the palace. He'll be safe there. The King would never hurt his son. Jamie's beloved by the people. But Johannes'll keep him there to stop him from running away from the kingdom or going off to destroy the portal. Unless Alrik ported him to Elvage with him."

The way Britta spoke about him took away any question I still had as to their connection. They were involved in some serious moonbeams, rainbows and heartstrings love. It was the stuff I'd read about, but never experienced.

I stepped over a jagged rock, adjusting to the steep incline. I wasn't exactly athletic, but I didn't want to embarrass myself in front of the seasoned climbers. Even Britta in her long dress was faring better than I was. This was their first experience with a human, and I was determined not to make a fool of my kind by breaking a bone on the first leg of the adventure.

15

TIGHTROPE WALKER

*N*ightfall came faster than I was anticipating. Probably because the few dusk hours where my eyes could tolerate their sun felt like noon to my senses. Their moon was massive, as their sun had been, but it had a red hue that gave only the bare minimum of illumination. Britta yawned, and I could see other signs that the travelers were tired, but we trudged on.

"Best ta travel at night." Tor took it upon himself to narrate for me, since I was the outsider in the band of thieves. Nik was a ways ahead of us, scouting the area so we didn't come across any nasty surprises. What those could be, I wasn't sure, and didn't want to find out. "Foss, yer awful quiet. Ya thinking we'll get tha same welcome with yer people?"

Foss had not spoken in nearly half an hour, now that Nik was not near enough to fight with. "I'm certain we'll get it with every nation we visit. We don't come with great news. We come to destroy an old artifact that they see as a service to the people. We'll be hanged for this if we're caught." He shook his head as he helped Jens push a road-block out of the way. It was scary how strong they were. Foss looked like a Mediterranean version of The Rock, and apparently had the strength to complete the picture. "No, it's best we move quickly and quietly. Do the deed and live with the secret, if we live at all."

"Well, aren't ya just a bucket of sunshine." Tor grumbled under his breath and broke wind at the same time. It was really a thing of misfortune that he volunteered to take the lead behind Nik. He couldn't walk a whole minute without oozing some noxious gas out his rear end. It was a good motivator to stay quiet. Didn't want any of that nonsense wafting into my mouth.

Nik came jogging back toward us with news that stayed our progression. His white-blue hair shimmered in the red moonlight, making it look like it had tiny glittering stars in the tresses. "Up ahead's a spindel lair. We can try to scale up or down the mountain if we don't want to chance it."

They debated this while I wondered what a spindel was. Since no one bothered to clue me in, I assumed I would not be granted a vote. We were high up – too high up on the mountain for comfort. I gulped and decided to keep closer to the inside of the trail.

I was right. Neither Britta nor I were asked our opinions when it was decided we would forge through, due to lack of proper climbing equipment. This bothered me not for my own pride, but for Britta's. She did not take offense at being discounted in such an obvious way, but I did on her behalf. I doubled the silent treatment I was giving Jens. Doubling the punishment entailed not speaking... even more. I decided I wouldn't even look in his direction. This did little to hurt him as I hoped it would, since he was behind me and there was precious little reason to look at him anyway.

We reached another roadblock due to a rocky avalanche that had made our path its resting place. The boulder was as high as my shoulders, and had a bunch of smaller, but still giant rocks atop it, making it impossible to move or climb over. The path we'd been walking on was wide enough for someone to always walk on my right, keeping me a healthy distance from the edge. The barrier left only a couple inches of space from the steep drop-off to tiptoe on.

This would be a challenge. I tugged at my necklace, my nerves bundling up inside me, making my hands and feet stiff.

Nik wasn't worried about maneuvering the giant obstruction. "I once fought a Were on a precipice not unlike this one. Not a scratch on me when I finally killed the beast. I could probably dance on that ledge with my eyes closed and be just fine." He tossed me a cheesy game show host grin that I tried to return, but my smile was faked and cracked with fear.

"Let's see it, then," Foss challenged, pointing to the less than half a foot of clear road right on the edge of the path. The drop was abrupt and several stories down, ending in a rocky death. "Dance us a jig up there, Nik. Give us a twirl like a good little barmaid."

Nik held his nose up in the air and stretched his long legs around the obstacle. He didn't even care that there had only been room for the balls of his feet on the ledge.

I cared. My palms were sweaty, and I wondered how to delicately tell them that I was afraid of heights. And falling off them. I didn't want them to think all humans were wusses, but I mean, seriously, climbing the rope in gym class was more than I could handle. I'd never been this high off the ground in nature. Never. Asking me to tiptoe on the edge was beyond my current capabilities.

I really felt like a dunce when Tor managed the feat. He had help from Foss, who held his sleeve from behind until Nik grabbed onto Tor on the other side. Not foolproof, but it worked.

Britta was like a friggin' ballerina twisting around the wide obstacle with her long legs.

"Go on," urged Jens from behind me.

"Um, I'm okay." My voice came out pinched and higher than I would've liked. "You go on ahead. I'll catch up." I cringed that he'd gotten me to talk.

"Nice try. It's easy, Loos. Just walk on your toes and lean toward the mountain."

"Really?" I snapped. "Is that all? Now do I walk one foot in front of the other?"

"That's how the cool kids do it. Come on."

"Don't rush me!" I looked at the narrow space and did my best to keep my racing heart inaudible.

"Useless females!" Foss growled.

Jens threw out his hands. "Don't rush you? Sure, take all the time in the world. We don't have a possible army after us. You've been chased out of town by the king before, right? Maybe you can toss your blonde hair and do one of your flirty laughs to distract him."

"Shut up!" I shouted, the panic gripping me by the throat. "I... I... I can't do this!"

Foss did not bother hiding his frustration. "Just throw the rat on your back and have done with it. Come on!"

Nik came back across the ledge and backed me into the side of the mountain before I fell over to my death from a panic attack. He put his hands on either side of my head and looked me dead in the eye. His gaze was so intense out of nowhere that my fear shifted to confusion. "Miss Lucy," he breathed, a calm smile lighting his features. I sucked in my stomach as he boxed me in with his body.

Then Nik did something that was so surprising, I could only gawk at him with my mouth hanging wide open like a guppy. Instead of speaking his instructions to me, he sang. A low, melodious voice that was meant for beauty floated around me in a dizzying improvised tune. I felt Jens stiffen to my right, but paid him no mind.

Nik sang, *"We're crossing over to the other side of the rock now. You won't be afraid, and you'll follow me wherever I lead."*

Then he leaned into me, still maintaining eye contact as if he was trying to enchant me with his ocean-colored orbs. He breathed heavy in my face, and then placed my hands on his waist.

"Uh, Jens?" I broke Nik's intense gaze and turned to the fuming man beside me. "I think your friend up and lost his mind. You want to deal with this?"

Jens spoke through his teeth as he snarled at Nik. "Look, Nøkken, we have to be able to trust each other on this trip. That won't happen if you try mesmerizing her. Or any of us, for that matter."

Nik released me and stepped back, puzzled. "Why isn't

it working? Have you trained her to resist us? That takes years."

Revelation dawned on me. "Oh! I'm sorry, were you trying to mind control me? I forgot about that part of your people. Go ahead. I'm ready. Mind control me into not being afraid of heights."

"Don't you dare," Jens sneered.

I palmed Jens's face to silence him.

He responded by licking my hand.

"Aw, gross! Sick, Jens." I wiped my hand off on my jeans and tossed my hair over my shoulders, readying myself for Nik's mojo. "Go ahead, Nik." I let out a nervous laugh. "I didn't realize that's what you were trying to do. Kinda freaked me out, singing like that. Thought you needed a head check."

Nik frowned. "Well, if it didn't work before, it won't now. Why isn't it working? I thought humans were easily suggestible."

I kept my voice a sugary brand of pleasant. "Huh. And see, I thought Nøkken were arrogant, racist fools. I guess we were both wrong to think an entire race could be reduced to a stereotype." I gave him a superior look as I tried to reassemble my bearings. I did not often have men singing in my face and looking at me like... well, like that.

Nik had the grace to look ashamed. "A thousand apologies, Miss Lucy."

"Just the one's all I need," I replied with a small smile.

"Really?" Jens did not mask his irritation. "Get back over there, Nik. You don't know the first thing about humans, or Lucy. I've got this."

I hated that he treated me like I needed to be handled. I

geared up to yell at him, but he held up his finger to silence me.

"Do you want to look weak in front of everyone? Do you want Foss to win?"

"I... no."

"Then you will do this." He grabbed my hand and led me to the blockade. "I'll hold your hand on this end, and Nik can grab you from that side. If you slip, one of us'll catch you." I'm sure my sorry puppy expression was visible, because Jens gave me more of the "man up" speech until I could take no more. I wanted to cross to the other side just to get some space from him.

I stepped forward and stretched my arm around the blockade. "Nik? Nik, I can't reach you." I closed my eyes and felt Jens grab onto my other hand. I wanted to bat it away, but decided death was worse than holding his hand for a whole minute. My feet shuffled around to the precipice and inched forward.

Jens huffed. "Loos, you're not moving."

"Yes, I am!"

"Are your eyes closed?"

"Of course!" I wanted to vomit, but luckily my stomach was empty.

"Open your eyes! What are you thinking?"

Foss opened his mouth to complain in his brusque way. "Just stick your rat in a cave or something, Jens. We'll come back for her once we've destroyed the other portals."

My eyes flew open and found Jens's emerald ones in the moonlight. "I don't like this!" I choked out, determined not to break down in tears as I balanced on the edge of the cliff. "I want to go home!" Yes, I know I sounded childish, but I didn't care. You try balancing on a mountain's edge with your butt hanging over the side and see how you like it.

"Are all humans this useless?" Foss questioned.

Jens softened, my fear bringing out a slice of his lurking humanity. "Hey, it's okay. Um, do you remember that awful restaurant in Idaho? The one with the menus shaped like cowboy hats?"

"Huh?"

"You and Linus got food poisoning from the chili cheese fries and spent the whole night taking turns barfing in the bathroom. You couldn't eat anything after that for days."

"I remember. Great, irrelevant story, Jens. I'm kinda hanging off a mountain here!"

Jens glanced around as if he wished he did not have to speak about this with so many witnesses. "I stayed with you that night and all the next day. You were delirious and I was invisible, so I took my chances and held your hand until your fever broke. I didn't let go until you were ready, and I won't this time. I've got you."

I stared into his impassioned eyes and saw in there years of commitment to my family that had not faded. "Please don't let me die on this mountain."

"Never," he promised solemnly. "I plan on your death being something involving a go-kart, a few dozen clowns and cheez-whiz."

"I don't want death by cheez-whiz!" I squeezed his fingers. "And don't be funny! I'm freaking out!"

He smiled as if we were old friends shooting the breeze. "Reach for Nik. Can you feel him yet?"

I stretched toward my goal and gasped. "Nik! Is that your hand?"

Nik's voice came back to me further away than I would've liked. "Yes! You're doing great. Keep moving."

I obeyed as fast as I could, but it was still a snail's pace. Jens tried to let go of me, but I panicked at the thought. "Don't you let go, Jens! I'm not ready."

He responded by clutching my fingers tighter and nodding. His voice was quiet, and spoke peace into my fear. "You have to trust me to know when it's time to let go."

I heard Foss say in exasperation, "This is exactly why I didn't want any women on the journey. They can't handle the mountains."

Oh, I wanted to kick his seven-foot-tall mountain climbing butt. "Do you think my wingspan's as big as yours? Shut your smackhole, Foss!"

"Drop her off the mountain!" Foss commanded. "Talking to a Fossegrimen chief like that."

Jens shook his head to dismiss Foss's grumping. "Don't worry, Loos. Just focus on moving your feet."

I begged Jens with my eyes not to leave me. I knew my mouth would never cooperate and admit that I needed him.

He nodded, as if he knew what I would never say and completely understood.

Nik's voice tried to soothe me from the other side. "Just a few more steps. You're almost there."

"Now, Nik!" Jens commanded as he let go of my hand.

Before I could give in to the terror, Nik gently reeled me over to his side until I'd cleared the avalanche. I was lowered to the ground to quell my shaking as Britta and Nik got in my face and began speaking in soothing tones at a rapid pace. "She's white as a sheet," Britta fretted, mopping the sweat off my brow with her apron. "You poor thing. This is more than you bargained for, isn't it."

I nodded as my chest heaved from relief and extreme dread at what I'd just done. Before I knew it, I was being hefted to my feet and wrapped in a warm hug. The smell of Jens was familiar and comforting. In the back of my brain it registered that he had spent half a decade with my family, so it made sense he smelled familiar, but in that moment, I clung to him and inhaled the soothing balm. I sucked him into my lungs and let him fill me with his strength and peace. His hand palmed the back of my head and gripped my hair, pulling at the roots.

"I did it!" I cackled madly at the success and brush with my greatest fear. "Did you see me? I was a ninja!"

Jens leaned back and beamed at me, and for the first time, I caught a glimpse of how scared he actually was for my safety. "Next stop, trapeze artist."

"No way. Not now that I know you plan to off me at a carnival with all those clowns." We laughed in each other's arms.

It dawned on me when neither of us was willing to let go that Jens had made himself invisible for my family. His job was to disappear. No one touched him. No one talked to him. It began to make sense that he was occasionally grouchy.

I rubbed circles into his lower back and buried my face in his chest. It was a heady thing for both of us, being in the presence of such comfort, and we did not consider breaking apart until Foss cleared his throat.

"We should get moving," Foss said, interrupting our newly acquired calm. "Do whatever that is on your own time."

Britta whirled on Foss as if she meant to give him a thrashing for breaking us apart prematurely.

Jens looked as embarrassed as I felt when we rejoined the group. He situated his red pack on his back and moved me to his left, so I was in between him and the mountain. Even now, he was taking every precaution to keep me safe. He nodded to me and tried to reassemble his stoic personality. "Let's go, Mox."

16

SPINDELS

"So I single-handedly destroyed a coven of Weres armed with only a dagger. Not a scratch on me."

This was hour seven hundred and fifty billion of Nik regaling us with his heroics. Or twenty minutes. I started to lose time whenever he talked about his greatness. It was… great.

"Funny how you never have a scratch from any of these battles," Foss interjected, "or any proof at all. Our slave trade is getting out of hand. Perhaps we should hire you to remedy that."

Nik smiled graciously, giving Britta a shot of his dazzling teeth. "Oh, I think I'll stick to defending the Nøkken borders. Wouldn't want to be a glory hog."

Sometime later (I really missed having the ability to tell time), Nik held up his fist, indicating we should stop. "Up ahead's the spindel lair. Did we decide on fire or trying our luck with stealth?"

"We didn't decide," Tor grumbled. "Ya keep arguing, and we land on the same thing. Fire's safer, but draws more attention ta where we are. Sneaking by the lair'd be tricky, but if it works, our location'd be secure fer now."

Foss and Nik began their usual disagreement, so I sat down and leaned my back on the mountain. I had not walked this much in… ever.

It was pretty dark out, though I welcomed this far more than the blinding daylight. Their red moon was a thing of beauty and grandeur. If mine was a Frisbee in the sky, the one in Undraland was a monster truck tire.

I was bordering on exhaustion, but did my best not to show it. Jens sat down next to me, leaving the others to their debate. He handed me his canteen, and I took a grateful swig.

"How're you holding up?" Jens asked, looking at my mismatched shoes instead of at me.

I shrugged. "Oh, you know me. Bulletproof."

"You don't want to weigh in on fire versus sneaking?"

I glanced up to the others, who were having a heated discussion in hushed tones. "Nah. I'll let Frick and Frack duke it out. I don't actually know what spindels are, so I can't imagine I'd have a useful opinion."

"Spiders. Well, mostly. Spindels are poisonous spiders with black hairy bodies the size of softballs." He held up his fist as a visual of the size.

I turned my head slowly to look at him. "Excellent. So, we're dying soon? Good to know."

"The poison doesn't kill you. It paralyzes you so they can lay their eggs in your body while you sleep. Then they hatch and the larvae feed on you."

My mouth dropped open. "What? Gross! What is wrong with your universe? That's horrifying! When do we get to meet some unicorns, or something awesome?" I shuddered at the thought of spiders crawling up my back and biting me all over.

"They're actually not a big deal because there's herbs that flush them totally out of your system if you come into contact with them. When we get to Elvage, Alrik can get us some. We're almost there, actually. Just another day's trek, and you can get some rest."

"I look that bad?"

Jens turned his head to look out into the night. He bumped his shoulder to mine. "You never look bad."

I was glad the sun was gone, so my confused smile would not be seen. "Thanks. You're one smooth talking garden gnome. In fact, you're the smoothest garden gnome I've ever met."

Jens grinned, the golden diamond-shaped tattoo on his cheek wrinkling around the crinkles next to his emerald eyes. "Good thing you've only met two other ones. Let you think the standard of amazing is me."

I nodded ahead to Britta, who was interjecting politely when Foss and Nik hit a wall in their back and forth. "What's the deal with your sister and Jamie? They're very cutie pie for each other, but it seems like it's all hush-hush."

Jens repacked his canteen and offered me an apple from his sack. "He's the Tonttu king's son. His wife was picked out the day he was born. Freya from the Nisse tribe of Tomten. As a group, they're a little more high maintenance, and Freya embodies that. Jamie's getting to the age where marriage is expected. They didn't do anything wrong, Jamie and Britt. He's my best friend, and she's my sister. Of course they would spend time together if they're around me. They're both solid Toms. Why shouldn't they fall for each other?" He shook his head. "King Johannes didn't like me before, but when he found out Jamie was in love with my sister? Let's just say it was a good time for me to take a security job working for your family in a whole nother world. The only job my sister could get was... you know, the worst one." His words were clipped when he spoke of the king. "Jamie's going to fulfill his family obligation, but it'll kill them both."

"That's pretty sad." I tapped the side of my shoe to his boot.

Jens nodded. "It's very sad. Britta's twenty-two, which is at the tail end of normal marrying age for our kind. I know that's weird to you, being that in your culture women get married or not at any age without it being a big deal, but here it's a stigma. In another year, she'll be seen as an old maid. Like, there must be something wrong with her if she's still single kind of thing."

A few beats of silence passed between us before I spoke. "Do you need me to tell you how messed up that is?"

"Nope. All I want is to see Britta happy. She's pretty independent for a Tom. Not many women choose to live alone. None are as handy with outside work as she is, either. She's had offers for marriage, but she turned them all down. For her, it's Jamie or no one."

"Good for her." I looked up at the woman in a new light. Though she looked oppressed with her quiet nature and Amish clothing, I admired her resolve to stay true to herself and not cave to society's rules when they crossed with her own. "You must be pretty proud of her."

I could feel Jens staring at me. "I am. Funny, but not many people get that. I kinda knew you would, though."

"Single girls unite?" I tried to keep any unhappiness out of my voice. Sure, Britta was an old maid at twenty-two, but someone was in love with her, and she had that bliss of being over the moon for someone. Her singleness was a choice. Mine was every guy on the planet's choice. I shifted uncomfortably on the rocky surface and fished for a change of subject. "So, spiders. That should be fun. Anything else I should know? Got any pterodactyls around? Space monsters? Killer tomatoes?"

Jens snorted. "Boy, Linus would love that."

My smile instantly mutated to a false one as I pushed through the thought of my brother at the dinner table. He had an aversion to tomatoes, calling them The Red Plague. He claimed he was allergic to them, but I still maintain it was placebo. He just hated tomatoes and pretended to have a stomachache whenever they were on the plate.

I didn't like talking about Linus or my parents anymore. Now I was the one with the placebo stomach pains at the mention of Linus's tomatoes.

I stood abruptly with my tour guide smile plastered in place and extended my arm to help Jens to his feet. "Ready to breakdance fight those totally harmless spiders?" I held up my hands like a ninja and jiggled my shoulders to demonstrate what a good dance fighter I could be.

The look Jens gave me was also wrapped in a smile, but beneath the layers, I saw pity. That accursed pity I could never manage to escape, even in the magical land of

Undra-Narnia. He was about to say something, but saw something behind me and tensed. "Don't move," he cautioned, smile still intact. "Just stand still."

The hairs on my arm stood up, and the urge to whip my head around like a maniac was overpowering. Jens inched by me with the grace of an actual ninja. There was a quick movement, a gasp and several more wafts of air hitting me from behind. I nearly jumped out of my skin (not a great thing to do on the side of a mountain) when Jens yelled, "Spindels! Run!"

I whirled around and saw exactly what Jens described: eight-legged furry creatures bigger than rats. A line of them was spilling out of a crack in the wall to our left like a waterfall. Black monster of Frankenstein critters scurried over my feet and up my legs. They were tripping and jumping out at us, separating Jens and me from the others, who ran further down the trail. "Follow me, Loos!" Jens commanded.

I screamed and covered my ears on instinct as I ran behind Jens. He knocked dozens of them out of the way, acting like a linebacker for me (or whatever the crap that position is that blocks the bad guys from taking down the quarterback. What do you want from me? Linus played soccer). Kitten-sized arachnids landed in my hair, their spindly legs tangling in the curls. I felt one scurry under the hem of my shirt and bite the small of my back. It was a small pinch of a needle with a cold chill that lasted long after I shook the fur ball loose. My scream was high-pitched, but only exhibited a tenth of the terror I felt inside.

We ran as fast as we could, but the spiders were ambitious. When we trampled through the last of the black mess of them, I did not slow until Jens began to stumble. He tripped a few times, but picked himself back up. He grabbed onto my hand and trudged a few minutes more to a little cavern where he collapsed. "Jens!" I knelt beside his heaving form and patted his back to calm him down.

"Go on ahead and tell Britt to run for Alrik."

"I'm not leaving you like this," I protested, surprised that he would even suggest such a thing. "They're not that far behind us, Jens! They'll be crawling all over you in minutes!"

He waved a shaky hand like I was being too dramatic. "We passed giftig bushes. They repel spindels. They won't cross the giftigs. I'm fine here."

"I don't want to just leave you here!" I protested, feeling all kinds of wrong as I watched his strong body slow down.

"You have to. I got bit a few times, and the poison's already moving through me. My knees are shaking." When he saw my horror, he put on a weak smile. "I'm fine. Takes 48 hours for the gestation to run its course. We're a day out from Alrik's village, so we've got plenty of time. Just go with the others and bring back Alrik as quick as you can."

I nodded and scrambled to my feet, bolting up the moonlit path and shouting with abandon for the others. I ran with renewed energy, despite having not eaten much or slept in who knows how long. The dark of night was disturbed by my brazen volume, and though I was alone, I couldn't really connect with any fear that wasn't related to saving Jens.

When I heard footsteps running toward me, I slowed,

heaving a sigh of relief when I saw Foss. "What happened? Where's Jens?"

"The spiders got him! Lots of them bit him and he can't walk. He sent me to tell you to run for Alrik, and I mean, run!"

Foss needed no other explanation. "Let's go, then."

I wiped the sweat from my brow. "No. I'm going back to stay with him. If more spiders come, he won't be able to fight them off." As the words came out of my mouth, I questioned them. Did I know how to fight them off? I mean, other than using a shoe, I'd never defended my territory from spiders before. Not like this.

"Is he on the other side of the giftigs?"

"Yeah, but I won't gamble on that. I'm not leaving him." My chin raised, daring him to argue with my resolute tone.

"Are you sure?" Foss gave me a hesitant look, which affected my volume greater than I meant it to.

"Run!" I shouted. "Don't stop. Don't look back. Run!"

He was startled by the crazed look in my eye. "Alright, little rat. He'll be fine. I'll go get Alrik right now."

"Do you think I'm speaking metaphorically? How are you not running? Do you need me to put the fear of God in you?" I stepped toward the enormous warrior menacingly, not quite sure what I might do to evoke a sprint from the man.

"I'm going!" He turned and ran up the incline as if I might unleash the powers of PMS on him.

I stumbled back down the path, my heart clenching in my chest when I found Jens collapsed on the stone floor of the small cave. He had looked so strong just moments ago when he helped me across the blockade. My wobbly knees were quaking from adrenaline, and the cold spot on my spine felt like it was spreading to my hips.

Jens groaned. "What are you doing? I told you to go with them!" His face was red, and little pink spots were bulging out on his cheeks and neck.

"Shut up," I snapped. I was too excitable to feel repentant for my attitude. "I can't believe you thought I would leave you here. You think you know me so well?" Sweat was pouring off me now, and my lungs were beginning to feel the cold that was working its way around to my navel. I shouted at him over his coughing, not even feeling remorseful for yelling at him in his pathetic state. "I stayed with Linus through every chemo treatment, every needle and every new doctor! I held his hand while he died! Now you'll shut your mouth and let me take care of you, or so help me, forget Martin Luther King! I'll end you!"

"There's nothing you can do, Lucy. Nothing you could've done for Linus, either. Only Alrik can help me now. You would've been better off going with the others." He coughed again, and I could see the color draining from his face as the sweat dripped off his chin onto the ground. "If something finds us up here, I can't protect you."

"Then I guess they'll have to deal with me. What else you got up here? Besides the radioactive spiders, I mean. Boxing kangaroos? Chainsaw-wielding elephants?"

Jens laughed, which set him on another coughing fit. "You shouldn't be here, Lucy."

"I shouldn't be a lot of things." I knelt next to him and felt his slick forehead, which was burning up. "Let's get that backpack off of you." His arms were stiff as I slid off his red pack and cast it to the corner of the cave near his feet. "Arms up," I instructed, working his moist black t-shirt over his head. I stood clumsily and hung it on a stone jutting out from the wall, hoping he did not notice my poor balance. He had endured dozens of spider bites, so the poison was stronger in him, working faster to take him down. Hopefully I'd scared Foss enough to make quick work of the rest of the journey.

I slumped down next to Jens, propping myself up on the wall next to his head. My hand found its way into his hair, brushing through the wet follicles to ease his shaking. "I know you're cold. Just wait till your fever breaks. Then I'll get you off the floor."

"I'm fine." He shuddered as he hugged himself in the rosy moonlight that stretched in from the cave's opening. He was lying supine on the rocky ground, tremors ripping through him at half-minute intervals.

"Wow. That sounds even more pathetic than when I say it." I looked over his torso and saw a couple more raised bumps, but the thing that gave me pause were the violent scarred-over slashes across his bodybuilder chest and stomach. I spoke in a quiet voice. "Jens, what happened to you?"

He managed a wan look of disbelief that conveyed he thought I was stupid. "I got bit by spindels. Are you just figuring that out?"

"No, idiot." I rolled my eyes and pointed to his wide chest. "Your scars. Did someone play Operation on you?"

He pressed his palm to one of the scars, an insecurity poking through as his eyes darted to my face, and then away. "Sort of. Trolls. A whole tribe of them was in the village, tearing it up. Everyone was fleeing, even the king, but I didn't feel like it."

"Didn't feel like it?"

"Fleeing's a lot of work. Packing up all your stuff. Running to the Nisse town the next mountain over. Like they'd really take us all in." He coughed a scary, rasping bark, so I inched closer, lifting his head onto my lap so his upper half was off the cold stone floor. Once he had his bearings back, he continued. "So I took care of them. It got a little bloody before the end. That's how I got most of my scars." He shifted on my lap, moving his head to rest against my stomach. "But not this one." He tried to lift his knuckle to show me, but he could only move it an inch up and down. Sure enough, there was a small crescent-shaped scar on the knuckle of his forefinger. "This one's from you."

"What? I never cut you before." I gently lifted his hand to examine the damage. His grip was almost arthritic with its unyielding tension. He held onto my hand like he was afraid to let it go. Like he was afraid to let me go, but couldn't find the words to admit it. I wanted to run my fingers over his abs, but decided that probably wasn't kosher in my world or Undraland.

"I got it fixing your car one night while you were sleeping. You really need to change your oil more often. That three thousand miles isn't a suggestion, Loos. Your engine's gonna go one day, and you'll only have yourself to blame." He coughed into my shirt, and then did something so precious, I had to smile. He burrowed his forehead into my abdomen like a kitten searching for comfort. I brushed my hand down the side of his tattooed face and tickled my fingers across the hairs at the base of his neck. His eyes were closed and his breathing shallow. "Mm. That feels nice."

I lifted his rigid knuckle to my mouth and kissed the scar in hopes of healing it. I whispered a few incendiary things to the man in my arms to see if he was awake, but nothing stirred up his fight. When I was certain I was alone, I tested my limbs by wiggling my toes and trying to move my shoulders. It was all doable, but everything was too stiff. I was losing mobility in my legs for certain.

The moon did its job giving me something beautiful to look at. I wondered with a strange peace if either of us would survive the spider babies nesting inside our bodies. The scenario was worthy of a good freak-out, but in keeping with the rest of my body, my insides felt numb.

When all was quiet, I heard movement outside the cave. My peace shattered in an instant as I wondered how I might fend off legions of spindels with half my body asleep and Jens completely incapacitated.

The movement reached the mouth of the cave, displaying two glowing gray eyes in the dark. When the creature stepped closer, I gasped with delight. "Come here, little puppy," I cooed in a sickeningly sweet voice. I clicked my tongue, luring the precious dog further in until I could get a good look at him.

Grayish white fur with black patches all over and the cutest little face melted my heart.

"What happened to your poor ear?" I asked, reaching out with a clumsy hand to pet the besotted creature. "It looks like someone took a chunk out of your ear here. Aw! Sweet baby."

The dog did its job and sniffed Jens and me from head to toe before deciding we could be best friends. He whined at me for food. "I'm sorry, buddy. I'm starving, too. Maybe when Uncle Rick gets here, he'll have tacos in his pocket for us. Maybe some burgers or a sloppy fistful of Indian food." I scratched behind his good ear. "Where's your family? You're all alone, too?"

It felt like he answered me with a tilt of his head, so I continued on, wondering if the spider bites were making me crazy. "There, there. It's okay to be alone. Stay here, and we can be alone together. Here, baby." I clicked my fingers over Jens's chest. "Come keep Jens warm. He's feverish up on his head, but ice cold on his body." I petted the large puppy, coaxing him closer to Jens. Finally, he rested his snout on Jens's icy chest, licking him a few times to show his acceptance into his new family.

"That's right... um, no collar." I fished around for the first name that popped into my head. "That's right, Henry Mancini. I'm your mommy, and Jens is your puppy. Take good care of him."

Ice crept higher up my spine, and I realized I could no longer wiggle my toes. I gave my dog a brave smile. "Don't you worry, Henry Mancini. Everything's going to be alright."

17

SELECTIVE RESCUE

*M*ovement outside of the cave woke me, but I could barely turn my neck to verify the source of the noise. Henry Mancini hopped to his furry feet and scampered to the cave's opening to check it out for me. He barked when Uncle Rick came into view, and though most of me was immovable, my heart lifted in my chest at the sight of his friendly face. Though, I admit, it was still strange to see him in the long wizard-type robes. When he would visit us in the real world, he usually wore Dockers and a hand-made orange cardigan no one had the heart to tell him was a woman's. He still had the cardigan on, but the wizard dress underneath really threw me.

"Hello, dear. Have you been enjoying the sights?"

I looked up into his eyes and tried not to break down with relief. Jens had not moved in hours, and I feared the worst. "Can you help him? Is it too late?" My mouth could barely move, but I managed to get the words out without sounding like I'd had a stroke.

Uncle Rick took out a pouch from his robes and dipped two fingers inside. He produced a thick mulch-colored paste that he proceeded to rub on Jens's gums and the inside of his mouth. "There we go. It works quite quickly," he said, putting away his pouch and sitting next to me so he could keep an eye on Jens's progress. He rifled through the red backpack, sighing with relief when whatever he was looking for was still there. "I see you made yourself a little friend." Henry Mancini was sniffing Uncle Rick's ebony hand and sneezing at the remnants of the green concoction.

"Henry Mancini. He's been keeping Jens from freezing over." I knew I should probably tell Uncle Rick that I needed some of the paste, but I wanted to make sure Jens had enough of it to cure him first. He'd been bitten so many more times than I had. "Are the others okay?"

Uncle Rick nodded. "Nik is busy telling any of my kind who will listen how he defended their borders once fighting off a menacing troll."

"Making friends, as usual."

"Indeed. We are a patient race, which is playing in his favor." I could hear the smile in his voice, but my neck was too stiff to turn my head to look up at him. "Tor's enjoying elfish libations, which are a bit stronger than your average drink. Foss and Britta are with Jamie, resting and preparing for the next task."

"Jamie? I thought he was still at his dad's palace. How'd you manage to get him out?"

"When I port myself, it leaves an imprint that those familiar with elfish ways can spot. I can take one person with me when I do it, if I'm strong enough. So I took Jamie with me, after he sent the message to Jens, fearing what his father might do to him." He scratched a gray patch behind his ear. "Understand, it was not my intention to abduct a member of the Tonttu throne. Jamie wanted to come along. I can't imagine Jens will be pleased, though."

"Jens loves Jamie."

"True, and part of that love is keeping Jamie safe. Jamie doesn't have much experience with long journeys such as ours."

"He'll figure it out. I haven't died yet."

"A fact that will please many, I'm certain." Uncle Rick's focus shifted to Jens when he saw movement. "Jens? Can you hear me, son?"

"That's some fast-acting stuff," I commented, relieved that it was working. "Did you give him enough?"

Uncle Rick nodded, testing the man's limbs for signs of life. The red bumps were already going down.

"Is there any left?"

"He doesn't need more than I gave him. Patience is the key ingredient now."

Relief flooded through me, and I didn't realize until then how scared I had been for the man in my arms. "C-could I have some?"

"I can teach you how to make it when we get to my house. I can teach you all sorts of herbal remedies. It would be my joy." He looked at me in the darkness with a glimmer of paternal pride. My face was shrouded in black, since the light did not shine on my upper half anymore.

"That sounds nice. But can I have some of it right now? Is it real expensive? You don't have to give it to me." I'm not sure why I was in no rush to be certain of my survival.

Perhaps teetering on the edge of death for hours had the same numbing effect that the spider larvae did. Deep down inside, I was ashamed that a small part of me welcomed the uneventful quietness of death.

Uncle Rick leaned closer, and then clicked his fingers in my face, summoning up a flame that danced on his fingertips so he could get a good look at me. I think I was immune to being surprised anymore. I mean, the man can teleport. Not much freaks you out after that. "Lucy!" he exclaimed, whipping out the burgundy pouch again. His fingers fumbled this time as he swiped the inside clean and jammed two digits in my mouth. His face was stern as he brushed my teeth and tongue with his fingers. "Why didn't you say something? Foss told me only Jens was bit! Why, Lucy? Why?"

I had a feeling I was only a sentence or two away from a stern "young lady", so I didn't answer. Conversation was kind of impossible right now anyway. The pouch was turned inside out and shoved into my mouth. Uncle Rick held the back of my head as I sucked the last of the paste from the rough fabric. My tongue went fuzzy, and then started warming. As I swallowed, the heat spread through my body at warp speed, killing off the larvae and warming my frozen extremities.

Jens was regaining consciousness and Uncle Rick was looking cross as he lectured me, testing my arms and legs for any signs of circulation.

The heat was delicious. It soothed my anxiety as it spread through me like honey, warming and healing as it went. My eyes closed as I enjoyed the blissed-out sensations coursing through my body. I went from rigid to oddly boneless and laid down on the ground contentedly once the weight of Jens was lifted from my lap. Uncle Rick was shouting something, but I was too cozy to care. I closed my eyes and smiled. If this was death, I would welcome it.

FIRST HUMAN FEMALE IN ELVAGE

*T*he fingers in my hair were pure bliss, and when I stretched my body, the bed beneath me was the softest I'd ever felt, like sleeping on a cloud. The warmth in the room was a welcome respite from the cold of the dank cave's floor. I took in a deep, cleansing breath and found that this Heaven smelled just like my room. When I finally opened my eyes, I realized my nose was buried in Jens's leg. The familiar smell was him, and in that moment between sleep and waking, I took great comfort in the scent that always followed me.

"Lucy?" Jens chuckled.

"Not yet," I protested, snuggling his leg like it was a teddy bear. I was so comfortable, and still in a hazy peace I did not want shattered so soon. The fingers in my hair gripped the locks and gently tugged, stimulating the roots and making me almost drool on his thigh. "That feels so good," I purred.

Touch was one thing I craved and did not get much of.

Sure, Tonya and I hugged. There was the occasional brush of the shoulder against a stranger, but other than those few things, no one touched me after my family died. I tried not to miss it, but I did. As Jens ran his fingers over my cheek, it connected with a part of me I had tried to kill off in my attempt to survive.

"You finally awake?" he asked, a smile in his tone. "Sorry about that. Our medicine works different on humans than it does on us, I guess. It killed the spiders, which is the important thing, but we didn't count on it knocking you clean out."

I turned into his leg and wiped my drool off on his pants. After everything we'd just been through, I figured he could take it. My eyelids were heavy when they opened. I rolled onto my back to squeeze out every bit of enjoyment I could from the cloud-like bed as gold dust sparkled around me. "Beautiful!" I breathed, entranced by the shimmering glitter in the air. "Am I dead?" It was the only explanation I could think of. I lifted my arm to brush my hair from my face and found that I was wearing foreign clothes. I wasn't even mad that someone dressed me without my permission. I was too content in the most comfortable bed in the universe. Too happy watching the gold dance around me as it floated weightlessly in the air. Too cozy lying next to my own personal guardian angel.

His voice came back to me less relaxed than it was previously. "No, you're not dead, but you almost were. Why didn't you tell me you got bit?"

My hand swished in slow motion through the air, separating the glittering particles that each went off on their own little dance in the world. The room we were in was painted cream and gold with pale blue accents. There was a vanity with gold trim in the corner that was so fancy, it looked straight out of an antique shop. Nothing felt real, so I enjoyed playing with the gold glitter hanging in the air. "What could you have done about me getting bit?"

Jens was silent while he thought on this. Finally, he responded with, "I don't know, but you should've told Foss. And when Alrik got there, you should've told him first thing."

"If I'm going to start telling Foss things, I'll start with a big long lecture on women's rights." I sighed. "I had one tiny bite, Jens. You had a billion. Not to question your stamina, but you looked like you were at death's door. You needed more of the mulch paste than I did. It's okay to say that I was right."

"No. We need you for the human gate. The portal needs to be destroyed by its own kind. What use would I be for that?"

I shrugged, unperturbed by his argument. "Hire a demolition expert."

"It's a little more complicated than that, smartass."

"Hey! I'd be nicer to me if I were you. I just saved your life by sending Foss to fetch Alrik." I grinned when he had no response to this. I was still on my back next to his knee, staring in bewilderment at the floating gold. "That's right. I'm leveling the playing field."

"How's that?" Jens asked uncomfortably.

"You're no longer this almighty force, and I'm not the weak human idiot you got stuck watching. I officially helped save your life." I batted at a few more particles, watching them dance like ballerinas through the air. "I rock."

Jens laughed through his discomfort. "Yes, I suppose you do. But no more. That gets to be your only time saving my life, got it? Next time, it's my turn to save the day."

"Whatever. You're my pretty princess. Just admit it."

He said nothing, but reached down and put his hand in my hair again, leafing through the tangles and making me swoon. Now that I was more awake, it dawned on me how weird it was that we were this close already. That it would occur to him to tickle my scalp, and that I would let him do it. Yes, it was strange, but part of me felt more at home with him than I usually did when I was all by myself. He was sitting up in the bed, leaning against the tall head-board, and I was content where I lay, snuggled up to his side.

"Jens, what would..." I stopped short and bolted upright, whipping my head around like a crazy person. "Henry Mancini!"

Jens laughed. It was the only sound that could distract me from my alertness. "I think you might be the first person this century to call out his name like that."

"Where's my dog?" I slipped off the bed, and for the first time, actually looked at what I was wearing. "And what is this? I know for a fact I have a proper change of clothes in my green backpack, which is somewhere in the abyss of your red bag." I was bathed and dressed in a cream-colored gown that kissed my bare feet. It was fitted up top and flowing on the bottom. Would've been pretty on anyone else. "Britta?" I asked warily, finally glancing up at Jens.

Jens nodded, his smile more laid back than I thought it

should be, given the audacity of the crime at hand. "She's afraid you're going to be mad at her."

I shook my head. "Why am I dressed for a Renaissance fair? And where's my dog?" I examined his clean black t-shirt, jeans and boots. "And why do you get to look normal, but I can't?"

His legs swung off the bed. He made his way over to me in the room with golden swirled walls that were so fancy, I was afraid to touch them. "You're dressed like this because this is Alrik's home, and you're wearing the clothes of his people. You're the first human in Elvage, so he's expecting a fair amount of visitors once you're ready. Important ones." He motioned to his jeans. "I get to look like this because guardian gnomes can dress how they like. No one cares if I'm ready for a ball. They care if I can scale a mountain in a pinch."

"Great. Where's my dog?" I looked around the room and tried not to get distracted by the glitter. The vanity and wardrobe were made out of blonde wood to match the flooring, but other than that, the room was bare.

"Your *wolf* is outside with Tor and Foss."

"Henry Mancini's a wolf?"

Jens sighed. "Do we really have to call him that?"

"Only if you don't want me to call you Jennifer. Of course you have to call him that. It's his name."

"Jens isn't short for Jennifer. It's our version of John, which is a man's name. If we were in Sweden, it'd be pronounced 'Yens'." He pointed to his chest. "Man." Then he did something that made me stop breathing. He wrapped his arm around the small of my back and drew me to him, pressing my body to his in a way that was firm and forceful. "Woman," he said, clutching me tight to him. He took my hand and placed it on his tattoo, the corner of his mouth lifting at my obvious swoon. "And don't you forget it."

I felt like I was on the cover of one of those dog-eared romance novels you always see at used bookstores. Gorgeous man, blonde woman in a dress with her curls swirling out behind her. Bells rang in my brain when he leaned closer to me, lifting me to my toes so he could stick his nose in my neck.

Delirium closed my eyes and anticipation made my heart flutter as he smelled my skin. In all my romantic fantasies, I never really thought much on a man's nose buried in the crook of my neck, but my legs turned to jelly when Jens kissed my collarbone. He moved his mouth up my neck and kissed my jaw, further melting me with his touch. My body formed easily to his, and my hand wound into his messy hair possessively. I had never been kissed like this. I had never been seduced, but my body under-stood the dance as my brain turned to mush.

A knock interrupted our moment. I wished I could unhear it so I could remain in the haze, but Jens stiffened.

"Miss Lucy? Are you well?" Jamie called from the other side.

We broke apart as if struck by lightning, both of us wary of the other. "I… I…"

Jens waved off my mumbling. "Forget about it." He turned away from me and shook his arms out, as if doing that would make his body comply with whatever his mind was telling it to do.

When sense reentered my brain, I moved past Jens, but

paused before opening the door. "Is this decent?" I asked him, unsure if I was wearing a dress or an undergarment of some old Colonial variety.

Jens leaned on the wall next to the door, feigning ease and mocking me with a touch of the lust in his eye he tried unsuccessfully to mask. "This is what we call a dress. Or what you refer to as a Halloween costume." When I glared at him, he rolled his eyes. "Come in, Jamie."

Jamie entered with Britta, who looked like she was afraid I might shout at her. "Miss Lucy," she said with a dip of her head. She was well over six feet tall, but her subservient demeanor made her seem smaller. She looked from my blush to her brother's avoidance and did her best to swallow a delighted smile.

"Um, thanks for letting me borrow your dress, Britta. And thanks for cleaning me up and everything."

"It's no trouble." Britta's shoulders relaxed. "Alrik bought the dress for you, actually. He said to let him know if you need anything at all."

"Where is he?"

"He's in the observatory, entertaining guests who are all anxious to meet you."

"Why?" My nose scrunched and that familiar pit in my stomach churned. I always felt sick to my stomach on the first day at a new school. I usually ralphed just before first period in the ladies' room. "You guys are the ones with the magic. I'm a normal person."

"Yes, but you're the first human woman they've ever met, so you've drawn quite the turnout." Jamie stood in the doorway, as if entering a woman's chambers was unbecoming to him. He wore a blue fancy George Washington-style coat over his clothes and had the posture of an old-fashioned gentleman. It was a little intimidating.

"May I fix your hair?" Britta asked in her mousy voice. Her dark green dress had an apron over it, and she wore her long brown hair in two clean braids on either side of her head under her white bonnet.

I ran my hand through the tangles, never having cared much what it looked like. "Um, sure. Is it a disaster?"

Her lie was easy to spot. "Oh, no! I just thought you might want your hair in the style of your uncle's people." She motioned to the vanity, and I sat obediently while she made sense of my blonde hair with a pearl-handled brush. She let it hang loose and tied silver and pink ribbons through loops she knotted in my hair.

Jens and Jamie were talking in hushed tones that made me nervous. I didn't like surprises, and everything about this place would be one.

When Britta was finished, I thanked her and turned to look at myself in the concave and cloudy mirror. I was astonished. With no product whatsoever, she'd made me look like a Renaissance princess. Or a fairy. Or whatever those women at the fairs were supposed to be. "Whoa! Is one of your magical powers hairstyling? How'd you do that?"

Britta smiled by way of an answer.

Jens extended his hand to hoist me up out of the chair, but when I stood, I did not drop his hand. Part of me held onto him because I was nervous. The other part... I wasn't ready to look too close at that yet. Suffice to say, Jens and I had been through enough in the past couple days to be at the place where we could lean on each other a little. He gazed down at me and gave me a look with a thousand emotions flickering through it, tinged with a hint of teasing. "Are you gonna hurl? You've got that look."

"Well, aren't you a charmer?" I straightened, trying not to feel like a child in the midst of the three tall people. Jens led the way down the golden hallway, down a flight of blonde-colored stairs, down three more hallways and to a set of doors that was shut. I could hear commotion on the other side.

Jamie held out his arm for me to take, but I did not move toward him. "I'm fine. Thanks." I looked to Britta, who was grinning at the place where my hand was still joined with her brother's. "But Britta needs an escort. I mean, a woman walking around without a man? What would the neighbors say?"

Jens dropped my hand and took a step back from me. "No. Do what you're told and go with Jamie."

"Come again?" I can't recall the last time someone ordered me so rudely.

"Go with Jamie. He'll bring you out and present you to the elves. His stamp of approval will help them accept you. Set you off on the right foot." When I didn't move away from his side fast enough, his tone turned sharp. "You can't hold onto me like that, Lucy. People are gonna get the wrong idea about us."

I recoiled from his acerbic tone. "What wrong idea? In the bedroom, you were just –"

"You were imagining things." He gave me a look of warning not to test him. "What? You really think you could keep up with someone like me? Come on, Loos! Rumors fly like crazy around here, and I don't want anyone in my business, least of all you."

"Jens!" his sister scolded, her face cross. The same emerald eyes stared daggers at him, angry and ashamed at his harsh words.

I wondered if Jens had a girlfriend. Everything he was saying was pointing to either to him being ashamed of me, or wanting to hide me to keep his options open. Solid guy. Boy, do I know how to pick them. "It's fine. Whatever. Pass me around." I tried to brush it off like a joke, but I could not keep the hurt out of my words. People certainly had gotten the wrong idea about us, if "people" meant me.

What had I been thinking? I knew next to nothing about Jens. We weren't even the same species. I took Jamie's arm without looking up at him and waited like a good little puppet for him to move us forward. I could tell he was watching me, but I ignored him.

"He's right, you know," Jamie said, bending down to speak quietly to me.

"Gotcha. I wouldn't want to ruin his game. Far be it from me to… whatever. It's fine. Loud and clear. Lucy Kincaid is bad for business." I slid emotionlessness onto my face, lest I let my hurt feelings be known. "I thought I wasn't supposed to hold onto you, though. That Freya chick isn't going to off-with-her-head me, is she?"

Jamie shook his head. "Elvage isn't Tonttu. You were a rarity there, but Alrik wants your status elevated here. It'll give us more opportunities if he presents you as the leader of your kind. We're both royalty now, and this is normal for that kind of thing."

Jamie started explaining the rules of proper Tomten

courting, making excuses for Jens, but I had no patience for it. I felt a little bad when I interrupted him mid-sentence with, "You know, I don't really care. Jens is bipolar. Message received." I forced out a laugh that made me cringe at its obvious fakeness when I heard it. "Boy, do I know nothing about men." I finally looked up at Jamie, who had that infuriating pity in his eyes. "Let's ripcord this nonsense."

"What?" Jamie asked.

I heard Jens huff behind us, and the sound made me furious. "She means that she wants to get out of here. Don't listen to her, Jamie. Get on with it."

I whirled around on Jens, shoving my finger in his closed-off face. "Give me some space and quit messing with my head. Go do your garden gnome thing and don't interpret for me. You're off-duty. In fact, you're fired."

Jens glared at me and postured, using his intimidating height to tower over me and gain the physical advantage in the conversation. "I don't answer to you."

I threw up my hands. "Well, you seem perfectly happy to answer *for* me."

"That's because no one can understand you here!"

"No kidding!" I yelled. "No one understands me at all anywhere! I've got nothing and no one, so quit being in my face!"

"You make absolutely no sense!"

I used wild hand gestures to make my point. "Get away from me! Is that easy enough for you to grasp?"

"You know I can't do that!" Jens shouted. His anger was a little frightening, but I maintained my ground with a sneer that matched his. "It's my job to keep you alive."

"Get away from me," I snapped, turning my back on him. "I wouldn't want to soil your perfect reputation, almighty troll-slayer."

"Lucy..."

"Let's go, Jamie."

Jamie pushed Jens lightly in the chest to shove him backwards, giving his best friend a look of disapproval.

The double doors opened, and Uncle Rick came out, an air of secrecy about him as he shut the entrance at his back. "Lucy, a word?"

Uncle Rick motioned for me to follow him down the hallway, so I obeyed. When Jens made to follow me, I barked, "Back up, guard. I'm allowed to talk to my uncle."

Uncle Rick waved off Jens and led me further back the way I'd come, peeking through doorways and adjoining hallways to ensure we were not overheard. The intense look in his gray eyes when he addressed me was not to be trifled with. "Lucy, I need you to do something for me without asking questions."

I nodded, already falling in whatever line he decided to place me in. "Sure. Anything."

"Good girl. Do you recall the time you got grounded for stealing my car keys when you didn't want me to leave?"

I exhaled. Really? That's what he wanted to talk about? "Again, I'm sorry."

He waved his hand to excuse my youthful indiscretion. "I wasn't upset then, and I'm not now. You took them from my sweater pocket without me even noticing. It was brilliant." He leaned in, lowering his voice to a whisper. "I need you to do the same thing now."

"Come again?"

"No questions. There's a man I'll introduce you to after the formal sit-down is over. Kristoffer. He's the keeper of the keys for the elfin guard. He's their Head of the Guard, actually. He works for the palace. Highly trained, so be the best pickpocket I know you can be." He placed his hand on my shoulder to ensure we were on the same page. "The consequences for getting found out will be dire, so best not get caught."

"What the crap, Uncle Rick?" I glared at him so he knew how much I wasn't thrilled with this idea. "Okay, fine. Sure thing. After the Q&A."

Uncle Rick nodded, his shoulders relaxing now that I was onboard. "Yes. I only need one key off the ring, so lift it, fetch me the black round key that looks like it fits a safe or something small. Then you can give him back his keys with no one the wiser."

"Yes, sir."

He gave me a look of pride I couldn't help but feel was misplaced. My parents had ripped me a new one when I'd fessed up two hours after I'd stolen Uncle Rick's keys and he'd missed his bus. What can I say? I was twelve. I didn't want him to leave.

Uncle Rick led me back to a tensed Jens and a patient Jamie. "Thank you, gentlemen. If you'll follow me."

Jamie turned to me. "Take a breath before we go in. Are you ready for this?"

"I don't think it really matters, does it? There's no ripcord, Jamie." With that, I let him wrap my unfeeling hand around his arm as we strolled into the gold cherub-bedecked grand room, hoping the day would be over soon.

19

QUEEN LUCY THE PICKPOCKET

When I was told we were going to the observatory to talk to some of Uncle Rick's friends, I assumed a handful of elves. I was startled out of my fight with Jens when forty-plus oversized people in ethereal robes stood at my brazen entrance. I shrank and plastered my hand to Jamie's arm, allowing him to escort me to the only empty seat in the room, which was next to my uncle, facing the audience.

The walls were painted gold, which made the gold dust that floated everywhere around us blend in seamlessly. The floor-to-ceiling tapestries were pale blue, like my dress. In fact, as I looked around at the gold chandelier, the matching chairs with blue cushioned seats, and the table in the back with a pale blue tablecloth laden with gold platters of tea and biscuits, I realized Uncle Rick had picked out my dress to match his house. I felt like a doll, and this room was my dollhouse.

I sat on the baby blue upholstered Victorian-style couch

with my back straight and hands in my lap. I had not worn many dresses, so every movement felt like it needed special attention. When I sat, so did everyone else. The lace curtains behind the heavy blue tapestries were drawn, and I was grateful I didn't have to meet my uncle's friends without being able to see them because of their crazy bright sun.

Jamie stood next to the settee I was positioned in and called the room to attention with his regal stature and formal address. "Ladies and gentlemen, I'd like to introduce you to Queen Lucy of the Other Side."

The room stood again to show me respect, and I had no clue how to respond. My wide eyes searched the room for Britta, who dipped her head to show me what I should do.

I gave them all a slight bow of my head, and they resumed their seats. *Queen Lucy, indeed. That'll take some getting used to.*

Jamie opened the floor for questions. Seven elves stood to address me, so Jamie took it upon himself to emcee the event. "Go ahead, Berit."

"Queen Lucy, are you a good representation of the height of your people, or are you unnaturally short?"

Oh, good. Science time. "I'm smack in the middle of the spectrum," I answered.

Jamie called on a woman named Agnetha. She stood and stared at me with beady eyes, cataloging my every measurement. "Does she have yearly fertile moon times?"

I quirked my eyebrow to Uncle Rick, who explained quietly to me, "She's asking how often you menstruate."

My chin lowered slightly as I answered, despising that I was being subjected to this line of questioning. "Yes. Once a month." My ears burned at having to talk about this in front of strangers. I was especially displeased that Jens was in the room. He stood at the doorway, watching the crowd and keeping tabs on my location.

How could I have thought I was anything more than the job to him? I chided myself on never attracting a boyfriend, or I would have had more experience with male attention and known the difference between someone wanting to be around you and someone having to be.

Ouch.

"Your body is responding to our sun and moon, so you won't have your normal cycle here," Uncle Rick explained. "She does respond to the fertile moon cycle, but it will become an annual occurrence, like the women here. That has to do with her environment, not the human body, though. Next question."

I hated, truly hated, that my uncle was talking about my period, and apparently knew more about it than I did. Although I admit, things were looking up at the thought of only being a murderous wench once a year.

"What's your educational system like?" the next elf asked. Thankfully, the next two hours of questions were much like this one, and not quite so personal. I started to get some of myself back after a while, and began talking with my hands again. Uncle Rick smiled down at me, relieved that I was not so resigned. I even regained my sense of humor when someone asked about our sewer system.

There was one person in the crowd who stood out to me. He was the only elf around my age in the whole room. The man looked to be in his mid-twenties, had black and silver eyes and watched me without movement. He was dressed in a black shirt and matching pants, and wore the same color collar around his neck like a dog. He was so still as he took in every answer, it made me fidget just being in the same room as him. When he stood slowly and with purpose to request his question be heard, I stiffened. Whatever this would be, for some reason I was nervous.

"Charles Mace, go ahead." Jamie turned to me. "Mace is Alrik's ward."

I looked up at Uncle Rick. "Like how Robin is Bruce Wayne's ward?"

He nodded, smiling at my odd reference. "Indeed. He's my son."

My question must have been plain on my face. Uncle Rick was black, and Charles Mace had skin like mine.

Uncle Rick placed his hand on my shoulder. "I adopted him when he was just a baby."

My mouth dropped open and my stomach churned as I sat with my hands politely folded in my lap. Uncle Rick had family that wasn't us? I looked at Charles Mace in a new light, guessing that I would probably run into this one again in the house.

Mace did not break his penetrating gaze, nor did he blink when he spoke. Such focused attention made me itch, and I fought with the urge to scratch my neck. Every movement I made was watched by the entire room, several people scribbling on parchment every time I shifted in my seat.

Mace cleared his throat. "Tell me about your mother and father."

I could feel myself pulling back. Ask about my time of

the month, sure, but don't go near the personal stuff. Iron gates slammed shut in my mind, throwing up a very secure mental block that kept me sane.

"No," I replied, causing a stir. "That's specific to me, and not all humanity. I'm not here to talk about my personal life. I'm here so you can learn about humans."

Uncle Rick stood and raised his hands to address his friends and colleagues. "I think two hours is enough questioning for today. Are you all convinced that she is of no danger to us?"

Danger? That's what this was really about? I looked around and saw them nodding. I'm pretty sure I was supposed to be insulted, but really, they were right. I presented no threat to anyone.

Uncle Rick motioned to the tea and treat table toward the back of the room. "Please help yourselves and stay as long as you like."

The people stood and milled around, drinking tea and eating circle-shaped purple cookies. I remained in my seat, afraid a sudden movement would restart the inquisition all over again. A few of Uncle Rick's friends came up to me to ask more questions, waving their cookies around as they talked. I did my best to accurately represent my kind, while Jamie and Uncle Rick flanked me as if I needed filters for the crowd.

A well-built gentleman with short brown hair cropped around his face was fifth in line. During the Q&A, he'd asked about my skill with a knife, a bow and my ability to fight off a predator. He was a little intense, with tight lips and a stern jawline, and was the only other elf besides Mace who wore pants as opposed to a Gandalf gown. He extended his hand when it was his turn to meet the human female.

Uncle Rick did us the courtesy of introducing him. "Queen Lucy, this is Kristoffer, Head of the Elvage Guard." The careful concealment of Uncle Rick's usual eye-twinkle let me know the snatch and grab show needed to start.

I fanned myself, feigning weakness from the warmth of the room that had too many bodies jammed inside. "Kristoffer? Very nice to meet you. I'm sorry, but could you ask your questions while we get some tea? That was more exhausting than I thought it would be."

"Of course, your majesty." He and Jamie both extended their hands to me, but I clung only to Kristoffer's beefy grip. When he pulled me up, I could feel which side he was favoring, and knew the pocket he had his keys stashed in. His talk was all business as we moved through the gold-dusted air. "I was hoping you could tell me more about your militia. If you're not skilled at using a bow, what sorts of weaponry do you use?"

Yikes. I thought it best to steer clear of talk involving nuclear bombs and whatnot. "Where I come from, Queens don't do much fighting. We have strong and handsome men like you who save the day for us, so we can live in peace."

His wide chest puffed out as he led me toward the table laden with refreshments, and I could tell my compliment was working its magic. "That's as it is here, as well."

I smiled up at him, unleashing as much charm as I could conjure up. "Well, whataya know. We've got something in common after all." I turned to face him, my hand leaving his and travelling up his forearm to trace a large vein in his bicep.

Pickpocketing is easier than people think.

By the time I'd given enough evasive and mildly flirty answers, I had his keys out of his pocket and palmed under a plate I picked up. I placed on it a purple cookie to have something to make the plate work as more than just a prop. The confection reeked of old lady perfume, and I couldn't imagine it tasted much different. I was starving, but wasn't sure perfume constituted satisfactory food.

Kristoffer finished telling me about his plans to reinforce the cells in the dungeon, and I held up a finger to pause him. "I have something I think you'll want to see. Plans for a similar revamp of our prisons. I think I left it in my bag. Will you excuse me? I'll be right back."

His business-like demeanor had long since cracked. He waved his fingers at me, his thin lips grinning as I walked away.

I escaped to the hallway and darted down another to make sure I was alone. I slipped into a room I assumed was an office, judging by the bookshelf, desk and lack of anything else to distract from studying. I set down my plate on the desk and fumbled with the key ring, trying to remove the black one without making too much noise.

Jens found me just as I slid the key Uncle Rick needed off the ring. I closed the loop back up, doing my best to ignore Jens's fuming at my side. "What do you think you're doing? You really think it's a good idea to go throwing yourself at the first bodybuilder you see? I got news for you, Loos. Everyone here's in good shape. We're all farmers and craftsman."

"Yes, that's exactly what I'm doing," I simpered, shoving the black key down the front of my dress and tucking it into my bra.

"What the... What are you doing?" he asked, stepping back to watch for anyone who might intrude on the privacy I still needed.

"I'm working. But good to know you think I'm a ditz who'll go for the first guy who pays me the time of day."

He rolled his eyes. "I know you're not a ditz, but you were throwing yourself at Kristoffer. He's not your type."

"I know he's not." I looked up at Jens's surly mug and took a step forward to close the gap between our bodies. "You are." Just as he'd done in the room upstairs, I leaned in and inhaled near a sensitive spot on his neck.

The man smells like sugar cookies. You can't not love that.

"We can't do this," he protested. The fight was weak, and I could smell a victory to go with my cookie.

I saw goose bumps erupt on his neck as I pressed my lips to his jugular, pulling him closer as my fist dug into the fabric at his chest.

Jens moaned, his hands pressing against the wall on either side of my head as I planted small, sensual kisses up his throat, dragging my lips from side to side across his jaw. "I've wanted this for so long," he admitted. "You have no idea how much I..."

His eyes were closed, and he was leaning into me, while still bracing himself so he did not fall for me completely. It was a beautiful thing, the moments before his crash and burn.

I almost felt bad when I pulled away and ducked out

from under the cocoon of his arms. Jens stumbled forward, nearly slamming his head into the wall. He righted himself as he fought to emerge from his haze.

"That," I spat. "That's what you did to me upstairs. Lame move, right? Don't you for one second think you can mess with me and get away with it." I picked the plate and cookie up off the desk and spun on my heel, walking back into the observatory, ignoring his angry shouts in my direction.

The keys were palmed under the plate as I approached Kristoffer, fake smile plastered in place. "I'm so sorry. I thought I had the plans on me, but I must've left them back home."

I set the plate down, keeping the keys tucked in my hand. To distract him while I placed the keys back inside his pocket, I touched his opposite arm again with my free hand. Pickpocketing has a lot to do with counterpoints. If you're going for the left pocket, draw attention to the right arm. You're welcome.

"Do you forgive me?" I asked, blinking up at him.

"Of course, your majesty." He smiled, completely unaware that the light cough I was faking as I turned my head to the side was to hide any noise the keys might make as they shifted in his pocket.

I pointed to the people congregating around the couch, waiting for me to return. "I guess this is where we say goodbye. Thank you, Kristoffer."

He escorted me back to the pale blue settee, and I sat with my hands folded in my lap and a key poking the underside of my right breast.

Jens stalked into the room and sulked near the back, glaring at me as he watched Kristoffer like a hawk.

Charles Mace stared at me without blinking as he waited in the line. The nearer he got to me, the more nervous I became. His gaze was so intense, I wanted to hide from it. He seemed an outsider to the others. Most treated the space he took up as uninhabited, but it didn't seem to bother him. I was his only concern, and every now and then his fingers twitched as if he meant to reach out toward me. For what? I don't know. I addressed every other possible person until Mace was standing directly in front of me, daring me to look away from his silver irises.

I visibly backed up, my stranger danger alert beeping ominously. His lips pursed as if holding back an onslaught of questions.

Jens postured and moved closer to me, sizing up the threat Mace presented. I turned and glared at my guardian gnome until he backed away.

Mace did not notice anything in the room, except for me. His was not a romantic gaze, but a calculating stare. "I have questions for you."

Uncle Rick answered for me. "You'll have plenty of time for that over dinner tonight. Right now, we have guests, so keep it light, son."

Mace nodded, still not looking away from me. "Will you be living here with Alrik?"

"I have no idea," I responded, my voice growing mousy in his intimidating presence. "I just woke up here."

Uncle Rick answered for me again. "Lucy will stay here with me as long as she likes."

Mace's angular jaw tightened. "Good." He looked like he

was struggling with himself. His volume dropped to a whisper. "We'll have much to talk about over dinner, then. I'm one-quarter human, but I've only known Elvage. I would love to know more about where I came from."

"Oh, sure. I'll tell you all about it." I was glad to know the source of his intensity. It made him give off less of a serial killer vibe in my mind.

When Mace seemed satisfied that I would not bolt if he took his eyes off me, he excused himself and exited the observatory. Jens followed him to the door and watched him disappear down the hall.

20

FIGHTING WITH JENS

*M*y stomach was in knots the entire afternoon, so I started the long process of settling in. I wanted to get Henry Mancini back from Foss and Nik, but that would involve going outside where more elves waited to bombard me with questions. Jamie took me back to my bedroom, where I shut myself inside and flopped on the bed. The beauty of the floating gold was not so enthralling anymore, now that my spirits were sufficiently down. The bed still felt like a cloud, so I stretched out on my stomach, digging my toes into the down of the mattress.

My door opened, announcing Jens's entrance. "Get out," I ordered.

"You know I can't do that. You may not understand it yet, but you haven't done much in the past five years that I wasn't right there for."

"New regime. Get out."

"What are you thinking, ganking keys from an Elvage

guard? What was that even for? Are you just bored, so you're trying to cause trouble? Do you know how harsh penalties are around here?" Then he did a high-pitched imitation of my voice, his hands splayed near his face in a feminine manner. "Oh, Kristoffer, let me stroke your giant man muscles. Oh, Kristoffer, you're so charming and funny. What is this? A cookie? I know so little about your mysterious land. Tell me more." He snarled at me. "Pathetic."

I kept Uncle Rick's secret and dodged that line of questioning. "Please just go."

He huffed. "Don't be like this. I didn't make the rules. I'm just doing my job."

I tried to maintain some semblance of a calm demeanor, so he wouldn't know how much he was getting to me. "It's been a long day, and it's barely halfway over. May I please, please have a little space? That's all I'm asking." I buried my face in my pillow. I was hungry, and my empty stomach was coercing more irritability into me than I would normally express.

"Look, I know I pissed you off, but you have to know we can't be together. If you had more experience with men, you'd understand how bad we would be for each other." He touched his throat and then rubbed the nape of his neck, trying not to tell me I had hit a nerve. "And that stunt you pulled kissing my neck like that? Never again."

I rolled over on the bed and stared up at the ceiling. "I don't think I could want to punch you more right now. I get it. Loud and clear. Crystal. I'm over it. It was a moment of insanity. Now do us both a favor and find a new address."

"Shut up. You're just mad because I turned you down. You're acting like a baby about it." He held out his hand. "Give me the key."

"What key?" I asked, meeting his fuming glare with an indifferent one.

"Kristoffer's key. I'll drop it back in his pocket, and he won't be any the wiser. Hand it over."

"I don't know what you're talking about."

He ran his tongue along the outside of his teeth before he spoke. "Give it. You have no idea what you're playing at."

I displayed my hands with a smile, proving they were empty. "I don't have any key."

He was steaming, his mouth opening and closing several times before he landed on what he wanted to say. He pointed to my breasts and shouted, "Don't think I won't go in there and get it myself!"

I met his fury with a hearty laugh. "You'll do no such thing. Run along, little garden gnome. Try that story out on someone else." I dropped my pitch to imitate his gruff cadence and said, "Lucy's stealing keys from trained military men and hiding them in her bra!" I laughed again, laying back down on the bed and examining my nails. "Classic. When you tell it, make sure you mention to my uncle that you tried to threaten me with getting to second base. I'm sure he'll love that."

Jens was almost purple with rage. "That's not what I…" He clenched his fists and let out a noise of frustration. "You're punishing me for turning you down."

"No, I'm punishing you for hanging around after leading me on and *then* turning me down. You know, in my non-experience, when a guy flakes on you, he usually has the decency to leave you alone with your embarrassment afterwards. I'll say it again. Get out."

Jens pulled at his hair, as if I was the one being the problem. "Fine. I'll go check up on that Mace character. I knew Alrik had a kid, but I never met Charles. I don't make many trips to Elvage. Most of my dealings with Alrik were on the Other Side." He shook his head. "I don't like the look of him, though. Something's off, so stay away from him for now."

"Just for that, I think I'll make him my new best friend. Don't tell me what to do."

"Are you really going to be this difficult? This is who you are now?"

"Who I am?" I shouted, so angry I nearly forsook my non-violent ways. "You don't know the first thing about me!"

He turned and yelled back. "I know everything about you!"

And you don't want me. You've watched me for years, but you feel nothing for me. I've always been and always will be asexual. It has nothing to do with moving around. Even if I'd stayed in one place, I would still repel men like the plague. Fine. Message received.

"Get out and don't come back!" I commanded, pointing my shaking finger to the door.

Jens gave me a look that showed me how little he actually understood me before exiting. When he left, a gust of tension flew out of the room with him, to my great relief.

I dug the key out of my bra and examined it, and then tucked it back in its hiding place. I lay on the bed and stared at the ceiling for hours, content with my solitude. I focused on deep breathing and clearing my mind as best I could. It wouldn't do to spend my time here with fury just underneath the surface. I mentally unwound each tightly knit bit of tension from my brain, breathing a little easier the longer I rested. Eventually I was able to be dazzled by the gold dust in the air again, and the sight gave me peace.

I'm thinking it was a few hours later when Britta came to see me. "Are you well, Miss Lucy?"

I let her in and shut the door behind her when I saw Jens in the hallway. "I'm fine. You can just call me Lucy, you know. We climbed around a mountain together. I think we're past formalities."

Britta smiled. "As you wish. Alrik sent me to fetch you for dinner."

Thank goodness. The last meal I'd eaten was the apple from the red sack a day or more ago. "Thanks. Anything I should know before I go down? Do you eat with chopsticks or have separate tables for men and women or something?"

"No. Just forks and knives. And men and women eat together, but usually there's a separate table for the higher society folk. Alrik believes in having one table, so I don't think that will apply today." She worried the hem of her sleeve. "I'm afraid I don't know everything about your culture, so I'm not sure what all's different. Jens never talked much when he came home to visit."

"Huh. How often did he come home?"

"First Sun's day of every month. Gone by the morning."

"Jeez! Were we that in danger that he only had one day off a month?"

"I can't speak to that. Jens never fit in very well at home, except with Jamie and me. After the troll incident, he was too famous too fast. The king hates him because the people adore him. Jens is a private person, so he took a job where he could be invisible."

"I think I prefer him that way," I groused, straightening my hair as I reached for the door.

Britta eyed me. "No, you don't."

I raised an eyebrow at her sudden gall. "I like you," I declared.

Britta laughed. "Glad to hear it. I very much like you, as well. Shall we?"

As we walked past Jens and down the hallway, Britta drifted behind me. "Um, I don't exactly know where we're going. You don't have to walk behind me, you know. Is that a thing here?"

"Your station is closer to Jamie's, so yes. I walk behind you in proper society."

I sighed and stopped, glaring at Jens to back far away. He obeyed and took several steps back. I turned to Britta. "No offense to your awesome society, but I don't need a lady's maid or whatever it is. I have no friends here. Could you just be my friend? Is that ridiculous to ask?" I felt so awkward begging her to be my friend, but pride be darned, I needed someone who would be nice to me. Someone I could survive this with.

Britta's smile was warm when she reached out and held my hand. We walked like that down the many hallways, and I felt like a little girl, out to braid flowers in my hair with the neighbor girl for the afternoon. Britta was a nice addition to my empty life.

Henry Mancini scampered to greet me with a wagging

tail and a silly, winded expression that told me Foss and Tor were giving him a good workout. "Hi, baby!" I got down on my knees and scooped my puppy to my chest. He squiggled and squirmed in my arms, trying to lick my face. My smile had gone unused in the past few hours, and it felt good to exercise it for him. "Did you miss me?"

Before I knew what was happening, Henry Mancini was ripped from my arms. "Hey!" I was on my feet, scowling at Jens. "He's mine!"

"Jens!" Britta protested.

"He's a wolf, Lucy! You can't let a wolf that close to your face. He's not a dog."

"He's mine! I found him, and he kept you alive by warming you up when you were almost dead! Give him back!" I was so near tears at him taking my dog away, I think it shocked Jens into handing him over.

"Fine! Jeez! Calm yourself down. Far be it from me to keep a wild animal from biting your face off."

I hugged Henry Mancini, who could sense my tension. He licked my face to comfort me. "He was all alone when he found me! He has no one! I'm his mommy, Jens. You don't just take someone away from their mother!"

Jens held his hands up and backed away, looking almost contrite that he'd confronted a crazy woman. "Okay. I get it. You can keep him for now, but if he starts nipping at you, I have to get rid of him."

"No! You won't burn him up, like you did my whole life. He's a person, Jens! He has feelings!" I knew I was being irrational, but I didn't care. In fact, given the amount of crazy I'd been subjected to in the new world, Jens was lucky this was the extent of my outburst.

Jens used his eyebrows to tell me how stupid I sounded. "I won't kill him. I'll just put him back in the wild."

"You'll do no such thing," I snapped, turning on him and stomping in the direction of the scent of food with Henry Mancini scampering after me.

21

CHARLES MACE

oss, Nik, Tor, Uncle Rick, Jamie, Britta, and Charles Mace sat at the long dinner table that was laden with two large roasts, potatoes, a wide array of vegetables and brown pretzel rolls. The gold and crystal chandelier hung low to illuminate the gold walls that matched the rest of the house. The room was long, but narrow enough to feel cozy and accommodate the large table that seemed perfectly suited for our sizeable party.

I walked past my uncle, placed one hand on his shoulder in a hug, and reached out to hold his hand with my free one. Once our grips locked, I pressed the key into his palm. I took a seat next to Uncle Rick, who was at the head of the table, and frowned when Jens squeezed in on my other side. Henry Mancini kept my feet warm.

"Pass the morötter," Nik requested with a finger raised to gain Tor's attention. Tor was ladling something that looked like a Brussels sprout soup over his mashed potatoes. The dwarf passed Nik the gnarled-looking purple carrots.

We all dug into the delicious pot roast, and I could not remember anything tasting so good. I cooked well enough, but I had nothing on my mom. She could work her way through any cookbook without breaking a sweat. There was no replacing her. As hard as I tried to be an adult and take care of everything myself, I was still only twenty and couldn't make a decent lasagna to save my life. I could do chicken, so those were the dinners I had. A roast? A roast is a beautiful thing. I fed Henry Mancini scraps from my plate, and I could feel his love for me growing. That's the thing about a good roast.

I was knee-deep in my second plate of food, ignoring the conversation around me when I noticed Mace staring. He sat across from me on Uncle Rick's other side, taking slow bites as he watched me debase myself in my gluttony. I wiped my mouth on the cloth napkin and kept my eyes on my plate. Everyone else was regaling Uncle Rick and Jamie with their adventures on the mountain. I had little to add to that.

Jens scooted his chair closer to mine, as if he didn't take up enough space. I continued to chew some vegetable that looked like a cross between asparagus and a tomato, and tasted something like both. I didn't ask questions. I was just grateful someone was feeding me. The flavors were amazing, exploding on my tongue and livening my senses, and by proxy, my mood.

Mace's fork was poised as if he meant to eat the food on it, but his hand forgot its mission. I could feel his eyes on me still, studying my every move.

Now Jens was fighting me for elbow room. I jabbed him off with my elbow, but he did not seem to notice my affront at his proximity. "Get lost," I grumbled, clutching Henry Mancini closer between my ankles.

He responded by leaning his torso into my personal space, as if he was shielding me from something.

I released my fork with a clatter and crossed my arms. "Dude! Back off."

Jens paid me no mind. "Rick, you want to tell your man to keep his eyes to himself?" He glared at Mace, motioning to me with his fork. "There's nothing for you here."

I wanted to snap at Jens for being rude, but the truth is that Mace was giving me a mild dose of the creeps. I kept my mouth shut, but kicked him under the table.

He didn't even flinch, which made me feel pathetic that I couldn't move him with my force. I instantly regretted my action. Martin Luther King, Jr. never would have kicked someone for being a jerk. I silently begged his forgiveness and vowed to use peaceful resistance next time.

Uncle Rick held up his hand to calm Jens. "Charles is of no threat to Lucy. In fact, if dinner is over, I would like a word with them both."

I shoved three more bites in my mouth before anyone could take my plate away and gave Henry Mancini a chunk of meat. I ganked another roll from the basket before Uncle Rick's housekeeper cleared the table. The housekeeper was graying, and kept from looking directly at the guests at the table. "Thank you, Delling," Uncle Rick said to her as the others excused themselves for the night.

"Let me take yer yap outside till yer done eatin'," Tor suggested.

I could only guess that he meant Henry Mancini. I gave my puppy one more snuggle before sending him off with Tor.

When Jens did not get up, I motioned for him to get lost. He responded by wrapping his legs around his chair and crossing his arms over his chest.

I counted to four before speaking, making sure to keep my voice quiet. "Are you trying to be difficult? Uncle Rick didn't mention you on the guest list to this conversation."

Uncle Rick spoke up. "Actually, I prefer Jens stays. It's his job to know about you, and this will affect you, for certain."

Jens shot me a superior look with a raised eyebrow and a triumphant smirk I kind of wanted to smack.

I plastered on a stewardess smile, making sure I spoke quietly, so as not to lose my temper at Jens. "Then I'll write it all down in a telegram and send it to him in Guam, where you can reassign him. You can even verify the note so he knows it's not my wild imagination running away with me." I waved my hands in the air as I spoke, and then brought them to cross over my chest, mirroring him.

Jens looked like he wanted to respond, but he swallowed down his retort, so as not to incriminate himself by admitting we almost kissed.

Uncle Rick leaned his elbows on the table and pressed his ebony hands together, resting his lips on his fingertips. "Are you both finished convincing me you're unhappy?"

"Did it get him reassigned?" I asked petulantly.

"No. Jens is permanent."

"Then, no. I've got a whole laundry list for you."

"Save it for later, dear. This is more important." Uncle Rick motioned to Mace. "Allow me to properly introduce you to Charles Mace. I was given the privilege of caring for him over two decades ago when he came to me as a boy. His mother was Huldra, and was banished when he was very young. His parents did not trust the Other Side, since it would be teeming with jilted and angry Huldras, so they entrusted him to me."

Something dinged in the back of my brain, but I could not place what. Charles's gaze had not left my face. He did not seem perturbed that his messy childhood was on the table for open discussion.

"The Huldra are a people with strict aesthetics. They look like taller humans, but with cow's tails about two feet long stemming from the base of their spine."

"Huh? Cow's tails?" Another ding went off, but I still could not place the connections my brain was making without any help from me.

Charles Mace reached behind him and slid a real, live cow's tail over the top of his pants to show me.

"Whoa! Cool!" I exclaimed. I couldn't look away from the odd sight.

Uncle Rick continued, smiling. "His father and mother went over to the Other Side. She got her tail removed and put her Huldra ways behind her. They started a new life and had two children, raising them in the human world. The boy was born with a small tail, and the girl was... you, dear. Completely and perfectly human."

I was very still, letting the floating gold cease motion around me. The dings in my head blared like sirens now.

My mother had a scar at the base of her spine that she said she got falling down the stairs when she was a teenager.

My parents had another child. A whole other kid I'd never known existed. My heart began to pound so loud, it was the only sound I heard, though Uncle Rick was still speaking.

Linus. He was born with a vestigial tail that they'd amputated when we were newborns. We always said that we would get matching tattoos to cover up his scar when we turned twenty-one. He was always a little sensitive about his scar, though no one could see it. It was the one thing he wished he could change about himself, other than, you know, the crapbag of cancer.

Now that I knew the whole picture, it seemed to me that Linus hated his scar a little too much. My breath caught, forcing my words to choke out of me. "Did... did Linus know?"

When Uncle Rick looked at me with that cursed pity, the blood drained from my face. "I told Linus who he was on his seventeenth birthday when he was in the hospital and they didn't think he would make it."

I remembered that birthday. Linus hadn't spoken to me for days. I blamed it on the chemo. It did funky things to your body and could crush even the brightest spirit. Spending your seventeenth birthday in the hospital is no one's idea of fun. That was when he started treating me like his kid sister, instead of his equal.

I stood up from the table abruptly, but my knees were unprepared. They buckled under me, but I was yanked upright before I could plummet to the ground. Jens sat me in my chair, but my spine felt like a noodle. Echoes of my father telling me to sit up straight in my chair at dinner taunted me, but I couldn't obey.

Uncle Rick and Jens were saying something. It must've been important with the way they were carrying on, but I couldn't hear a word. Incoherent noise with no meaning reached me, burying me deeper in my fog.

Home. This place wasn't my home. I didn't belong. I wasn't related to Uncle Rick by blood. I tried to piece together that Charles Mace was my brother, but my sand-castle of sense crumbled every time I tried to put structure to it.

Suddenly my feet felt wrong here. I put all my brain-power into telling my legs to move, and finally they obeyed, pitying me as they went.

"Lucy, sit down," Uncle Rick insisted.

Jens tried to lead me back to my chair, like I was a senile old woman caught roaming the streets on her own at night.

I pulled away and reached for the door. "Air. I need air." Bull. I was going to run. As soon as my legs cooperated, I was going to bolt. I didn't care where or how, but I knew I needed Henry Mancini to come with me, and he was outside.

Jens held onto my triceps, searching my face for signs of life. "No, Loos. Just take a breath."

I felt cold all over, but somehow managed to struggle out of his grip. "I need air! I can't breathe in here!" I turned the knob and flung open the door, stumbling back and falling on my rear at the burst of unnatural sunlight that temporarily blinded me. My eyes shut tight as I moved to my hands and knees on the wood floor. I smacked the ground when Jens reached for me. "Don't you touch me! You knew! You knew all of it! Did Linus know about you?"

"It wasn't my decision!" I could hear the plea for clemency in his tone.

I let out a single cry of despair, and then slapped the ground again, my eyes still shut. "No! I will not cry in front of you!"

Uncle Rick and Charles were talking at me, but I could not understand the mix of voices all colliding with each other in dissonance. It was Jamie's voice that reached me above the din.

"Miss Lucy! Close the door, or you'll hurt your eyes." Jamie ran in and shut the door before me, taking in the men all shouting, and me shaking with heartbreak and rage on the floor. Instead of asking for explanations, he scooped me up off the floor like a child, lending me one arm for support for me to lean on and the other as a shield around my shoulders. "You should all be ashamed of yourselves! When you are ready to apologize for upsetting this woman so, she'll be in her chambers."

Jamie walked with me up to the bedroom, where I climbed under the covers and shut out the world.

22

SHARING A BEDROOM WITH JENS

J slept. I don't know for how long. When I awoke, there was no bustle about the house, so I guessed it was nighttime. Dim light filtered in from the window under the shade, illuminating touches of the room. While I slept, someone had put Henry Mancini in bed with me. For that, I was grateful. His fur was warm, and his snout rested across my arm as he slept peacefully.

Linus had kept a secret from me. A big one. He broke our pact, our us-against-the-parents deal we made when we were kids that we would never keep secrets from each other. We'd pricked our fingers and swore a blood oath, making it official. We were dramatic six-year-olds, but leaving your friends as often as we did made us cling to each other all the more.

I turned over in the bed and found a head of messy black hair leaning against the bedside. Jens was sleeping upright sitting on the wood floor, which I couldn't imagine being very comfortable.

Good.

I kissed Henry Mancini and slipped out of bed, tiptoeing toward the door. I tried to think thoughts of invisibility, but one of the floorboards gave me away. A hand shot out in the dark and wrapped around my ankle. I tripped and fell, smashing my knee into the ground. "Ow! What was that for?"

"You can't sneak off, Lucy," Jens scolded, releasing my leg when he was certain I wouldn't run. "Sorry. You alright?"

I crawled away from him in the dark, kicking at him for some distance. "I'm fine. And I wouldn't leave without Henry Mancini, so you can unclench."

"You cracked your knee pretty good. Let me take a look." He lifted my dress over my knee to examine it, but I yanked it back down.

"I'm wearing a dress, Jens! Hands off. Jeez!"

He lifted his arms in surrender. "Sorry. I wasn't thinking. Did I hurt you?"

I gesticulated wildly. "Are you serious? That's all you ever do! Go back to sleep. I just wanted to get a glass of water."

"I'm sorry, okay? When Linus got sick again when he was seventeen, I..."

"*He* wasn't seventeen. *We* were seventeen! You had a secret with my best friend in the world, and you both kept it from me for years! Why was I kept in the dark by everyone I loved? Why?" I stopped my tirade and shook the crazy out of my head as best I could. "No. We're not doing this. I'm getting water, and you're going back to sleep." I rubbed my sore knee, waiting for the sting to fade before I stood.

Henry Mancini hopped off the bed and scampered over to lick my purple toenails.

Jens petted Henry Mancini, earning a few licks to his palm. "So, that's how you're playing this one? Shut it all off and bury it where everything else got shoved?"

"I could crawl into a hole of despair, cry until I die and see if that pays the bills. I never tried that one before."

"Can't you have a normal conversation without sarcasm?"

"I don't know. Can you talk out of your mouth instead of your butt?"

"I guess you can't. You're such a child."

I laughed bitterly. "A child. You're funny. No, Jens. I'm old. I'm too old to have patience for people who can't handle their own feelings. I didn't imagine what almost happened here yesterday."

"Nothing happened!" he argued, clearly agitated.

"That's why I said 'almost'." I shook my head at him, donning a superior tone now that I'd regained the upper hand. "Wow. That hit a nerve. Do you want to talk about it? Or are you going to use sarcasm to cover over that place inside where you keep all the bad things buried?"

"Now who's talking out of her butt?" he jabbed lamely.

"Now who's the child?" I pointed out, gladly earning the glare he shot at me. I reached down to pet Henry Mancini, but my hand landed on his instead. "Don't touch my dog," I said as I cast his grubby mitt aside.

"He's not a dog. Henry Mancini's a wolf." Jens turned his wrist and caught onto my hand, holding it in the dark. I could hear his breathing grow heavy as we glared at each other.

Then slowly, without warning, the mood shifted. The anger fused with intensity, and hanging between us was something raw and unbalanced. His grip on my hand tightened as he moved into my body space, leaning me back onto the floor. The motion was so smooth and swift, I didn't have time to resist it. I lay beneath his hovering body and felt neurons firing from head to toe, transferring energy and multiplying it without my permission. My arm was pinned to the ground next to my head, but instead of feeling helpless, I was emboldened.

Jens sniffed my hair, and then pulled up, studying my face for some sort of answer to all of his unspoken questions.

I let go of the ripcord and bunched my hand in his shirt. "Stop pissing me off," I growled, and then yanked him down.

Jens gave in to my gravitational pull. I gave in to the need I had been trying to live without. The instant his lips crashed onto mine, I felt an eruption from inside my chest. Passion, emotion, fury and something beautiful bloomed and blossomed and burst again and again as we kissed.

I wrapped my legs around his waist and rocked us until I was on top, and he was my prisoner. I shoved his hands to the floor beside his head and reveled in the surprise mixed with unbridled lust on his face as he jerked his chin up to beg for more of my mouth. His need was captivating and oddly heady, so I indulged him.

I indulged myself.

Neither of us liked the submissive role on the floor.

Jens pulled a fast one and rolled me so I was beneath him again, but instead of attacking like the animals we were in the moment, he slowed. His kisses were filled with just as much passion, but he took the time to relish every brush of our lips. Each movement was a plea for understanding, for acceptance, for something he needed only from me.

I gave it to him. Whatever it was. Whatever he needed. I gave it all up for the taking. He kissed me in lengthy strides, and for once, our mouths worked for our benefit. He kissed the snark straight out of me. He took away the anger I could not put words to. He put value to the parts of me I secretly tore down and treasured the bits of me I was unsure about.

He kissed me slowly until I was trembling beneath him, a jumble of emotions and stimulated nerves. "Better," he whispered into my cheek as he allowed me a moment of reprieve from the intensity. "Better than I ever imagined it."

"I give it a seven," I responded once my voice came back to me. We both sounded like we'd run a marathon.

Jens snorted into my neck, collapsing on top of me. "Sorry. You can't make jokes when I'm like this. Seven out of how many?"

"Indeterminate."

"Oh, man. That's a five-syllable word. I haven't scrambled your brains enough." He kissed me again, a savoring one to remind us both that what just happened had indeed occurred. He made a noise under his breath, a sort of "mm", like I was a delicious dessert he could not get enough of. I was very aware that I was wearing only a thin dress.

"That was better than I imagined it, too, for the record."

He rolled off me and propped himself up on his elbow, his other hand tracing the contours of my face. "You fantasized about kissing me?" Henry Mancini whined for attention, so Jens gave him a clumsy pat.

"No. Well, yes, but I meant for my first kiss. Spent a lot of time picturing it. I'm glad it was with you. That was incredible."

Jens covered his face with his free hand. "I forgot that was your first kiss. I'm sorry, Loos. There were no flowers. No romance. I pretty much just attacked."

I smirked, giving him one light brush with my lips. "That's the thing about chemistry. Explosive if you do it right."

23

HALFY

I woke up the next morning in the bed and peeked over at Jens, who was asleep on the floor between me and the door. Watching him breathe in and out was comforting; it assured me that it really had happened, and that he wasn't flaking out on me this time. He was so sweet in sleep, his lips parted and arm splayed across his toned belly. I didn't mean to rouse him just by staring, but he rolled to face me.

"Morning," he said, his voice gravelly. He stood and stretched before sitting on the edge of the bed, cracking his neck twice. "You sleep well?"

I sat up and kissed him in lieu of an answer.

He moaned into my mouth, and I thrilled at the sound. He tipped me back onto the sheets, starting the day with a solid make-out, which, really is how every day should start.

He grabbed onto my leg and hitched my knee over his hip, eyes still closed. His large hand palmed my calf muscle and squeezed as he emitted that "mm" noise again. "I like you in a dress."

I kissed his swollen lips. "I like *you* in a dress."

He snorted and rolled onto his back, the perfect picture of restful slumber. He breathed so peacefully that I was content just to watch him.

Then he pounced. I squeaked as we wrestled, fighting to be on top as we rolled around on the bed, laughing and kissing each other in our cozy little bliss. The fighting was the best part about the kissing, and we did both well.

The knock on the door a few minutes later was a bummer, and I was gratified to catch the murderous look Jens threw at the door for interrupting our time. "One second." He untangled himself from me and sat on the edge of the bed, taking a few deep breaths to slow his racing heart. "It's not kosher for a Tomten and his charge to be sharing a bed, so try not to look so... like you've been rolling around in the sheets with me."

I hopped out of bed, straightened my hair and opened the door. "Good morning, Jamie," I beamed.

Jamie's expression of concern mutated into confusion at my giddiness. He looked to Jens, who stood from the bed a little too quickly, straightening his shirt. "Oh! Um, good morning, Miss Lucy. So sorry to interrupt." His eyes lit up with joy and teasing when he addressed his friend. "Jens, did you sleep well, brother? Alrik would like to see you both downstairs for breakfast in the observatory." He leaned down to pet Henry Mancini, and I saw Jamie's small red pointed hat fastened to his wavy brown hair.

"I slept fine. We'll be down in a minute." Jens tried to avoid his best friend's knowing look. "Don't start, Jamie."

"Shall I send word to Jeneve that she's off the hook for good now?"

Jens shook his head in warning at Jamie, his eyes wide.

"Who's Jeneve?" I asked, running the pearl-handled brush through my curls.

Jens answered with "no one" just as Jamie answered "my sister". Jens sat on the edge of the bed and shoved his feet into his boots and began lacing them up. "Drop it, Jamie. She doesn't understand our culture. It'll seem weird to her."

I bent down and kissed the top of Jens's head, earning a giddy grin from Jamie. "You always seem weird to me. I highly doubt Jeneve will be the tipping point."

Jamie waved off Jens's discomfort. "Surely you know about how Jens saved our village from the tribe of murderous trolls?"

"I do." I clasped my hands under my chin and faked a swoon. "My hero!"

"Oh, shut it. Adoration from you is just unsettling." Jens stood and stretched, avoiding my eyes.

"Aren't you going to wear a little garden gnome hat, like Jamie's?" I inquired, still fuzzy on the details of their culture.

Jens scratched his rippled abdomen, drawing my eyes like a beacon. "Nah. That's for proper folk. Trust me, no one expects me to be proper. They expect me to slay the trolls and beat up the bad guys."

Jamie opened the door and continued his story as we walked down the hall. "Back then, the reward for anyone who vanquished the trolls was a small fortune and the king's daughter in marriage."

Well, that was worth stumbling over my own two feet. Jens righted me as Henry Mancini batted the hem of my dress. "Don't get worked up. I'm not married."

"Oh. Okay. Confused me there for a second. You can see how gravity would be my nemesis after that."

"I took the cash reward, but turned down the offer for his daughter. Serious slap in the face to the king. That, coupled with the fact that everyone got a little carried away in their gratitude is why King Johannes has it in for me. Plus, Jamie's my best friend."

"I'm the black sheep of the family," Jamie admitted with a small amount of pride. "Royalty is supposed to sit around all day and reap the benefits of the labor of the people. I do not believe in that. I don't live in the palace anymore. I have my own home, which you've been in. I raise my own crops and have a marvelous time doing it."

"But you're betrothed to that other Nisse woman," I observed. "So you must still be seen as a ruler of value, right?"

Jamie's smile died. "Yes. And when the time comes, I shall fulfill my duty. Father thinks it'll smooth over relations between our regions. Plus, he does not wish me to marry below my station. Sets a bad precedent for my more valuable siblings."

Jens rubbed a stiff muscle on his left bicep. "If I would've just sucked it up and married Jeneve, my family's position would have been higher, and Britta might've been an option."

"Jens!" Jamie protested, shocked that Jens would speak about their hidden love in front of me.

"Oh, is it a secret?" I asked, my fingers tracing the gold-painted hallway walls as we walked. "I mean, it's written all over your faces."

The prince shook his head at his friend. "You know it wouldn't have mattered, even if you did marry Jeneve. Father will have what he wants, so he's traded me like a sack of flour. It's my birthright. Besides, if you had taken Jeneve for your wife, the fortune you won would be long gone by now. Father doesn't realize how much it takes to satisfy her, because our money comes from the people. I would never have let you marry her, so there's no use dwelling on it."

Jens offered a weak smile to his friend, clapping his hand down on his shoulder from behind. "Sure, but then we could've been brothers."

Jamie turned and gripped the nape of Jens's neck, and then pulled him in for a loud kiss on both cheeks. Very Italian, and totally adorable. "Jens, we *are* brothers."

"You two are precious," I commented as we reached the observatory.

"Go on in, Jamie," Jens instructed, pulling me aside before we entered. Henry Mancini jumped up for attention, which Jens gave him in the form of a scratch behind the ear. "Things are different here than where you come from. We can't hold hands or kiss in public or be... you know. That kind of public stuff just isn't done here. If it is, people will assume we're getting married or something. The king's already tried to have me killed three times for turning down his daughter. If word gets to him that I'm... you know, what happened last night? You'll be on his short list, and it'll be bad for you. And for me, since I protect you. That's why I was a jerk to you yesterday."

I shot him a simpering look. "You know, you could've just explained that yesterday. Didn't have to go all stereo-typical cool guy on me."

He smirked. "But I am cool." When I had something to say to this, he held up his hands. "You're right. That was lame. Do over. Hey Loos, as much as I want you all the time, we can't be public about it in Tomten or Elvage."

"Alright. So no tantric sex in the observatory in front of your friends and my uncle? Boring!" I pulled on him, but he didn't move. "Come on."

"Hold on. I'm picturing it." He closed his eyes with a devious grin.

I walked into the observatory with Henry Mancini, ready to stuff my face with scones, tea and whatever else my uncle's housekeeper cooked up. My appetite was curbed, though, when I saw Charles Mace added to the band of thieves. The bliss of the kiss faded and crumbled in parts as the night before slapped me in the face.

Brother. Charles Mace and I shared DNA, which made him my brother.

Mace was staring at me in that intensely focused way, as if studying me would bring him closer to the parents he couldn't remember. I wanted to avoid him, but instead I decided to face the weirdness head-on. Taking a deep breath, I walked right up to him and stuck my hand out in greeting. "Hey. Yesterday was kinda crazy, huh?"

He took in every facet of my very normal hand and finally grasped it, his expression that of wonder at the contact. His tail swished behind him. "Yes." His silver eyes cataloged my every breath. "I've so wanted to meet you, ever since I learned my parents had other children."

Henry Mancini barked at our contact, making his opinion of Mace very clear. "Hush, now," I chided the pup. Turning my attention back to Mace, I said, "How long have you known?"

"A few years."

We were still shaking hands, which I tried not to feel weird about. "Ah. Did you handle it as gracefully as I did?"

The corners of his mouth lifted, his thin lips similar to Linus's. "I believe I broke Alrik's favorite teacup."

"Good for you. He deserves it for keeping us in the dark for so long." As much as I didn't want to admit it to myself, Mace looked unbalanced. Crazy, even. Maybe it was the silver touch to his eyes, or the black hair that was a little too long and worse than a good Johnny Depp-type of messy. Perhaps it was the dog collar, or the fact that he wore a black shirt and pants, when no one else was dressing emo. He had hunched shoulders, and a tall, lanky form that was given to hovering. Then there was the unblinking way he stared at me. They were all signs that he'd grown up without a sibling. There was no one to tell him to stand up straight, get a girlfriend and stop being weird. Poor guy.

I dropped his hand, since the handshake seemed never-ending. "Just so you know, if I'd caught wind of any of it, I would've pitched a good old girl fit until they introduced us. I had no clue of any of it."

He rolled his shoulders back a little and gave me a small smile. "A 'good old girl fit'? What would that look like?"

I rattled my fists in the air, shook my head and mimed screaming to conjure up a nice representation. "You know, like that. Maybe with a 'how dare all of you' thrown in for good measure."

"I tried every trick in my book, including a version of your girl fit, and nothing worked. I've so wanted to meet you." He swallowed, daring me to look away from those strange eyes. "I very much wish I could have seen them. Our parents."

The way he said "our" made my heart clench in my chest. My mom had another child. My dad had hidden an entire life from us.

I thought I had all the time in the world with them to ask questions of how they met and personal details that might've led me to Undra. Linus was a limited edition, but they were supposed to live forever.

"Mom would have liked you," I admitted, another clue sliding into place. "Her paintings. She was always drawing different kinds of eyes. Ones that don't exist where I come from. I guess they were yours. I can't imagine someone forgetting eyes like those."

It was as if I'd told him he'd won a thousand dollars. Not a million, but a solid thousand. A big, no holds barred smile broke out on his face, chasing away the cagey expression he'd worn non-stop since I first laid eyes on him. "She did?"

"Yeah. Stupid me never asked about them. But they were yours. Unmistakable."

Everyone else was milling about the room, eating and talking, but Uncle Rick and Jens were sitting at a table in earshot.

Charles lifted his hand as if he meant to touch my hair,

but retracted, realizing that was not kosher. "We look nothing alike," he commented, mildly amused.

"I don't really look like Linus, either. He was taller with darker blond hair." I whirled on Uncle Rick, face stern. "Why didn't Mom and Dad ever talk about this? Why were Linus and I kept in the dark?"

Uncle Rick dabbed his mouth with a pale blue cloth napkin before answering with a guarded expression. "Because the pain of leaving a child behind was greater than they could bear."

Mace's expression closed off again.

Though I did not know him, my heart went out to the poor guy. What a crappy situation. I reached out and patted Mace's back.

Charles stiffened at the contact, as if I'd shocked him. Slowly, he relaxed, offering me a bewildered smile as he leaned into the touch. He had all the haunted markings of an outcast.

Something swished and caught my eye. Sure enough, Charles Mace's tail was protruding from under his shirt.

I tried not to stare, but I mean, come on. It was a man with a cow's tail. I had to remind myself not to grab it so I could get a better look.

Uncle Rick stood and called the meeting to order. Instead of finding a seat in the mix, I sat on the outskirts with Mace, determined not to abandon my new... brother.

Brother. I could say that, right? I wasn't betraying Linus by calling a spade a spade. Right?

Charles and I sat next to each other on a blue and gold loveseat that needed to be restuffed. I could feel the wood on the edge. He watched me in his unsettling way and slowly moved his hand to mine, lifting it and cradling it between his as if I were made of glass. "May I?"

"Um, hold my hand? Sure." Henry Mancini growled, but I shushed him again. He whined and circled three times before curling up on my bare toes to warm them.

The gold flecks floated around us as we listened to Uncle Rick tell the same story he'd told us last night. Jens was next to Uncle Rick, leaning back in his chair casually, but I could tell that he was on high alert, glancing over at me every few seconds.

Once Uncle Rick caught everyone up, he continued on to new information. "I fear we may run into the same problem we did with the Tomten, that they will not want their portal closed and we will not get our chance. That's why I've decided to move in stealth. It'll take much time for word to spread to this region that a portal has fallen. King Johannes's pride runs deep, and he's got a grudge against King Hallamar of Elvage he's quite attached to. Letting loose a disgrace like this would be quite uncharacteristic of the Tonttu king. So we have a little time to plan our attack." This brought about a few noises of appreciation. "To close the portals, you must tear them down using Pesta's rake, which thanks to Lucy and Jens, we have." He nodded to me, as if I'd done something impressive. "For those of you not in the know, each land's portal can only be destroyed or accessed by its people. So elves cannot use the Nøkken portal to the Land of Be, and so forth. I will be the one using the rake on the portal for Elvage."

I felt Mace stiffen around my hand. His hawk-like angular face was very focused on every detail of the plan.

I kinda wanted to flick his tail.

"When it comes time for each of you to destroy your portal, you must take the rake in your hand and knock down the bone frame *without* passing through. If you pass through it, your arm and soul are forfeit to her, and she'll be in possession of the only weapon we have to destroy the portals, so do not attempt it." Uncle Rick took a sip of his tea, as if he had not spoken of amputations. "We must limit her access to new souls."

I raised my free hand and waited patiently to be called on.

Uncle Rick had a gleam of happiness in his eye when he saw my other hand sandwiched between Mace's. "Yes, Lucy?"

"Is Charles coming with us?"

"Astute question, dear. Yes. Charles is my charge, and he's decided to help us."

I wasn't terribly fond of Charles being referred to as a charge and not his son. It felt distant, and I couldn't imagine the hurt I would feel if my dad called me that.

Tor grumbled, "What use can a halfy be?"

Uncle Rick continued on as if Tor had not spoken. He started with the order of nations we would travel to, and various obstacles we might face. Mace was watching me, which I tried to be cool with.

"One key problem we'll have after we destroy the next portal is the increase in security around the others. I specifically chose each of you because so few are opposed to the Land of Be. Each of you is irreplaceable. We must have one from each land destroy their own portal. So work as a team and leave no one behind."

Henry Mancini licked my ankle, so I stroked him with my other foot. He could feel my discomfort surrounding the plan.

So could Mace. He stroked my knuckles with his thumb and wrapped his nearest arm around my shoulders. I know it was a sweet thing for him to do, but it felt strange. Linus and I were thick as thieves, but he didn't hold my hand and put his arm around my shoulders when we sat around watching TV together. I tried to relax into the nonthreatening touch, determined to fit in here with my new... brother.

"Lucy, Jamie and Jens will meet with King Hallamar this evening. I trust you all slept well?" Heads nodded in response. Uncle Rick continued. "They will keep him and a few of the more important names in Elvage distracted while we do our deed at the portal. We rendezvous at Drucken Tavern under the name Holden."

I turned to Jens, asking him with my eyes if he knew where that was. He nodded, but his mouth was taut with tension and displeasure.

Tor spoke up. His wiry red hair was shoved in a netting of some kind. It looked like a bird's nest made of red dreadlocks. I kinda wanted to shove pencils in it. "Ya haven't told us why we've got a halfy in on the plan. I thought ya just needed one from each race. But now we got three Toms and a halfy."

"And two females," Foss added. "One the size of a rat."

Mace swallowed, but took no obvious affront to Tor's slight on his ancestry.

Britta had been attentive and silent the entire time, but

somehow the fact that she was a woman trumped all potential usefulness in Foss's black eyes.

At this, I snapped. "Tor, I'm a halfy, too, so if you can't handle Charles on the journey, you don't get me. Good luck tearing down the human portal without a human who has ties to Undra! And Foss? Shut your smackhole about me and Britta. I've had enough of it, and she doesn't deserve that. You heard Uncle Rick. We do this as a team. Get onboard, you jag." I glared at Foss, who leaned forward and leveled an intimidating stare at me, expecting, to his folly, that I would back down.

Foss growled, "Control your rat, Alrik."

Uncle Rick's voice was kind, as it always was, but his eyes had a note of scolding in them. "Foss? Lucy? I trust you can overcome your differences with grace. And Torsten the Mighty, I perceived you to be of the highest intellect, athleticism and judgment of your kind, which is part of why I chose you to join us. Yet you seem to be under the impression that half-breeds are inferior to the purebloods."

"Aye, sir. They are. They don't have the full access ta their kind's magic."

Uncle Rick motioned to Mace, who stood, taking my hand with him as he moved to Uncle Rick's side. I could tell he wanted me to vouch for him, and I wanted to, but really? I just met the guy yesterday. When standing next to him and letting him hold my hand was all that was required, I relaxed a little.

"Lucy just learned that Charles Mace is her brother. Charles is one quarter human, one quarter elfish and one half Huldra, same as Lucy. This gives him the ability to destroy not one, but two portals." I could see light bulbs flashing over their heads at this reasoning. "Even if portals were not our mission, I would still call on Charles as one of my most useful assets."

The others sized up Mace uncertainly. "You wish me to be elfish?" Charles questioned, his lanky posture adding to his borderline unbalanced menace.

"I do. They seem to need further proof. And I admit, I rather enjoy the sight of a speechless dwarf. A true rarity in nature." Uncle Rick encouraged his surrogate son with a wave of his hand.

Mace dropped my grip. "My birth father was a wind elf, but I was raised by Alrik, a water elf, so I'm schooled in both arts." Charles mimed opening the window like a grand magician or something. Like a child at a magic show, I was fascinated when the window started shaking against the pane ominously.

The shutters banged open against the outside of the house as if his hand had actually touched them. The curtains blew out of the room as alien wind was introduced. The mid-morning sun struck me with its brilliance. Normally, I would have just shut my eyes, but I had been looking right at the window when it opened. The shock of the light made me stumble back. I heard a chair scrape the floor, and before I hit the ground, I felt Jens at my back. He steadied me, so I hid my face in his shirt. Henry Mancini yapped around me, but I couldn't see him. I couldn't see anything.

"You know she can't handle our sun!" Jens yelled. "Jamie, shut the windows!"

I heard more banging and assumed Jamie was obeying.

Jens palmed the back of my head to keep my face buried in his black shirt.

Jens was arguing with Mace, but the sun was so over-whelming that I was still trying to get the flashbulbs of light to calm down inside my eyelids, and didn't hear much of their fight.

Foss's gruff cadence could be heard above the ruckus. "There's no way we can travel with her! Useless female!"

Uncle Rick let out an attention-arresting whistle, quieting the riotous mules. "We need Lucy to come with us, and I'm working on a solution to her aversion to our sun. Patience, everyone." He produced the key I'd given him and moved toward Charles.

Jens and Nik both let out shouts of protest. "No, Alrik!" and "You don't know what he'll do!" reached my ears.

I heard a click and a whimper from Mace. Uncle Rick's voice was dripping with emotion. "It's done, son. You're free."

I heard Mace's choked cry and knew the two were embracing. "Thank you, Alrik. You can trust me."

"I know, son. I know. Now go help your sister."

A hand from behind me went over my face and palmed my eyes while I stood in the arms of an angry Jens. "You should've told us, Rick! We deserve to have a say in you unleashing a Huldra!"

Tor held up his hands. "The men can't control us with their whistle. Only the women carry that magic."

Jens stared down Alrik with a sneer. "I know you, Rick. You wouldn't have kept Charles so hush-hush if he didn't have something up his sleeve. He's the son of Hilda the Powerful! They collared him for a reason."

Charles gripped my face and tried to remove me from Jens, who only held me tighter.

Henry Mancini was going nuts, barking at the two men I was sandwiched in between. Britta was yelling at Jens to let me go. Tor started shouting, "Get the halfy! He'll rip off the human's head!"

Mace's voice was laden with emotion as he pressed his body against my back. "I'm Huldra, Jens, not a monster. I can fix her! If you trust Alrik, then trust me."

"Get your hands off her!"

Anxiety flooded me, and then it happened.

Mace let out a beautiful melodious whistle in my ear that, I swear, had three different notes flying out simultaneously throughout the entire tune. I had never heard a whistle like that. I knew the sound was loud, and delivered right into my ear, but it was not intrusive. Instead I found myself leaning into it. I pulled away from Jens so that only Mace was clutching me. He held my waist with one arm, and gently stroked my cheek with the other. The whistle was so magnetic that I found myself leaning up on my toes and pressing my ear to his lips to absorb every note. I'd never understood the Pied Piper of Hamlin before, but now I knew he must have been Huldra.

When the tune ended, I was released from the spell. I slumped against Mace despite myself and shook sense back into my brain. My eyelids opened slowly, and for the first time, I saw Charles Mace clearly. Lots of baggage. No real home. His collar was gone, and for once, he looked like he was allowed to be himself.

Charles moved to the window Jamie had shut and pulled back the lace curtains. He pushed out the shutters, letting the luminous sunlight into the room. Protests ensued, but the sun was not repellant this time.

I walked toward the window and shoved my hand in the golden glow, relishing the heat I'd been missing.

Mace addressed the room. "That was three different commands. One modified her sight. The second calmed her down. The third healed the blast to her eyes from when she looked at the sun before. I can do anything a full Huldra can do, but I can also work two kinds of elf magic: water and wind."

"Three in one," Uncle Rick added, beaming with pride at his protégé. "So now you know he won't be a handicap on the group. In fact, he's made Lucy more useful, since she can now walk around in daylight. Lucy? Do you have any objections?"

I turned from my spot in the glittering sun and smiled. "Can he kill spiders?"

Mace nodded slowly with a look of confusion at this inferior talent I insisted upon. His collar was gone, and he looked a new man, radiant with the joy of freedom.

"I'm fine with it. Put it to a vote?" I suggested, unwilling to let myself have the final say in anything in a world where I couldn't see without help.

Uncle Rick took the floor back. "All those in favor of Mace joining the group?"

All hands went up, except Tor's. He crossed his arms petulantly and stared Uncle Rick down. "I won't vote fer it, but I accept yer choice. If ya say he's good fer it, I won't stand in tha boy's way."

"That settles it. Lucy, you're set to meet King Hallamar

shortly. Can you be ready to leave soon? Send your bags with Britta, and she can bring them to the tavern."

"Sure thing." Bags. That's funny. All my crap is inside Jens's Mary Poppins backpack. I stared out the window in amazement at the nature I could finally get a good look at while Uncle Rick carried on talking to the others about traveling to the tavern.

24

AWAKENING THE BEAR

The trees were so tall and thick; I could scarcely understand how houses were built around them. And such grand homes, too. Some were three stories tall and narrower than I would have thought could be architecturally sound. The gold dust was everywhere, not just in the house. I wanted to dance in it and roll around in the moss-like grass.

Mace stood behind me, watching me watch the world he was accustomed to.

I motioned for him to stand next to me. "What's that?" I asked, pointing to an oddly-shaped tree with golden leaves.

"Those are *knut träd*. Thousands of years old." He touched his neck where the collar had been and smiled at me, relief still washing over him in waves. "Thank you. Alrik said it was you that stole the key from Kristoffer. I can't believe you did that for me."

I didn't look over at him because I could tell he was still staring at me. I didn't have the heart to tell him I hadn't known what the key was for, and that I was just doing what Uncle Rick told me to. I shrugged. "Well, thanks for using your Jiu-jitsu to Kung-Fu me new eyeballs. I really hate being cooped up."

"You also hate when people have to do things for you. I can tell. This way you won't be so dependent on Jens."

"You caught that, did you?"

"Hard to miss. What's Jiu-jitsu? And what's Kung-Fu?"

I tried to explain it, but I think I only confused him more. I turned around and saw everyone grouped up in deep discussions about provisions and the trek. I knew nothing about any of it, so no one asked my opinion. "Feel like a jailbreak?" I asked conspiratorially.

Delight flooded Mace, who nodded. "The back entrance. No one's there this time of day."

"Keep it casual," I warned. I was so tired of being followed and cooped up and told what to do. I had been living and operating as a full-fledged adult before this. Now I had a short leash, and did not care for it.

Mace and I strolled toward the hallway with Henry Mancini tagging along at my heels. As soon as we cleared the observatory, I broke out into a run. Mace grinned as we raced for the win and burst out the back door.

I welcomed the sunlight that greeted me and bathed me in its beauty. I dared it to be too much for me this time, now that I had Mace in my artillery. I ran with my elfin-Huldra-human brother through the trees with trunks so thick, I swear a car could have passed through if it was hollowed. Mace led the way to a creek with water so blue, it looked like someone dumped a bucket of dye in it to get it that explosive cerulean color. I stuck my toe in to see if it would dye my skin, but it did not.

Once one toe was refreshed, both feet wanted in. "Come on!" I waved to Mace, who shook his head with the most natural smile I'd ever seen on the man. "Oh, but it's so cool. The water's perfect."

"I believe you."

I looked down and saw opaque rocks catching rainbows from the sunlight in their hard surfaces. I bent down to pick one up, frowning at how wet my dress was getting. "Yikes. You think Uncle Rick'll be pissed I'm ruining my dress?"

"Pissed?"

"Yeah. You know. Be so mad, he pisses himself?"

Mace laughed at my crude terminology. "No. He bought you a few dresses. I imagine he won't piss himself, if I understand what that means."

"I'm sure you can figure it out." I watched his easy smile and the shoulders that had once been hunched relax. "You're happy," I observed. "That's good. I've only ever seen you with that intense face you do." I mimicked his penetrating stare.

Mace started collecting a few opaque stones. "I was nervous to meet you. I thought you might hate me. I've known about you a lot longer than you've known about me. More time to obsess about why my parents left me, and what made you worth sticking around for."

"Oh." I dropped the hem of my dress in the creek. When he put it all in such blunt terms, I realized my selfishness in all of it. I only thought on how my parents' previous life affected me. I smacked my inner teenager in the forehead. "Jeez. I don't know what to say to that."

"I don't assume you have the answers to questions meant for them."

"I don't hate you. I can't imagine they did, either." I ran my big toe over a smooth stone, marveling at the glassy texture. "You were a kid. Sounds like they were when it all went south, too." I gave him a good look, now that he was standing up straight and not lurking. "How old are you?"

"Twenty-five."

"I'm twenty."

"I know."

I tried not to scowl, but I knew my attitude was evident on my face. "Of course you do. You, Alrik, Jens, and the stinking tooth fairy. Everyone knows everything about me, and I know nothing about anything here. I couldn't even see without help." I tipped my head toward him. "Thanks for that, by the way. Cowering like a child in front of seasoned warriors sucks." I clinked two of the stones together to test their strength. "I'm out of my element here, so you're not getting a good picture of me."

Mace squinted at me. "I think you look just fine from where I stand. Forget everyone else. You have to if you want to survive here."

"Yeah. What's all that nonsense about half-breeds? That kind of talk would not fly where I come from."

"So you don't mind that I'm not a pureblood?" he asked, his insecurity poking through as his tail rose behind him. His shoulders sagged, and though he was easily six and a half feet tall, he looked small in his shame.

"Your blood's as pure as mine is." I shrugged. "Most of

your world's things that matter have zip meaning to me. So, unless you're a Dodger's fan, we're square." I tried my hand at skipping the glass-looking rock, pleased when it made three whole jumps before sinking.

"I don't know what you're speaking of."

I sighed. "I know. No one does."

Boots stomping in the direction we came reached me, and Henry Mancini did not bother alerting me to the intruder. That's how I knew it was Jens. I looked up and saw his grim expression. "Uh-oh. Garden gnome on the warpath. Hide your valuables."

Mace greeted Jens with a nod of his head, which Jens ignored. "What do you think you're doing out here?"

"Am I your prisoner?" I asked politely.

"No, but…"

"Did you tell me not to leave the house as long as I live?"

He snarled at my disinterest in his fit. "I'm about to."

"I'm not in any danger. I took a chaperone," I said, pointing to Mace. "And I can see the house from here." I motioned to a chimney in the distance.

"No, you can't. And that's not even Alrik's house! You have no idea where you are!"

"Oh. Whoops." I put my hand on my hip. "You know, I lived without supervision before all this. I can come and go as I please." I motioned to myself. "Grown woman, here."

"Teenaged pain in my ass! Take this seriously!" He huffed at the edge of the creek. "And you've never lived without supervision. I was watching out for you every day for the past five years."

I placed two fingers to my lips and spoke to him like I

was the schoolteacher, and he was the child who needed things explained very slowly. "You were silent then. Let's revisit that, shall we?"

"You make me crazy!" he raged. He took a step forward, and I backed up instinctively. "Don't you dare run!"

"Get away!"

And then the water mutated. I'm sure there's a more technical term for it, but that's all I could think at the time. The water around me gathered up and rose in an instant, forming a wall between Jens and me. Jens growled, "Damned water elf!"

I let out an indelicate screech and fell backward into the water. Henry Mancini growled at the water wall and tried attacking it to save me.

I looked up and found Mace standing at my side. His expression was pure fury. He was glaring at Jens with his hand up, controlling the liquid divide between us. Then it dawned on me that by fighting with the pit bull, I'd unwittingly awoken the bear. "Mace! Mace, it's alright. That's just how we are." I struggled to my feet and tugged on his sleeve. "Charles, calm down!" I gently pressed my hands to his chest to remind him I was in one piece, and that he was overreacting.

He tore his searing gaze away from Jens and looked down at me with those inhuman eyes. He wrapped one arm around my hips in a lax half-hug. "He should not speak to you like that."

I waved my hand at Jens, as if it were all just a big joke. "Who, Jimmy here? That's nothing. You should see when it's my turn to yell at him. Cries like a baby, he does." I worked up a semi-convincing smile. "That's just how we are. Probably seems weird to you, but it's normal where I come from. They don't have that same iconic view of women you people do here."

Mace's expression twisted in confusion. "That's how you do things? That's normal for you? What kind of a place do you come from?"

I shrugged. "The real world. When people are mad at each other, they duke it out. That was just Jens telling me he cares about me." I winked at Jens, adding fuel to his fire. "See how worried he got when he didn't know where I was?"

"I don't understand," Charles admitted. "But you're okay with it?"

I rubbed his arm to calm him down. "Of course. Jens just worries too much."

"And you don't worry enough," Jens growled. "It's like you're asking to get lost or abducted out here. You know nothing about this world, and yet you're perfectly fine running off whenever you feel like it. We're going home right now."

"You gonna add a 'young lady' to that?"

"How about 'childish brat'?" he snapped, pointing behind him. "March!"

"Say pretty please." Henry Mancini licked Jens's boot to calm him down.

Jens was livid. It was kinda funny. Not the whole Mace freaking out thing, but Jens thinking he had any sort of control over me.

Then he lunged forward and grabbed me around the waist, throwing me over his shoulder. That was not so funny.

Jens summoned Henry Mancini, and then exhaled deeply, tugging on his ear. By Mace's confused exclamations, I deduced that Jens had turned us invisible.

I responded to being carried so degradingly by singing the Partridge Family theme song. His back muscles tensed, and I could tell he was finally trying to control his temper. I lifted up the hem of his shirt and gave the middle of his back a few little kisses to make up for worrying him.

"Knock it off, Loos. I'm still pissed."

"No, you're not. You were worried about me."

"Sure. Without you, I'm out of a job."

I smiled. Even in my upside-down state, my blonde curls dangling and bouncing with each step, I took comfort in the fact that anyone worried about me. It had been a while since anyone cared to ask where I was, when I'd be home, or expressed any interest that my well-being affected them. I hugged his ribs, kissing him all over. "Okay, okay. I forgive you," I said, snuggling him as best I could.

He scoffed. "You forgive me? That's rich."

"I just can't stay mad at you. You're such a lovebug. A big, giant Care Bear." I dragged my fingernails across his belly, enjoying the shudder that relaxed his nerves.

"Knock it off." He tromped over a large stump, clicking his tongue so Henry Mancini could still find us. "You heard Alrik. You're meeting the elfish king soon. You need to get ready, and then we have to go. I don't have time to go around trying to find you in the woods with some guy." He sneered in Mace's direction, who could not see his disdain.

"Some guy? I was hanging out with my new brother!"

Mace walked beside us, thoroughly confused. "This is all normal talk, Lucy?"

"Yup. This is how Jens tells me he missed me. Now he's taking me back to his cave for a throw down."

"Shut it, Loos. He doesn't understand your sense of humor."

Mace took affront to this. "I'm not completely obtuse."

Doesn't understand my humor? We'll see about that. While my arms were around Jens's torso, I gently began working off his belt, holding the metal buckle from clanking too loud with one hand, and holding up his pants with the other. I had to work hard to keep my giggling under wraps as he stepped over the threshold to my uncle's home.

Jens marched us into the populated observatory, un-invisibled us and hiked me from over his shoulder to the floor, drawing the eye of my fellow adventurers. "I found her," he declared. "You deal with her, Alrik. Make her understand that she can't just go wandering off."

Uncle Rick was about to address me in a kinder manner than Jens would have liked, but his eyes were drawn upwards. "Jens, what... what happened out there?"

Mace grinned and then looked at me with appreciation.

"What?" Jens demanded of the laughter and knowing looks popping up throughout the room. He took a step forward and heard the jangle of his belt. He looked down and found his pants undone and sagging slightly, exposing his boxer briefs to everyone. He turned red and hiked his pants back up, fastening his belt as he glared at me. "Real funny, Loos. Get upstairs."

I obeyed, scampering up the steps and grinning at the outcome of my little prank. I sauntered into the room and was about to shut the door in his face so I could change, but he followed me inside. "I know you gave all the guys down there a free show, but I don't do that sort of thing. Out you go. I have to change."

He stood in the center of the room, fuming at me, a giant wet spot marking him across his shirt from my river-wet dress. "You... you..."

I stood up on my toes, yanked him down by his collar and kissed him lightly on the lips. "I'm sorry," I admitted behind closed doors. "I shouldn't have run away like that. I was just feeling a little cooped up. Wanted a chance to hang with Mace on my own and get a feel for him."

"I don't like him," Jens ruled. He pressed his forehead to mine, and I could feel some of his tension dissipating.

"Then why did you show him your underwear?"

"Crap. That was good." He cracked a smile and backed me toward the bed. I toppled backward onto the mattress, eyes wide as he loomed over me. "Enjoy your moment, Kincaid. Payback's coming."

Then he kissed me. It was urgent, laced with frustration. I could feel how scared he was that he'd lost me in every kiss, and I began to understand that someone here actually did care about me. I had nowhere to go that was mine, but Jens was mine, and somehow without my knowledge, I had let myself become his.

QUEEN LUCY OF THE HUMANOIDS

*D*inner with the King of the Elves was weird. First off, there was no table and no real food. There was only a tea service, and the tea tasted kind of like sun-dried mulch with an afterthought of honey mixed in. Jamie and I sat in tall-backed ornately carved wooden chairs across from King Hallamar and Queen Sorena. We were in a room with so many golden decorations, it was hard not to feel overwhelmed. Grape clusters as large as giant platters hung from the walls, and gold vines twined across the ceiling to give visitors the impression of being outside while they were still inside. There were three white birds with gold wings that flew around to different nests in the ceiling. Various rich-colored paintings of heroic elves in the throes of battle bedecked the walls in enormous gold frames, giving me a preview of what the elves judged as aesthetically pleasing.

Kristoffer was Head of the Guard, so he was standing at attention near the pillar-flanked door, sneaking me half-smiles every now and then. Jens was with us, too, but it was custom that he remain invisible. That way I could be safe, but it would not break the opulent mood with the sight of commoners.

Don't get me started. Martin Luther King would have had a field day.

I'd made my opinion known to Jens and Jamie on the way over in no uncertain terms. I believe the phrase "bigoted aristocratic smackholes" was thrown around at one point. Apparently Toms, male Huldras and dwarves were lower class in this society, while Fossegrimens were feared in all societies. Since I was a fairly new species to them, I was like, Queen Lucy of the Humanoids or something. It was hard to keep up.

I sipped tea as I'd seen done in Jane Austen movies my mom and I watched together and nodded politely to the conversation, keeping my opinions to myself unless asked a direct question. Not my first time being the new kid in town. I refer back to *Rule #1: When in doubt, shut your mouth.*

It helped that I was the oddity. The king and queen looked at me as if I was a giraffe in their room, strange and fascinating in my differentness from their normal. They were enraptured at my smaller stature, confused that I was clearly not dwarf. Everything I did, they took notice of, so I did very little to compensate.

The royal couple was almost seven feet tall, slender, had brown braided hair and sat erect like they'd sewn a yardstick into their flowing gold robes. They had those kinds of teeth you know have to be veneers, so you try not to look directly at them. The woman had spindly tattoos on her fingers that wrapped around her wrists and vined up her arms. It sort of looked like henna, but the ink was green. I wanted to ask about them, but knowing me, I'd be accidentally calling her fat or something.

It was three long hours that we were sipping tea refills in the dining room when I felt an invisible hand on my shoulder. I tried not to jump when Jens whispered in my ear, "Say something. This is moving too fast. You need to take up more time."

Really?

I could smell something beefy wafting in from the kitchen area. Despite how much I'd consumed last night, I was ravenous. My mom used to comment that each new day was a challenge to Linus and me to see if we could consume an entire hippopotamus. She was not wrong.

I cast around for something to say during the next lull. It was hard to tell when there was a lull, since the king and queen seemed perfectly content just sitting and staring at me. I straightened the gold and pale blue gown Uncle Rick gave me to wear. It was so fancy, I was afraid to move around too much in it. "That's a lovely painting," I said of the portrait of an elf, a huge golden boar and a guy with a funny little hat like Jamie's. They were all fighting against a giant bald janky-toothed man with black bark-like skin and red marks peppering his body. He looked like a comic book monster villain.

"Ah," said the king. "That's from back when King Johannes and I got along. Though Jamie's always welcome in my kingdom." He nodded his head to Jamie, who smiled kindly.

"You've always known what was important in running

your kingdom. Father's forgotten that, but I have not." Jamie made it clear that his affiliations with the rest of Undraland were not his childish father's.

There was another traffic jam worth of pausing, so I searched for something else. "What can you tell me about the artist who painted that?"

There we go. Look at me, conversationalist extraordinaire. The two rattled off various facts about Oden the Meticulous.

"I suppose if you're going to be labeled as meticulous, painting's a good profession to get into," I commented. It was as if I'd told the first joke that ever was. The two laughed like they'd never had occasion to before. Even Kristoffer's professional demeanor cracked at my "hilarious" wit.

When that reached a head, Jens flicked my ear, reminding me to be charming. I smiled. "I know so little about your world. Can you tell me about Prince Jamie? He's been too humble to say much about himself."

Jamie gave me a modest smile from his seat next to mine as the king spoke. "Jamie comes from a long line of Tonttu Tomten. He's the third born and chose to live amongst the people instead of above them at his proper place."

It was hard to tell if King Hallamar admired Jamie or was scolding him.

The queen chimed in, her voice low-pitched like a sexy jazz singer. "Are you not betrothed to Freya of the Nisse? I can only imagine the good that will do your region." She turned to explain what was common knowledge to me. "There are three Tomten tribes with three kings who do their best to rule together, but separate. Jamie's Tonttu tribe is known for farming. King Gunnar's tribe to the North handles the upkeep of the cities. Then the Nisse tribe looks after day-to-day commerce."

Though he sat with perfect posture, Jamie was at ease in the overly formal room as he spoke to me. "My father's tribe is seen as being of lowest value, since we don't protect or trade in anything other than food. However, our warrior Jens the Brave changed public opinion when we had a mess of trolls no one could get rid of. Even the Nisse's best men were slaughtered in a failed attempt, but Jens went out and destroyed the beasts single-handedly. Our tribe has been seen to be of greater value since then."

Queen Sorena sipped her tea. "How is Jens these days? I know of eleven petitions in my immediate circle for women that wanted him as their Tomten."

I was about to say, "Why don't you ask him? He's standing right behind me," but Jamie shook his head infinitesimally. I was kind of shocked and impressed that the guy who guarded my family was in such high demand. I made a mental note to stop firing him.

Jamie answered for Jens. "Jens is well. He works for Queen Lucy, which is why she's been so well protected. He fended off an attack of Weres recently. Pesta must've forgotten to use the peaceful souls, and filled the bears with horrific ones again." His tone was light, like chiding a well-meaning two-year-old, but I saw his steel cutting with the kindness. "It's rumored Jens fought off a pack of Were-dogs, too."

King Hallamar laughed at what he assumed was a joke.

"Oh, you know how the gossip spreads. Weredogs. Have you ever heard of such a thing?"

I looked the king dead in the eye and watched his merry expression die. "There were *three* Weredogs. They were sent by Pesta to attack me, and Jens ripped them apart with his bare hands." I dared Hallamar with my eyes to question that. "I don't rely on gossip, either, which is why I'm grateful I saw Jens do it with my own two eyes. I had to leave my world because Pesta was closing in on me. She's getting desperate, which is why she resorted to Weredogs. There aren't many bears in the area I was living in."

Jamie closed his eyes as if I'd just dropped a precious china cup on the floor. I felt the hand of my guardian gnome on my shoulder and shut my mouth.

Jamie popped in with a "delightful" little conversation changer that somehow spun me as a nature-loving loyalist to whatever it is they stood for. Something about the wisdom of elves. I kind of stopped paying attention when we hit hour four, and there was still no food to speak of.

What I wouldn't give for Tonya and her hot dog casserole right now.

Tonya. I wondered if my alleged death sent her into Danny's arms. Good for him. Though, she could do better.

The gold and glass double doors behind the Queen opened, and I almost salivated at the thought that I might be fed soon. Someone in an official-looking uniform entered, summoning Kristoffer and the king out into the hallway so they could speak in private.

"Is something the matter?" Jamie inquired politely, setting down his teacup on the narrow glass table in front of him. His acting was flawless, like he was bred for pleasantries laced with deception.

"I can't imagine there would be." The Queen glanced over her shoulder to see her husband speaking in hushed urgency with Kristoffer and the guard in the hallway.

Jamie spoke for me, since I was not sure how to play in his game. "Queen Lucy usually travels in secret to keep Pesta from finding her location. She is of utmost importance to her kingdom. Pesta is angry Queen Lucy won't let her build a portal to Be in her land, so she has sent Weres to attack her several times."

My spine straightened at the lie that I somehow had a vote in what Pesta did.

Queen Sorena appeared troubled, but I could smell a self-soothing lie coming. "Werebears are peaceful. Pesta only sends the best souls to inhabit her creatures. You get the occasional fluke, but on the whole…"

Jamie's face was solemn. "That is not the case on the Other Side. Pesta has no treaty with Queen Lucy, and she's going about it the wrong way."

Queen Sorena folded her long fingers in her lap. "Indeed. But Pesta has been sequestered to the Land of Be for years now. Surely there's no need to fear her. She's not known for targeting specific people. The palace of Elvage is a fortress." Sorena smiled demurely at me, her posture so straight, I did not understand how she'd maintained it for four hours. "You are safe here, Queen Lucy."

"Thank you, your majesty."

King Hallamar came back in, his chestnut brow furrowed. "I'm afraid we'll have to cut our visit short, your majesty."

Oh, me. Right. "Is something the matter?"

"No, no," he assured me a little too eagerly.

Jamie stood, offering his hand to me. "Has Pesta found her? Are there Weres spotted in the area?"

The king rubbed the back of his neck like he did not want to tell us the problem, but for my safety, he clued us in. "It's the portal. I must see to it. One of my guards informed me that there's been some sort of disturbance. I'm sure it's nothing, but I must go there straight away."

I took Jamie's hand and stood, bowing with him when the elves bowed to us. "Is there a path you recommend we take? I have to get out quick if Pesta knows I'm here."

Their expressions fell that I was leaving so soon. I can't imagine I'd said one interesting thing the entire time I'd been here, but the way they looked at me, I'm guessing it was sort of like having a unicorn over for tea. The unicorn doesn't have to say anything; it can just sit there and drink tea while you gawk, enthralled at the magical creature.

Hallamar had his hand on his wife's back. Her brown eyes clouded with concern as she spoke. "You're leaving? We've only just begun to know you. I would be honored if you stayed longer. I could show you more of the kingdom. I'm sure the disturbance is of no import."

I smiled at the gracious hosts. "Thank you, but I should be going. This has been great. Real nice. Thanks for tea and the company. Elvage is incredible. This gold dust you've got everywhere? Off the charts nuts."

Queen Sorena lifted her heels off the ground as she spoke, hoping to catch me in a lengthy conversation to deter my leave. "It's remnants of elfish magic. A trace left behind when large amounts are used."

"That's incredible," I complimented her people. "Thanks for everything, Sorena. I hate to go, but I'm just worried Pesta will come after me. I wouldn't want to cause drama in your beautiful land."

Kristoffer stepped forward with his barrel chest, the need for my safety trumping his desire for me to stay. Good man. "If I may," he said, excusing his interruption. "You should take the Fallsbury passage. This time of day, there won't be many to slow you down." Then he did something so embarrassing, I blushed about nine shades of red. He got down on his knee to bow to little old me. I resisted the urge to confess that my title was completely made up. I tried my best to be cool when Kristoffer took my hand and placed a kiss atop it. "I hope you find rest from the Weres, Queen Lucy the Fair."

Queen Lucy the Fair. Well, that was adorably cute. A far sight better than Lucy Goosy.

I bowed to the elves again, and then exited on Jamie's arm. As soon as we cleared the room, we picked up the pace.

26

FALLSBURY PASSAGE

"It won't do to run, Miss Lucy," Jamie instructed, donning his forced smile as he greeted a few elves who bowed to him as we passed.

"Isn't it all about to break loose?"

"Yes, but there have been no mention of Weres, only that there was a disturbance with their portal. We don't want to look like we have too much information, now. Do we?"

"I guess not." I held tighter to him when four men in the guard's uniform ran past us toward the castle. "They're going to discover the busted portal soon, and it'll all hit the fan. I'd like to be gone when that happens."

Jamie looked around the sky as we walked at a pace that was too slow for my taste. He patted my hand as we strolled in the direction of the woods that were thick with knotted trees and aggressive root systems. "We will be. You played your part well. The king and queen won't suspect you of breaking the portal. Besides, you and I were with them at the time. Perfect alibis."

"I was pretty nervous. Things aren't so formal back home. I've never met an honest to goodness queen before. Super cool."

"What sort of aristocracy do you have?"

"My country has a president, but I'll never even come close to meeting him. Good thing you'll never see where I lived. Not very impressive when you compare it to kings and princes and whatnot."

"Is that what you want? To be a princess?" His curiosity was endearing; it matched his reserved smile perfectly.

I tripped over my robes that had been hemmed to fit my shorter height. Jamie steadied me, and we continued our walk toward the woods. "Right now I'd settle for four walls that were mine. Four glorious walls that never leave me." I sighed wistfully as I daydreamed about the simple things that were never attainable for me. "A home with a white picket fence and a garage. Maybe a little bed for Henry Mancini." Jamie waved to an elf as we passed by a well. "And I'd sit at my kitchen table – not a kitchen nook, a real table – and do my math homework over breakfast."

Mom could make blueberry pancakes. Dad could make a fire in my very own fireplace. Linus and I would have a pancake-eating contest, make ourselves sick, and then hold our stomachs all morning and blame the other person for our malady.

If I could dream up a home I'd never have, then I should be allowed to imagine who I'd want there with me.

I could tell Jamie was watching me as we walked into the thick tangles of trees and underbrush, so I purposefully kept my gaze straight ahead on our destination as I talked. "Extravagance is nice, but when you've never had the simple things, it's kind of all you want." I cleared my throat. "You don't live in your dad's palace. You chose your own house, so I bet you know what I mean."

"I do. One day, perhaps we'll both get what we want," Jamie said.

I seriously doubt it. I want my family back, and you want to be with Britta. "Maybe. But can you even admit what you want?"

Judging by the pallor of his face, I could tell I'd hit too hard. His thick lips were drawn in a tight line as he lifted a low-hanging branch out of the way. "I take it Jens has been telling stories again?"

"I guessed. It's pretty obvious. Britta's a cool person. I can see why you'd be attracted."

Jamie picked up his pace, taking us deeper into the forest, and cutting out a portion of the daylight from our path. We climbed over obnoxiously intrusive roots and brush. "It's not proper for us to talk about such things."

I gave him a withering look as I picked up the hem of my dress to keep from tripping over it. "Newsflash, you don't have to hide anything on our little trip. We're not actually in proper society right now. I don't think Nik, Tor or Foss really care who you've got the hots for."

"Your phrasing is very telling." He climbed over a felled tree with a trunk as wide as a yardstick. "I'm afraid it doesn't matter who I've 'got the hots for'. My choices have been made for me." Then in a quieter voice, he added, "But I suppose my heart is still my own. There's no crime in wanting something."

"No crime at all." I tried to keep the conversation going, but the many-layered dress was not meant for climbing over felled trees. I tugged, ripping a small piece of the pretty fabric. "Ah, man! It's like the dress knows it doesn't belong on me, and is trying to get away to a better owner."

Jamie bent down and wiggled the torn off piece free from the root it snagged on. "I don't like the idea of leaving a trail for the Mouthpiece to follow."

"The what?"

"The Mouthpiece. Pesta's mouthpiece? You know, the Undran Pesta sends her soul into when she wants to move around outside the Land of Be?"

I pointed to my blank expression. "I've got no idea what you're talking about." Then I snapped my fingers in time with the click that happened in my brain. "Wait, I remember. Yeah, yeah. The dude who's not really a dude, but acts like a puppet for Pesta to operate. Go on. I'm paying attention."

Jamie searched around for any other part of me I might be leaving behind before he continued on our journey. "Pesta can't leave Be. That's part of the agreement, but she figured out how to send her soul out into Undra. So she's technically not breaking the treaty because her body's still in Be. Father was not pleased about that. Neither were the Fossegrimens or pretty much anyone in Undraland." He shook his head, offering his hand to me to assist me over an uneven surface. "She chooses someone who's weak, and they let her in. For all intents and purposes, she becomes them."

"Um, what? And you guys allow that? What's the point of pretending she's chained to Be, then?"

Jamie answered my blunt question with kindness. "The Mouthpiece has none of her powers. They can barely access their own. All the same, I'd rather the Mouthpiece not find you if she's already sent Weres out for you." He dropped my hand so I could pick up my long dress and jump over a protruding root. "Alrik was smart to declare your presence among the Elves so loudly, holding a conference with you as the special guest. The Mouthpiece wouldn't dare attack you in the open, especially now that you're beloved by Alrik and me."

I clasped my hands together under my chin. "Aw! You belove me? I belove you, too."

Jamie laughed, confused but amused at my humor. "That's quite an honor. Thank you, Miss Lucy." He laughed a couple more times at random as we walked. "Hallamar and Sorena took a shine to you, which helps deter any uprising the Mouthpiece might try to start against you in Elvage." He gave me an approving look. "You did quite well back there."

"Thanks. Who's the Mouthpiece? Does it change whenever she gets bored?"

Jamie shook his head. "No. Once she's in a body, her soul's chained to it until they die. If Mouthpiece vessels started dropping all over the place, no one would let her in again. It would be bad for her plan to leave a body under suspicious circumstances." He scratched his chin as an orange bird the size of a puma flew overhead. "The vessel is a Fossegrimen named Rasmus. I know what he looks like, so you needn't fear. I'll make sure we aren't followed." He tugged on my hand. "Up and over this one. Do you need help?"

"Man, your world's confusing." I sized up the felled tree in our path. "I think I've got this." I put my hands up as high as they could reach, but I was still a few inches shy of spanning the width of the horizontal trunk. No sooner did I get a solid footing than two strong hands gripped my waist. I shrieked as I was lifted off the ground. "Jens!" I cried when his face appeared.

"Forget about me? I've been with you the whole time."

"Oh, sorry. I guess I did. I'm not used to the whole invisibility thing." I mentally ran over everything Jamie and I had talked about and ruled with relief that none of it would be embarrassing if he heard it.

The fact that I could not pick and choose what Jens was around for hit me all at once. I'm sure it should have much earlier, but I was dealing with a lot of new stuff flying at me, so the obvious stuff kinda slipped under the rug. "You were with my family for five years, right?"

My left field question caught Jens off-guard. "Yeah." He handed me to Jamie, who lowered me down the other side of the felled tree.

"You were there when I ran out the lease on our last apartment?" I asked as the three of us trudged between the mangled trees.

His answer was hesitant this time. "Yeah."

That was a blow. "Like, keeping watch from outside?"

"Sometimes."

"And sometimes you were... You saw... You saw?"

"I wasn't planning on bringing it up if you weren't, but yeah. I'm the one who told Alrik and made him cross over and get you."

I straightened and forged onward through the trees and

underbrush, wishing I had the ability to turn invisible and run away. "Gotcha. We almost there?"

Jens walked on my other side with obvious concern. "Don't be like that."

"Be like what? How am I supposed to be? No one was supposed to see that. It's private."

"It's my job!"

"Yep." I tried to outpace him, but his legs were far longer than mine. As my steps quickened, so did his. I was a wash of angry and humiliated, so I did the only logical thing I knew of. The method taught me by my parents from childhood. *Rule #4: When you want out, run.* So I picked up my skirts and bolted forward in the direction I was pretty sure we were supposed to go. I was livid when Jens ran with me. "Let me go!"

"You know I can't do that! Just calm down."

I ran faster, and Jamie trotted behind us. We reached the place where Uncle Rick had left horses tied up for us. They were brown, big and beautiful, but I couldn't appreciate them at the moment. I wished I was a cowboy, so I could hoist myself up and ride away as fast as I could to escape the man who'd seen me at my worst.

"Lucy, I've never told anyone but Alrik what you almost did. If it helps, the weekend he came and stayed with you in your new place, I wasn't there."

I tried to climb up on the horse, but there was no saddle and thus no stirrups to step into. As with the rest of Undraland, everything was a foot taller than normal, including the horses. Plus, I was in a heavy dress, not chaps or jeans or whatever John Wayne wore.

When Jens put his hands on my waist to lift me, I

whirled on him. "Don't you touch me!" I tried three more times, growing angrier as hot tears threatened to appear and give me away. When I realized there was no way I could get up there on my own, I nearly screamed in childish frustration. "I'll walk."

"Get back here. Come on, Loos. You have no idea where we're going or how many miles it is. You can't walk there."

I did not respond. I knew if I spoke, it would either be juvenile or reveal too much hurt. I'd already unwittingly shown enough emotion in front of him.

"Miss Lucy, may I escort you?" Jamie asked, grasping at a way to be helpful.

I slowed my escape and turned. "Is it really miles to the tavern we're meeting the others at?"

"Even on the horses, we won't make it there until nightfall."

"Are you telling me the truth?" I questioned. "You're not just being the wingman?"

Jamie held up one hand in promise and placed the other over his heart. "I assure you, I have no wings."

I nodded and went back to the horse, hating that I needed help to get on. Jamie lifted me and placed me atop one. I wasn't really sure if I was supposed to ride sidesaddle, but it didn't seem very safe without an actual saddle. I positioned myself the way John Wayne would have, not Princess Buttercup, despite my current wardrobe.

Three people, two horses. When Jens looked like he was about to slide on the horse behind me, I growled at him, barked like a dog and gave him my best don't-you-dare stare.

"Would you do me the honor of riding with me, Miss

Lucy?" Jamie asked graciously, trying to avoid another fight between Jens and me. Wingman, indeed.

Jens gave me a hard look before he backed off. "Making sure you're safe doesn't just mean protecting you from Weres. It also means that sometimes I have to protect you from yourself. You have no right to be mad at me for seeing what I saw and calling Alrik."

Deep, deep down, I knew I shouldn't be this mad at him. Right after everyone in my life died, I went home from the crematorium to an empty apartment. I locked myself inside for weeks until the rent ran out. The last few days I was there, I had a Mexican standoff with the largest kitchen knife we owned, a bottle of pills and vodka, and a rope I'd gone so far as to hang in the doorway of my parents' bedroom. For days I stared down the pills. I'd dump them on the floor, count them out and give each one a reason why I shouldn't kill myself.

Pill one: My family would be pissed if they were alive to see this.

Pill two: It would be the fourth death Uncle Rick would have to suffer inside a month. Probably not nice to do that to him.

Pill three: I didn't want to die without seeing the Polyphonic Spree in concert. That just seemed like a complete waste of a life.

Pill four was where I always drew a blank. Three reasons to live were all I could muster. It had been enough in the end, but only just. There were several days that I'd come very close to ending it all. There were more reasons to die than to survive.

Then Uncle Rick came. He took me out to dinner. It

was the first meal I'd had in who knows how long, and when we got back, all my belongings had been moved to a one-bedroom apartment in a new town. He'd put down first and last month's rent, set me up with the job bagging and checking at the grocery store, enrolled me in community college, kissed my cheeks and left. I was alone until Tonya and Danny moved in.

None of that was for Jens to see. It was private, and part of me that was supposed to be only mine. Job or not, no one wants to be seen as an emaciated suicidal mess crying on the floor of an empty apartment with no one who cared enough to pick her up, or even visit.

27

MERRY BAND OF THIEVES

I gritted my teeth against the horse's wide gallop for the first half hour, and then my body adjusted. I relaxed against Jamie's chest, and at one point even closed my eyes as the rhythm of the hooves lulled me to rest. Thank goodness I wasn't driving this thing.

Jamie held the reins with his arms on either side of me. He said nothing of my anger, and after a while his gentle demeanor quieted my rocking emotions so I only felt sad. Sad for all the loss, sure, but it was more than that. As the sun began to dip below the rolling green horizon, I let the horse and the steady heartbeat of the man pound out my sorrow and frustration with the hand I'd been dealt.

Jamie rested his cheek to my temple. "Sleep, Queen Lucy. Jens means you no harm. A finer man I've never known."

I said nothing to this, but instead closed my eyes. I had never fallen asleep on a real live man before. Sure, Linus and I had to bunk up most places we went. Our family generally migrated to one-bedroom apartments. There was no cuddling your brother, though. We had a strict get-out-of-my-space policy, and as a result had grown to be uncommonly motionless sleepers, except during the occasional nightmare. Leaning on Jamie was a comfort I would never admit to needing in that moment, but I was grateful for him all the same.

However many hours later, I felt my body being jostled in a different direction than forward. I opened my eyes to find Jamie lowering me off the horse into the arms of Jens. Part of me wanted to protest, but I was too tired for another round with him. Instead I leaned my head against his shoulder and whispered, "I don't want to fight anymore."

"Okay, Loos. Let's get you up to the room and we can talk about it."

"I don't need to talk. I get it."

He carried me into the Drucken Tavern, and I was too worn out to care how I looked or the crazy things the wind always did with long, wavy hair. Judging by the stink and the clientele, I guessed we were in Tor's land. The candlelight fell on a dozen or so dwarves in various stages of drunkenness, all with shorter statures and red or black dreadlocks down to their elbows.

The grisly innkeeper checked an old piece of paper before handing us a key. "What's that one ya've got there?" he asked Jens, showcasing three missing teeth up top. "That's not another halfy, is it?"

Suddenly, I was wide awake. I shimmied out of Jens's arms and stalked to the rude dwarf. "Excuse me?" I said, taking in the 4'9" stout man behind the rickety wooden counter. I could smell his stench from where I was next to Jens.

Jamie postured. "This is Queen Lucy, human female from the Other Side. She's the first of her kind to venture to the Warf. You will show her respect, Orton."

Orton took off his hat and bowed his head, looking like he might piss himself. His red frizzy dreadlocks were matted at the top of his head, looking like insect nests might be holing up in the crannies. I lifted my chin with pride as he stumbled over his apology. "I meant no disrespect, yer majesty. Queen Lucy of the Other Side, please take my best room. We've got oak-matured Gar you'll like, and I'll have the maid bring ya up some supper straightaway."

"What did you do with the halfy?" I asked, my tone ominous.

"We don't let that kind in here, yer grace. Ya don't have ta worry 'bout him soiling the place. We run an upscale establishment here, we do. Not like those quacks in Elvage."

My jaw didn't move as I pushed out the words. "Where is he?"

Orton motioned back out the door to the night. "He's in the barn with the horses."

Maybe it was the late hour. Maybe it was the smell or the long ride here. I don't know. But something in me snapped at Mace being segregated from the others and shoved in with the animals. "You put my brother in the stables?" I asked through my clenched-together teeth.

Orton's ruddy face drained of all color, making his smattering of freckles stand out all the more. "Yer brother? No one told me ya were related ta the halfy. I wouldn'ta..."

"Wouldn't have treated my brother like a dog? You're lucky I don't unleash my human powers of..." I tried to think of something scary enough. Angry girl face? Vicious rhetoric? No, it had to be something with an actual threat behind it. "You're lucky I don't unleash the powers of Vin Diesel on you!" Jens snorted behind me, but I didn't care. I kept my nose in the air as I spoke. "Please send word to Alrik's room that I will be sleeping in the barn with my brother."

"What? No, no. Yer grace, please. I meant no harm!"

"No. If my brother isn't good enough for you, then neither am I. By morning, word will spread that you made Queen Lucy sleep in the barn with the animals. Hopefully this is the last time you'll act so hatefully toward someone who's different than you."

Orton stammered incoherent apologies, offering me everything short of the sun and moon to stay in a proper room and not in the barn.

Life certainly had some strange twists and turns. There had been quite a few times when my family had to bolt in the middle of the night and crash in a skeezy motel for a week while Mom and Dad found us a new apartment. There had been quite a few that had no rooms for rent, or some that charged us an arm and a leg for the most disgusting, filthy room imaginable. We took rooms filled with who knows what kind of gag-inducing fluids in the sheets because that was all we could get.

This was payback. If my family were here, they would cheer me on.

Jens sighed, and I realized my victory was short-lived. We stepped outside into the night air that had the beginnings of a chill to it, and I began to regret my decision. The temperature swings were pretty drastic. Summerishly warm during the day, and chilly fall temps at night.

Martin Luther King, Jr. Martin Luther King, Jr.

I turned to my ever-present shadow. "Look, you don't have to go with me, Jens. There's no danger."

Jens rubbed his hands over his face. "You know I go with you. It's fine. I get it. Probably would've done the same thing if it was Britt."

"Mace can keep watch. I'll be safe."

He rolled his eyes. "Oh, that makes me feel so much better. The only male Huldra who somehow has a mind-controlling whistle. Sure. I'll leave you alone with him. No problem."

"Okay, Sarcasmo. That was me trying to let you off the hook. Take it or leave it."

"Leave it," he ruled, adjusting the red pack on his back. "Goodnight, Jamie. Tell the others we'll see them in the morning."

Jamie stood straighter. "I'm going with you. I couldn't possibly go against Queen Lucy's decision. It'll get around that I favored the racist, and I cannot have that. People are starting to see your land and mine as a united front, what with me escorting you through Undraland. Best it stays that way."

I turned and hugged Jamie around his middle since I only came up to his shoulder. "Don't be a fool. Britta's up there, and she's been worried sick about you. This is your one shot to actually spend some time with her away from your dad's prying eyes." I shook my head into his chest, taking note that he was growing decidedly less rigid around me the more time we spent together. "Plus, if you stay in the barn with me, people will think we're doing it. That won't help you much back home."

His finger went under my chin and lifted it so I was looking up at him, his brown eyes taking in the details of my face in the moon's red light. "I've never met a lady who spoke as plainly as you do. I'm not sure I like it."

I smiled up at him and winked. "I'm not sure I care if you do." I shrugged. "Whatever. I talk normal for where I come from. In my experience, it's the not talking about it that gets people into trouble."

"Fair enough." Jamie looked around to make sure no one was around to see, and then kissed my forehead. Warmth spread through me at the affection that was both platonic and familial all at once.

"Go get your girl, tiger." I chucked his arm, and we shared a smile of mutual appreciation before he trotted off into the tavern.

Jens wrapped his arm around my back and walked with me to the stables, his demeanor suddenly tenderer than his usual abrasiveness. "You sure you want to sleep in the barn?"

"I'm sure I would never leave my family out in the cold. It's all of us or none of us. That's the deal."

"You sure attached to that Mace kid pretty fast."

"Kid? Isn't he your age? How old are you, anyway?" A flash of dread washed over me. "Alrik's three-hundred-something years old. Please tell me you're younger than that."

He chuckled. "I'm twenty-eight. I've got three years on Mace, so I have the right to call him a kid."

"Be nice to my new brother, okay? I need this to work."

"I get it. I will." When I gave him a look of disbelief, he grew defensive. "When am I not nice?" Jens opened the stable doors and called out to Charles. "Mace, you here? It's just us."

I heard hay moving, and then saw silver and black eyes glinting off the dim lantern light. "Lucy?" Charles stood and ran toward us. "I'm so glad you made it! I was worried they'd taken you hostage or something."

He hugged me tight, and I could feel his worry. "Nope. Just the longest tea party of my life. I can't believe they made you sleep here! And where's Uncle Rick? Isn't he pissed?"

"I don't understand what that word means. I thought I did, but now I don't know. Alrik checked us in and then split off with Tor. He's trying to feel out a few contacts he and Tor have here to see if we can get some help."

If I'd ever called my dad Rolf, there would've been a swift reckoning. I didn't completely understand Charles and Uncle Rick's dynamic.

"But why? Isn't it best if no one knows what we're doing?"

Charles pulled back and looked at me with wonder, like he was afraid I might not be real. "Word's spread to the dwarves that the portal in Elvage was in jeopardy, so they're placing a security detail around theirs. We'll need someone on the inside to help get Tor close enough."

Jens stiffened. "In jeopardy? Didn't Alrik destroy it?"

"No. Alrik got two whole bones knocked down, but

then it was too well guarded to destroy more of it without being seen. Almost didn't get away fast enough, but we cleared the area with the others just before the army descended. We're lucky we got out of there when we did. The portal's still working, though. Every single bone has to be torn down for the pathway to be finished."

"I'm just glad you're okay," I admitted, hugging him in the lantern's light.

Mace's head rested on mine, and I could tell he was happy. He gave a contented sigh when he kissed my hair. "I am, and you are. You should go on up to bed, dear sister. I'll see you in the morning."

"Oh, no. I'm not staying in there if you're out here. I'm sleeping in here tonight. So is Jens."

Mace looked horrified. "But, no! You can't sleep out here. It wouldn't be right. You're Queen Lucy! Go back inside. I'll be fine. Trust me, it's nothing I'm not used to."

I glared up at him. "If they won't have you, they don't get me. Let's see him try to book a room after word spreads that he made Queen Lucy and her family sleep in his barn. Superior butthole."

"But I... you shouldn't... No, Lucy. You'll catch your death out here on a night like tonight. It's already getting cold. It's not worth it. Alrik's been trying for ages to get them to accept me. It's no use."

I tossed him a simpering smile. "Oh, Charles. I'm way more stubborn than Uncle Rick. Don't you know that by now?"

"No. I won't let you." He tried to appear firm, but I could sense an easy takedown a mile away.

"It's done. You better not've taken all the good hay."

Jens poked his head out from one of the stalls. "Get in here, Queen of the Barn."

Jens was always doing that. Disappearing and then reappearing when I wasn't expecting it. There was a joke on the tip of my tongue about enjoying a roll in the hay, but I didn't think it was appropriate in front of Mace, who I was still feeling out.

I turned around when I heard Nik and Foss arguing out in the night. The barn door slammed open, letting in a gust of chilly, yet fresh air. The horses really smelled like, well, animals. "Hey, guys. If it isn't my favorite band of thieves. And Foss."

Foss and Nik entered, followed by Jamie and Britta. Jamie grinned at me. "It seems we've all decided not to abandon Charles Mace to the barn."

"What?" Mace looked around at the tired smiles in confusion. "No. It's not worth it. You all need to be sharp tomorrow. You need your sleep."

Jamie placed his hand on my back. "It's like Queen Lucy said. It's all of us or none of us. Band of thieves."

Charles Mace dropped his mouth open as Britta and Jens laid out a large area of bailed hay, and then Foss and Nik spread out three thick bearskins on top of it. It wasn't the most comfortable thing in the world, but we were together, the whole lot of misfits. I ended up jammed between Jens and Foss, smiling when I saw Jamie lie down next to Britta, even though they kept a respectable distance.

Foss took his sheathed long knife off his belt and pressed it to his chest. "In case you or Jamie need to be kept in line," he explained of the knife.

"Huh?" I rolled on my side to face him.

"I know of Jamie's curse, and yours." He spoke as if he was jabbing me with uncovering a truth I was trying to hide.

"My curse? What the smack are you talking about? Right now my only curse is you."

His upper lip curled at having to speak to me like a person instead of a slave. "Your mind wanders while you sleep," Foss clarified. "Jamie, too."

Jamie answered through gritted teeth. "My mind doesn't wander if I'm near Jens or Britta, and I'm lying in between both of them. You've no need to stab anyone in their sleep, Foss, least of all Lucy."

I huffed. "Dreaming's normal in my world. And just because my mind wanders while I'm unconscious doesn't mean you have to cuddle weaponry like a teddy bear. Unclench, Foss."

Foss snarled, looking like he wanted to prove his information was legit. "I have it on good authority the curse is dangerous. Jens, your rat's not making any sense."

I kissed my finger and pressed it to his sheath. "Well, maybe you're stupid."

Jens wrapped his arm around my middle, drawing my back to his chest in a hug that had a warning of protection to it. "I'll make sure no one attacks anyone tonight, alright? Jamie's fine. Lucy's fine. Foss, go to sleep."

Foss cuddled his blade possessively, eyeing me with a note of hatred, readying himself even in sleep to attack if I breathed in an offensive way. I studied the horizontal tattoo marks up his forearms, wondering what significance they held.

Jens whispered in my ear, "Goodnight, baby. Don't worry about Foss. He always sleeps with a knife."

"That makes me feel so much better." I shifted my body so I was thoroughly entrenched in Jens's embrace. Several minutes of quiet later, I could still feel Foss watching me while I drifted off to sleep.

28

REBELLIOUS

"*I* leave ya alone fer one night, and ya cause an uproar," Tor complained loudly. His gruff voice roused most of us, but I was determined not to move just yet. Despite the worst mattress in the world, I'd actually slept quite well. I stretched my arm and realized why. Jens had spooned me all night long. Actually held me in my sleep. For all of the fighting we did, that solitary act covered over a multitude of sarcastic remarks and pithy comebacks. Even though I'd only just met him, he was familiar already, and I warmed to him easier than I would've thought. I rolled over and kissed his malleable lips until he awoke, his face grumpy in the early morning hour.

"Good morning, sunshine," I sang quietly, grinning when he responded with an animalistic growl. "You're pretty when you're angry."

"Don't start with me. I'm pissed you made us all sleep out here. My back is sore."

I cuddled into him, smiling at how grown up it all felt.

Tor intervened by yanking the thick blanket off all of us, introducing us to the crisp morning air. "Up, ya lazy lot. Don'tcha know we got things ta do?"

Henry Mancini entered after Tor and Uncle Rick, bounding up to me and licking my face to tell me how much he missed me.

Uncle Rick brought a basket of hard biscuits and a dozen apples that we all bit into with vigor while he spoke. "It took all night, but we were able to find a sympathizer to the cause. As you know, we have Tor to take the rake and destroy the portal, but we need a dwarf on the inside to get him close enough. The area's heavily guarded. Gerik will get Tor closer to the portal. Then we'll attack them to give Tor time to tear the bone structure down."

"Whoa, what?" My mouth was wide open. "No one said anything about fighting."

Foss and Tor looked at me like I was an idiot. Like they wouldn't have shown up for the mission at all if there weren't promise of bloodshed. Foss shook his head in my direction. "Useless rat child."

I ignored him. "I mean, these are Tor's people. They're just doing their job. Do they deserve to die for protecting something they don't understand is hurting them?"

Uncle Rick had a look in his eye that I'd missed from my own father. It was that of love and indulgence. "If only the world could get by without bloodshed, Lucy dear. We won't aim to kill, only to distract them and get Tor out. We're lucky to have so many Toms to vanish us from view. You and Jamie will go on ahead to Tokem's Peak and wait for us there."

"Sir?" Jamie questioned, clearly not liking the fact that he was on babysitting duty.

"Lucy is not to fight," Uncle Rick ruled. "She doesn't believe in it anyway, but even if she did, it would be unwise. She represents a new country, and Jamie, you represent the Tomten. If either of you are seen on the field, it will cause distrust to break out, if not full-on war between nations."

I could tell Jamie hated this idea, but could say nothing against the logic.

Jens wolfed down his second biscuit. "I'm her Tom. She doesn't travel without me."

Uncle Rick waved off Jens's protest. "Tokem's Peak is not far. It'll be safe for her there. Besides, we need you and Britta to vanish us. As it is, you'll each have two of us on you, not counting Tor, who you'll also have to vanish."

Tor grumbled. "I'm not riding on yer back, Jens."

Jens turned to his sister the same time I did. Even though she was six and a half feet tall, in that moment, she looked impossibly small. "No," Jens ruled. "I'll take two of you. That'll be enough."

Tor shook his head, his red dreadlocks swishing. "Ya know it won't be. It's up ta Britta, not you."

Britta's wide green eyes that matched her brother's eventually took on a measure of bravery. "I'm honored," she ruled, chin high.

Though her brown braids were disheveled and she had a rumpled look about her, Britta was to be admired. It was then I noticed Jamie inching closer toward her side to quell his anxiety. He shook his head. "It does not sit well with me that I flee while Britta stands and fights."

The pride Uncle Rick had for Britta could not be missed. "If Britta is caught, it will not reflect poorly on your kingdom. She's always been a bit rebellious. And I will stay with her, no matter what. Charles and I are capable of more than people give us credit for. We only failed at tearing down the Elvage portal because we couldn't afford to be found out so early by my own people. The dwarves won't easily recognize the elfish magic as belonging specifically to me."

"Alright, old man." Jens tried to bring levity to the moment, but each bite of the hard biscuit he ate looked like it was an effort to choke down.

"Wash up," Tor instructed. "We leave within tha hour."

29

JAMIE'S SECRETS

*B*ritta looked oddly right in the leather armor they all wore. She had shed her Amish bonnet, showing off more of her heart-shaped face. She had her own long knife she was more than comfortable with, plus another shorter one strapped to her triceps. She emerged from the stall where she and Jamie were invisible and saying their sad goodbyes in private. I was happy they were dropping the pretense that they weren't completely smitten with each other.

Jens would not look at me. He was dressed in jeans, a black T and leather armor, which consisted of a breast-plate, and arm and shin guards that slid under his pants. I'd never seen him more beautiful.

Jens bent at the waist and picked up Henry Mancini, giving him a good nuzzle that melted my heart. My man and my dog. Totally precious.

Out of the corner of my eye, I noticed Nik's fleeting stare land on Jens's backside. It wasn't a misplaced gaze; I recognized the same tempered attraction that swelled in me when I got a good look at the wonder that was Jens. Nik cleared his throat and looked away. Judging from the embarrassment coloring his face and the way he tried to immediately busy himself with other tasks, I guessed being gay wasn't a talked-about thing in Undraland.

I was permitted to trade in my Halloween costume for my jeans and Chucks, thank goodness. Climbing up Tokem's Peak was no time for wearing a princess dress. I hugged Uncle Rick, who did his best to quell my worries. I kissed Tor and Nik on their cheeks. They both let their chests swell at "the fair maiden's sendoff," as Nik put it.

Tor grumbled as his cheeks turned pink and he wiped off my kiss. "Alright, alright. No use getting all feminine. I'll be back soon enough."

Foss and I exchanged looks of disdain for each other, which was the most I was willing to do. I really didn't like him, and he looked like he would have preferred kissing an actual rat to a sendoff from me.

"Try not to get Jamie killed up there, little rat," Foss groused at me.

I saluted his scowl. "Try not to die out there." I hoped that sounded sincere. "You'd be really hard to drag off the battlefield."

He sneered at me and turned away.

Love you too, arrogant prat.

Then there was Charles. I'd only just discovered him, and now I was supposed to just let him go. It was clear he dreaded leaving me just as much, his black and silver eyes following me every time I moved an inch. "I wish I could vanish you," he admitted. "I would take you away from any hint of warfare to keep you safe."

I slid easily into his wiry arms, leaning up on my toes to kiss his cheek. "Be careful," I warned. I'd never sent anyone off into actual battle before. I'd spent a weekend packing up care packages for the troops over in Iraq once, but I hadn't known any of those soldiers, and Iraq was so far away. This was happening not three miles from where I stood, and I was holding an unseasoned soldier in my arms. My new brother. "Be careful. More than careful." I kissed his other cheek.

Charles turned his head and planted a small kiss to the side of my mouth. "I *will* come back to you. We only just found each other. Don't you think I would move heaven and earth to return to your side?"

Emotion rose in my chest and choked my throat. *Jeez! These guys with the language.* So gallant, it was hard to process. "Is there no other way to do this?" I asked of Uncle Rick.

My uncle shook his head in answer with a sad look on his face. "I'll do everything in my power to make sure we all return to you, Queen Lucy the Gentle."

I was used to saying goodbye to Uncle Rick. Though he was a permanent part of my life, he was always leaving prematurely. He liked to rip the Band-Aid off before I could count to three.

Uncle Rick took my hand and led me away from the others, who were still readying themselves. "Listen to me, Lucy. No matter what happens, I need you to stay with Jamie. He can be impulsive, and I need you to be the adult and stick to the plan. We will rendezvous on the far side of

Tokem's Peak. Set up camp there and lay low. Do not let him wander off to look for Britta. We will come for you. Tell me you understand this."

I nodded slowly, sensing the other shoe was about to drop.

Drop, it did. "There's something you should know about Jamie." Uncle Rick kept his voice to a whisper, making sure no one overheard. "When he's subjected to stress, he tends to lose himself."

I chose my words carefully. "What does that mean exactly?"

"His mother was cursed by a Siren when he was in the womb. She died in childbirth, and he carries a portion of the curse with him to this day. Undrans don't dream. It's not in our makeup. But Jamie does. When he's had stress in his day, he grows violent in his sleep, his body taking on a life of its own."

My eyes were wide, but I had no response to this. There was too much to say to pick just one rant.

Uncle Rick held my shoulder. "When his betrothal was announced to the public, I have it on good authority that in his sleep, he choked his guard out and attacked another before they could wake him. It's one of the reasons why he chooses to live alone. You've no doubt seen the locks on his door to keep him confined. Jens started a rumor there was a wolf about to explain Jamie's howling when he tries to break out in his stupor."

I whisper-shouted at my uncle, vaguely recalling Helsa mentioning something to Jens about a problem the Tonttu were having with a wolf. "Hello! We let him sleep next to Britta last night! Might've been nice to know."

The scratch marks on the inside of Jamie's door now made sense.

"Jens and Britta know all about it. He's no danger to her. She's a great calm to him, and he only loses his mind when he's very upset. I only mention it because I cannot imagine he will do well knowing she's in a battle. Try to keep him awake until we reach you. His fits only happen while he's asleep, so you need not worry if you can keep him awake."

"You're sending me into the mountains with Jekyll and Hyde? Thanks a lot! If he falls asleep, how am I supposed to make sure he doesn't fall off the side of the mountain or something?" More scenarios presented themselves to my imagination, each one more gruesome than the last. "What if he tries to kill me? I know I talk a good game, but I can't exactly overpower him."

"Jens trained him to go limp when you pinch a pressure point on his hand." Uncle Rick picked up my hand and pinched the flesh between my thumb and forefinger, and then rolled his pincer grip up the length of my hand toward my wrist. "Feel that? Pinch him there, and then rub upwards toward his wrist, and it should make him go back to sleep."

"Should?" I put my hand to my forehead as I tried to process it all. "Okay, fine. Thanks for the heads up. No wonder Foss slept with a sword last night." I stepped back and glared at my uncle when he tried to hug me. "You know, I'm starting to wonder when your protection will actually make me safer."

I could tell that this cut him, but he took the stab with a gracious bow of his head. "I'll see you soon. If you keep to the path, you shouldn't have any trouble. Make good use of your time and get to any point of elevation before nightfall. Do you understand?"

"Split personality sleepwalker. Kung-Fu his hand. Get on the mountain before nighttime. Got it." I spun on my heel before he could attempt another hug.

Henry Mancini was licking Jens on the cheek, enjoying being held by his co-owner. Jens nuzzled his neck, and frankly couldn't have looked cuter if he tried. He handed me my puppy, but did not look at me. Instead he went to Jamie and spoke to him in harsh whispers while Jamie answered in morose nods.

Tor came from his conversation with a blushing Britta, walking toward me with swagger and purpose. "It's custom fer the warriors ta be kissed farewell by the maidens of the land." He presented his cheek to me. "Do yer duty, lass."

"I just did!"

He pointed to his lips like the cad he was.

I gave him the squinty eye. "Is that even true? Or are you just trying to sucker Britta and me out of some loving?"

"Whatever answer gets me tha kiss fastest," he insisted, inching his ruddy face closer to me.

"Be brave, giant dwarf." With that, I planted a loud smooch on his puckered lips. "Player."

"Yeah, I am!" he bellowed, howling his laughter. Jens shoved Tor, but Tor was unabashed in his accomplishment at getting two women to kiss him off for battle.

Jens resumed his stern whisper fight with Jamie, so I busied myself relacing my beloved Chucks in an empty horse's stall. Britta sat down next to me in the hay, concern etched all over her face. "You'll be safe with Jamie," she assured both of us. "He's of the highest quality."

"Can I tell you a secret?" I kept my eyes on my shoes as I retied the left one. "It doesn't really matter. If I die, there's billions more humans who can do the job better than me. I'm no queen, and I have no experience with warfare. It'd be nice to make it through to the end, but all you need me for is to destroy the human portal, which isn't even built yet. Alrik can find someone to replace me, no problem."

Britta was horrified in that way very kind people are woebegone if you tell them the slightest unhappy truth. Sweet girl. "You must not say such things!" she exclaimed, her hand flying to her heart.

"Logically, you know I'm right. I'm not trying to be a downer. I'm just saying that if something does happen, it's fine." I lowered my voice. "So if certain people start feeling guilty over things they can't control, let them off the hook for me."

Britta shook her head. "You didn't know Jens before you came to our side. When you were going through your depression after your family died, he was rarely here on his monthly visits. He went straight to Bedra and lost himself in their lavender powder."

"Is that a euphemism for sex?" I should've known better than to use the S-word in front of her.

Britta's face turned crimson, and she lowered her voice. "Lavender powder comes from the smärtfri plant that was cursed by the Huldra. You inhale it to ease physical pain or to forget your life for a while. It's not permanent, like leaving for the Land of Be is. It's just a temporary escape. It's quite dangerous, though. Very addictive. He… Jens had a bit of trouble with the powder before he started working for your family." She watched me re-tie my right shoe curiously. "I could always tell when he was worried about you. On his one day off a month, he'd spend it completely high." Britta waited until I was ready to make eye contact. "If anything happened to you, I'm certain he would be lost to us forever. You must take care in the mountains with Jamie." She picked up my hand and pinched the same spot Uncle Rick showed me, and then rubbed upward to my wrist. "Right there. Try it on me, so I'm certain you can do it if you need to."

I obeyed, realizing that Jamie's well-being was of the utmost importance to Britta. It wasn't just because she wanted to be with him; her love stood steady even when she knew she could not have what she wanted. Even if Jamie lived through this and went home to marry the other woman, his survival was worth more than her own in her eyes. She was concerned for him, and not for herself, though she would be doing the fighting. It was the best kind of love.

"Hey," I said, placing my hand on her back to soothe her. "It's alright. I'll watch out for Jamie and keep him safe until you come get him. Don't worry about that. I'll keep his secret, too. No big deal."

Emotion swelled visibly in Britta, and before I knew it, I was in her long arms, clutched to her chest. "You're exactly as Jens described you, and I'm grateful for it."

Jamie moved over to us, offering us both a hand up. "Are you ready to go, Miss Lucy?"

I nodded. "Do it to it." I walked over to Jens and took my green backpack from him. He put Henry Mancini down to tag along with Jamie and I, and then leaned in for a kiss.

I backed away on instinct. "Don't."

"What? Are you still mad at me for something stupid?"

"No, but that was a goodbye kiss. I don't want any part of that. I don't do goodbyes. Not to you, at least. Just high five me and go do your thing." When his mouth dropped open in disbelief, I shook my head. "I'm serious. See you in a few." I slung the pack over my shoulder and whistled to Henry Mancini. "Jamie, we're out like stripes and polka dots." I opened the barn door and marched out into the warmth of the sun, not looking back at the thunderstruck Jens.

CURSED

"I don't really want to talk about it," I said for the third time.

"But his face! It looked like you'd just slapped him."

I gripped the rock wall and tried to heft myself up, yet again. "Well, I didn't. No point in getting all weepy with him just because we have to spend a whopping day apart. He's fine. I'm fine. It's this stupid wall that's pissing me off."

Jamie sighed. "If you'd just let me help you..."

My shoulders sagged in defeat. It was so dark out; I could barely see more than a few feet in front of me. Henry Mancini was getting impatient, and so was I. He nipped at my heels, agitating me further. "Do you think this is easy, pup? Just be patient. I can do it. Foss is wrong about me. I'm not a useless rat." I gripped the almost flat side of the mountain and tried to find purchase on it somewhere so I could go up to the path above us. It was a good two feet taller than Jamie, but if we could get up there, it would save us nearly a day's walk around the mountain's path that wound slowly up.

After my fourth fall, I gave up. "Fine. I can't do it. It's impossible anyway. If you want to try lifting me up, I guess that would be okay. But then how will you get up?"

"I'll manage." Jamie smiled and placed his hands around my waist, hoisting me up like I was a toy. Henry Mancini came up next, and before I'd dusted myself off and turned around to offer a hand up, Jamie was already on his knees behind me.

"How did you do that?"

Jamie chuckled. "How useless do you think Tomten aristocracy is? Jens is my best friend, you forget. He's an excellent teacher."

We walked down the rocky path, grateful that we'd skipped the extra travel time. It was well past nightfall, so we walked slower to avoid, you know, falling over the side of a cliff. I tried not to think about how high up we were. It helped that I couldn't see much. "When is it safe to set up camp?" I asked nonchalantly, as if I had tons of energy and didn't need to rest at all.

The hesitation in Jamie was clear. "I guess now is fine."

We felt around for the nearest cave and ducked inside. I pulled out two apples and stale biscuits for us, and we munched in the dark while we tried not to let our anxiety take us over. The air was crisp, but the dark inside the cave was suffocating. I was grateful for the slice of illumination the giant red moon provided us.

The discomfort was thick between us, so I decided to step on the elephant in the room's toe. "You're afraid to sleep in front of me, aren't you."

He looked down at his crusty biscuit dejectedly. "Jens told you?"

"Uncle Rick did. It's fine. I know about the pressure point. I'm actually not tired yet. How about I take first watch? Then if you go all serial killer on me, I'll catch it in time."

The shame was palpable in Jamie, even in the dark. He said nothing and refused to look at me as he drank from his canteen. Henry Mancini licked his hand, knowing exactly what Jamie needed in that moment.

"You don't like that I know your secrets," I stated. "Jens watched me for years, so he knows all mine." I poked at a rock to make sure it didn't move on its own. "I hate that."

"Jens is a good man." Jamie lay down on his back and stared up at the ceiling of the cave. "He was only doing his job. You shouldn't hate him for that."

I shrugged, leaning against the dank wall, my legs next to his torso. His head rested next to my hand, which had fallen to my side. "I don't hate him. It just sucks, is all. Hard to be a creature of mystery when he's seen me at my worst."

"And yet he's still smitten with you."

My nose crinkled. "I hate to break it to you, but he's not smitten. We fight all the time. We're easing into it."

Jamie chuckled, his tension lessening. "I hate to break it to *you*, but that's what Jens looks like when he's smitten. His mind's been made up for a long time about you. The 'easing in' is for your sake alone."

"I guess I'll have to take your word for it. I'm only just meeting him for the first time."

"That's where you're wrong," Jamie informed me with a

hint of teasing to his tone. He kept his eyes on the ceiling. "You've met Jens before all this. The day after your eighteenth birthday. You were getting your car fixed."

I could hear every breath echo on the walls of the cave. "Come again? I think I would've remembered meeting him."

Jamie paused before revealing a secret that didn't belong to him. "He was in the waiting room, fully visible, pretending he was there for a tire rotation. You wore a green shoe and a pink shoe, jeans and a brown shirt that said 'What Moose?' on it. You were reading Pride and Prejudice and he asked you to pass him the Motorists Monthly magazine from the rack. You said, 'At least they got their alliteration spot on.' And then he said, 'I could say the same for your book.' You said, 'Touché', and he hid behind his magazine for the entire hour that it took for them to fix your car."

My mouth was hanging open. "Um, that sounds pretty specific. Were you there, too?"

Jamie laughed softly. "No, but I felt like I was. For the next month, he told Britt and me the story dozens of times, obsessing about what he should have said. Apparently your brother laughed at him for being such a coward. The Linus one, not the Charles one." He sighed, shifting on the ground and petting Henry Mancini, who was snuggled between my legs and his shoulder. "Give Jens a troll, and he'll fight it without a blink. Give him the girl of his dreams, and he'll run away like a scared little boy."

"Wow. I... um, I don't know what to say to that. Is that really true? I don't remember it."

"It's very true. He got in a lot of trouble from Alrik and

your parents for appearing in front of you." He nudged my leg with his elbow. "Does that level the playing field a little, now that you know one of his secrets?"

I smirked, touching the toe of my shoe to his hip. "A little. Thanks."

"Why don't you tell me one of your secrets?"

I scoffed. "You've already proven yourself a terrible snitch. Why should I?"

I could see Jamie's hand gesturing about. "Because it would be your choice to share something instead of me just knowing."

Considering this, I tried to think of a good enough secret that I was willing to share. "I had a plant," I began.

Oh, boy.

"A little fern that I bought when I moved into the apartment I was last at. Before my best friend Tonya moved in, I lived alone for a few weeks." My voice lowered, as if the night might laugh at me. "I used to talk to the fern and pretend it was my dad."

Jamie was quiet, which was better than being laughed at, for sure.

"I promised myself that I would put down roots. That I would save up and buy an actual house with a white picket fence and everything that's normal. I'd plant that fern in the front yard so my dad could see where I landed. Until that happened, I was determined to keep it alive until my dream came true." I ruffled Henry Mancini's ear. "Fat lot of good that was. Burned to the ground the day I met Jens. All my normal always goes up in flames."

"And you blame Jens for taking away your fern father?"

I huffed. "Not on purpose. It's just a lot to take. I'm not

mad at him anymore. It's just sad. My first promise to myself when I started out on my own, and it's a lost cause. I couldn't keep my family alive. I couldn't even keep a fern alive. Sucks."

He paused out of respect for my fern, which I appreciated. "I'm very sorry to hear about your fern's passing." He covered the toe of my shoe with his hand and squeezed.

"Thanks. Okay, your turn. I want a juicy secret this time."

Jamie's large hand ghosted over Henry Mancini, who had turned his head and rested his snout on my leg. "How about a secret only a few people know? Would that work?"

"Sure. Give it a crack. I'm all ears."

He was thoughtful and quiet as he spoke through the darkness. "I can trust you to keep this between us? Jens, Britt, Alrik and my family know, but no one else."

I reached down and patted his forehead. Then my fingers drifted into his curly brown locks to soothe him. "Cross my heart."

"I'm guessing you know I killed my mother when I was born?"

"That's a terrible way to put it, Jamie."

He shrugged. "She was cursed, and it passed onto me."

"Uncle Rick mentioned something about that." I'd never put much stock in curses, but here in this mythological place, I'm guessing they were as real as anything.

Jamie's voice spoke to the ceiling, sounding like his mind was picturing his memory in vivid detail. "It's customary for the king to ride out with his men into battle. Inspire them and let them know they're not alone. When I came of age in my eighteenth year, I was sent into battle in his stead. My father has always been finding ways to kill me. This betrothal? It's to wage war on the Nisse people."

"How's that?" I scooted closer so his head was resting against my hip as I played with his hair.

"Freya knows nothing of my affliction. Not many do. On the surface, this is supposed to be a move to unite our two kingdoms, but father knows I will attack Freya in my sleep. He knows I would kill her. I've told him as much, but he insists it must be done. We need more land for farming, and this is how I'll fulfill my duty to my people. I'll kill her in my sleep, Nisse land will belong to me, and I will be hunted for the rest of my days as the Nisse try in vain to take back their land." He paused and focused on the feel of my fingers in his hair, trying to relax through the painful story.

"And if you just turn her down and don't marry her, that'll cause a big rift too, right?"

"Indeed. Either way, division. Both times, my fault. Cursed, I am. To the very end of my days, it seems."

I thought on this a moment. "Wow. I don't know what to say to that. I friggin' hate your dad, that's for sure. Who would use their kid like that?" The stillness in the cave became awkward. "Look, I know your culture keeps men and women separate, but mine isn't like that. Can I hug you? It seems like you need it."

Jamie sat up slowly, and in the faint crimson glow from the moonlight, his modest smile endeared me to him. "I would be honored."

"I'm so, so sorry," I crooned as I wrapped my arms around him. My head landed on his shoulder when he enveloped me in his embrace. He was so big, and in that moment, I felt small and safe.

I missed my dad. Though Jamie was not that much older than me, the comfort in his embrace filled that void. I held onto Jamie, grateful I was not alone in the dark of my life anymore.

I whispered, so as not to break the tenderness of the moment. "When the time comes, I'll help Jens sneak you out. You and Britta both. You two can come live with me. We'll figure this out."

His chest moved with the wave of a chuckle. "You sound exactly like Jens. I think I'm past hope at this point. Curses are not meant to be so easily undone. But I appreciate your concern for my happiness."

"Hey, don't knock it. I'm pretty stubborn when I want something."

Jamie leaned on the wall of the cave and ran his hand over my hair as I shifted next to him in our friendly snuggle. "Very well. When we get to your land, what will I do there?"

"I imagine you'll lay low for a while until you get the hang of things over there. Learn how to blend. Make up for lost time with Britta."

"Ah, but that's where there's a flaw in the plan. Her parents left for the Land of Be before they gave her permission to marry. She's stuck as I am stuck. No man would be able to marry her without her father's permission."

My nose wrinkled. "That's not a thing where I come from. Get yourself a job, and you can marry her as soon as Jens gets you papers that say you live there."

He frowned. "I'm certain you are oversimplifying things."

"Nope. You can marry whoever you want, Jamie. I'll be there to make sure it happens just as easy as that. You can have Queen Lucy's blessing. How about that?"

He tucked my head under his chin as he pondered my promise of a better life.

"Her parents left her knowing she could never get married? That's cold."

"Indeed. Yet she's remarkably warm-hearted for being dismissed so. She was always playing with knives with Jens instead of stitching and learning to bake bread." He had a small smile when he spoke about her outcast ways. "Most men were put off by that, but the first time she and Jens took me hunting, I found I couldn't look anywhere else for happiness. She's simply the perfect woman, salty bread and all."

There was a rustle outside the cave, and Henry Mancini was on his feet, snarling at the entrance. "Is that them?" I whispered.

"No." With calculated movements and tensed muscles, Jamie reached for his pack and pulled out a machete in a leather sheath. He slid it out, and my skin turned to ice. "Hold still."

I ceased all movement. I may have even stopped breathing. I watched as Jamie slid between me and the disturbance, machete clutched to his chest. Henry Mancini barked at the entrance to the cave, marking us as his territory.

It happened so fast, I could scarcely process it. Twigs were snapping, and then the largest bear I'd ever seen rounded the corner. His fur was black and shiny in the moonlight. His paws were almost as big as my head. His mouth had foam dripping down his chest like honey. The eyes. The terrifying yellow eyes gleamed with rabid insanity directly at me.

He roared, and I screamed.

WEREBEAR

*I*t was a blur, all of it. Henry Mancini made the first move, but he was quickly cast aside and thrown into the wall with a sickening thud. "No!" I cried out for my dog.

Jamie was on his feet, machete in his war-seasoned hands. He backed me to the wall where I stayed as he advanced on the Werebear.

One slash parried a deadly attack with the Were's claws. Over and over, they battled, claws against steel. The bear was getting closer to hitting his mark, and I knew if he did, Jamie would not recover.

Jamie managed to stab into the bear's thick fur, drawing enough blood to give him a moment to catch his breath.

"You're too close to the edge, Jamie!" I warned, pointing to the steep drop-off.

"I'll draw him away so you can run! Go, Lucy! Go!"

"I'm not leaving you!"

Then the bear roared so loud, the terrifying sound completely swallowed my ineffectual scream. The beast was wild before, but he was furious now. He lashed out and scraped against Jamie's stomach, drawing out a similar howl from the prince. Jamie dropped his machete to hold the bleeding wound.

I had nothing. No weapon. No way to defend myself or help Jamie. My eyes fell on Henry Mancini's motionless body, and something primal in me awakened. I had never thrown a real punch in my life, but I could not passively resist this bear, no matter how much I wanted to. The beast would kill Jamie, and he would never get his chance to marry Britta.

I picked up my backpack, swung it around and knocked the bear over the head with it. This only served to irritate the already livid beast. He whirled on me and stood up on his hind legs, roaring against the light of the moon. I inched in front of Jamie and picked up his machete. It was heavy, and felt impossibly useless in my hands. "Don't make me do this!" I begged the bear, as if he could be reasoned with.

I wanted to run. I wanted to pee myself, close my eyes and cover my ears in a ball on the floor. I wanted to escape.

If only I had those kinds of options.

On his way down to all fours, I lunged forward with an unheroic screech and plunged the blade deep into the bear's belly. His movements only made the steel cut more. The beast flailed, and before I knew it, I was being flung into the cave wall next to Jamie.

The machete was sticking out of the bear's furry stomach, blood drooling and spurting out at the entry point, but he was not dying as quickly as we needed him to.

Jamie and I both lunged forward when the bear reared up on his hind legs again to howl at the pain, the moon, me, and the limited cards he'd been dealt.

Our fingers wrapped around the hilt, locking with the other's, and we drove the blade into the belly of the beast until it would not go any further. There was fire in Jamie's eyes, and terror in mine as we yanked out the machete and stumbled back to give the bear his space to die.

Like a drunken fool, the bear crashed down to all fours and swayed from side to side as he bled out on the rocky path. Jamie whispered a prayer of release for the soul that had been trapped inside the bear and forced to do such harm.

The bear breathed his last in a sweeping gust that came out almost a relieved sigh, and I looked away as Jamie checked to make sure he was dead. My shaking hands found Henry Mancini rousing on the floor. My knees buckled, and I fell next to him. I gathered him to me, checking his vitals as best I could in the dim red hue. "It's okay, baby. It's okay. I'll fix it. I can be a good mommy, I swear!" Flashes of my fern taunted me, questioning my ability to nurture.

Henry Mancini responded by licking my fingers and whining pitifully. I clung to him as if he was my lifeline, begging him to forgive me for the horrible thing I'd just done to the bear.

After everything I'd been through, I had just taken a life. For better or worse, I was a murderer now.

Jamie made several noises of relief and discomfort, so I took my puppy with me to go check on him. The gashes were not deep enough to be deadly, but they would leave marks. I fished around in my green pack with fingers as dexterous as sausages and pulled out my first aid kit. "Let's go outside of the cave so I can g-get a good look at your cuts." I shivered from adrenaline, trying unsuccessfully to offer up a somewhat professional bedside manner.

He obeyed, but we both gave the bear a wide berth. Jamie yanked off his beige shirt and cast it to the ground.

"This is ruined, right?" I asked, picking up his tattered garment.

"Yeah." He was breathing hard, his muscles tensed against the pain.

I balled up the torn shirt and used it as a compress to stop the bleeding. "Lay down. It won't do to have you fall off the edge of the mountain right after saving us from that bear."

Jamie complied, grimacing at the cold stone that kissed his back. "I didn't save us. You did."

"We both did," I amended, checking his wound for signs of clotting. I dabbed the edges of the lesser marks with an iodine swab, frowning with frustration when rain droplets fell where I was examining him. "Is it raining?"

Jamie's hand shook as it reached my face and wiped away tears I did not know were there. Seeing the evidence of my fear, I let out a solitary sob before I could stuff my emotions back down. "You almost died!" I cried as I flung my arms around his neck.

"Shh. It's okay. I'll be just fine, thanks to you."

Henry Mancini attacked the wild animal for causing us such trauma, biting at his motionless leg.

Then a loud scream interrupted the quiet of the night. "No!"

Britta charged up the path, her emerald eyes wild with fright, braids swinging out behind her. When I released Jamie and sat back on my heels, the front of my shirt was covered in his blood.

"It's okay!" I called out, hoping she would slow down and watch her step. "He's alive, Britta."

She would not accept my assessment until she confirmed it with her own two eyes.

The two finally let down their defenses and indulged in their very first public kiss. I was the only witness. Jamie pulled himself to sitting so he could wrap an arm around her. The way he looked at her made my heart lurch in my chest. There was adoration. There was tenderness. Most of all, there was pure love blooming between them. I stepped back and waved the others forward as they rounded the bend.

Any hope of putting on a brave front was shattered when Jens ran to me in a fashion similar to how Britta ran to Jamie. "No, Lucy! What happened to you? I'll fix it! I'll fix it!" He all but pushed me into the cave before I could correct his assumption that I was covered in my own blood. He backed me into the Were without realizing it was there in his frantic state. The bear's black fur was hard to spot in the dark cave. "Get back!" he yelled, pulling out his machete.

"It's dead. Don't worry." He had a crazed look about him that made me want to speak very quietly and move with care around him. He had remnants of that same glitter under his nose again, but I was too discombobulated to ask him about it. "I'm fine, Jens. It's not me. This blood's from Jamie. He's hurt."

"Jamie?" Jens whirled around and saw his sister kissing Jamie on the ground and crying into his mouth. "Jamie!"

Nik, Foss and Tor came into view, followed by Charles and Uncle Rick, all showing various signs of being wounded in battle. They rushed as fast as they could without causing further injury to themselves, asking questions and well, pretty much just getting in the way.

I held up my trembling hands. "Okay, everyone. Get in the cave and take a seat." I went to Jamie so I could examine his wound again. Henry Mancini yapped at Britta, who would not permit an iota of space between herself and her injured love. "Britt, you can stay, but you have to back up. I need to look at this."

"Yes. Thank you. How can I help?"

I fished around in the first aid kit and took out my sewing kit from underneath the gauze, threading the needle carefully in the dark. There was no way to properly disinfect it, so I sprayed a little iodine on the tip and hoped for the best. "You can hold his hand and keep him quiet."

Luckily, Britta obeyed, overlooking my rudeness.

"There's only one cut too deep to heal on its own, so I have to sew it up. Just be very still. I'm not great at this."

"I trust you," Jamie said, his solemn tone akin to that of swearing an oath.

I wanted to vomit all over Jamie's chest, but choked it down so I didn't have to disinfect him all over again. He gazed upon Britta's face as if it belonged to an angel, despite my tugging and piercing his skin.

I don't know how I managed to finish suturing in a true line, but I did. I'd learned this particular skill practicing on oranges. Jamie's skin was not the same. If I'd done it wrong on the orange, I just got a little juice on my hands. If I did it wrong on Jamie? Well, I tried not to picture the damage of infection or ripped stitches. I dropped my needle four times due to my hands shaking before the job was complete. Then I turned on the group, who were surprisingly amicable, awaiting further instruction or explanation. "Anyone else?"

Nik raised his hand like he was in class. "Could you look at my leg? I got nicked with an ax."

Foss scoffed from his place in the corner of the cave. "Figures your one useful skill is sewing."

I was a little unbalanced, so I didn't acknowledge Foss had even spoken. I had just helped kill a bear. I didn't want to picture the damage I could do to a Fossegrimen prick.

Nik did indeed get nicked. It was a deep gash to the left of his shin on his right leg. I started the process all over again, glad that there was not enough light to highlight my tears.

Nik managed a cocky smile. "I was hit by an ax so large, I don't know how a Daydwarf managed to swing it."

Tor grumbled at this. "Dwarves are made of strong stuff. If ya can swing an ax, so can we."

"What happened was that I was running toward the portal with Britta and Foss. I almost was successful in taking out a legion of Daydwarf guards, but I had to slow down for Britta's sake, you understand. I had to jump clear over a felled Daydwarf and knock another clean out. It's a wonder I got sliced up. But that's what happens when I can't fight to my full ability." He regaled me with about five more minutes of stories highlighting his heroics. I should have been annoyed, but the sound of his voice was a good distraction from the screaming I was doing internally.

I packed up my things with clumsy hands and moved into the cave. As soon as I tried to sit down, my stomach roiled, informing me it had reached its pain threshold. Jens was saying something, but I couldn't hear it. I ran back out of the cave and vomited over the side of the mountain. It poured out of me from the very soles of my shoes, thrusting out violently onto the path below. I threw up so hard and for so long, I could think of nothing else. It was not until my body was empty of nutrition that I heard unhappiness coming from just a few feet away.

Jamie was loudly vomiting to my right over the side of the mountain as Britta and Jens held him.

"What happened?" Jens asked once we were all huddled together in the cave. Tor and Charles had gathered up stones and branches and put them in a circle down a ways from the cave to make a fire. Uncle Rick was quiet, occasionally sneaking glances at Jamie and I. Foss and Nik were busy slicing up the bear to make steaks for everyone to eat.

Uncle Rick suggested we wait out the night in the cave. Everyone was exhausted, and Jamie and I were sick with some weird flu or something. Whatever it was, I hadn't barfed that much in my whole life. Jens, Uncle Rick and Charles were conversing in hushed tones by the fire as the steaks cooked, stealing worried glances at Jamie and I that they shifted to encouraging ones when they saw us looking. I heard foreign words like "laplanding" being thrown around, but I was too beat to ask questions.

I had long since given up a tough façade of being able to muscle my way through the events of the day. My heart was heavy, my stomach was sick, and I was so weak from both that I lay on the floor of the cave to get an early start on a nap. Jamie was dragged in and laid next to me. My eyelids were weighted, but even through my near-delusional haze, I could tell Jamie was not doing well. He was white as a ghost, covered in sweat with dark circles under his eyes. His breath came out in shallow puffs that looked painful. I wanted to comfort him, but I could barely lift my stiff hand.

"We shouldn't linger here. Eat what you can, and then we keep moving," Foss ruled.

Jens shook his head, his messy black hair making him look a little crazy. "No. We can't move them yet. They're sick."

Foss lowered his voice. "You know what this is, Jens. You know why they're sick. Rest won't help them."

Jens stared at the partway gutted bear, dread plain on his face. "It's just a flu. It's just a flu. Totally normal on the Other Side. Rest. Rest and fluids. She's fine. It's just a flu."

Foss chewed a mouthful of meat as he spoke, his tone grim. "Your charge won't be the same after she transitions. Best say your goodbyes now."

Jens quieted to a whisper. "It's just a flu. It's just a flu."

Britta fretted over us with motherly affection I had not known in over a year. Cool compresses were placed on our foreheads, and she kissed my cheek as she sang a soft lullaby I had never heard. I wanted to weep at the pathetic state I'd deteriorated to in such a short time, but I could not muster up the energy required for that task. Everything was a task, so I gave in and was pulled under, grateful for the dark that swept me away.

Love *Undraland*? Leave a review!

NØKKEN

BOOK TWO IN THE UNDRALAND SERIES

Enjoy a free preview of <u>Nøkken</u>

HAZE, HALFY AND HIM

*T*or's booming voice infiltrated my delirium. "I know, but we have ta get moving. They'll wise up and search the mountains fer us soon. How well do ya think they'll fare then?" I could picture his red face and ratty dreadlocks as he spoke. We were on the mountain, still tucked in the cave after Jamie and I had killed a Werebear together. We were sick with some awful virus that I prayed would pass before I ralphed again. I had nothing left in my stomach, but the green around the gills feeling was still lending its oppressive vibe.

Jens argued, "But their fever's not even broken yet! Moving them now? I don't like it."

"It don't matter whatcha like. Lucy and Jamie'll be easy targets when scavengers come fer this dead Werebear."

Foss chimed in, "Which could be any moment, mind you. Take the prince, leave the rat. I'll buy you a new one."

"But what happened?" Britta demanded an answer. "She's got a couple bruises, but that's it."

Charles sounded grim. His words delivered a weighty blow I was too much a foreigner to properly understand. "There's no way she and Jamie could be exactly this sick out of nowhere at the same time."

"If you want me to say it, I won't. It's impossible," Jens ruled.

"There's a dead Were right in front of your face, Jens." Mace lowered his voice. "You know what this is. You just won't admit it."

"There's nothing to admit! She's a pacifist. There's no way she could have killed that Were with Jamie. You don't know her like I do."

"Maybe *you* don't know her as well as you think you do," Mace countered, playing the antagonist. "It's obvious to everyone but you that she laplanded with Jamie."

Jens lashed out at Mace. "Hey, newbie. Why don't you shut your trap and make yourself useful helping Britt and Alrik with the stretcher?"

I wanted to get up and join them to see what I'd missed, to tell Jens and Mace to stop fighting, but my body was uncooperative. I could crack one eye open, but that was all. The rest of me was totally useless.

I'm sure there was more talk happening, but I couldn't understand a lick of it as my brain floated in and out of consciousness. The next thing I registered was being picked up and laid somewhere cold and sweaty and hairy - Jamie. There was a faint notion that I was somehow floating with him on a stretcher of some sort, but I was too out of my body to investigate further.

After that, I have no idea how much time passed or

what happened. All I could hope was that Jens was nearby to keep my useless body from further harm.

* * *

DAYLIGHT FELT warm on my skin after the... night? Week? Month? I'd been cold. I turned over on my side and snuggled into the growing warmth next to me, wrapping my arms and legs through it contentedly.

I inhaled the scent of oatmeal cookies.

Ah, Jens. My guardian garden gnome I hadn't actually known all that long. Now, despite the arguing, I was growing attached to him in a way I was not quite ready to examine. I missed sleeping next to him, even though we'd only done that once.

I nuzzled his neck with my nose and planted a kiss on a sensitive spot I knew would make him tingle. Before we could get into another fight, I wanted to enjoy the peace of his protection.

"Uh, Lucy? What are you doing?"

"I missed you, Jens." I murmured sleepily.

"Did you, now?"

His teasing voice was a sweet sound to the nothing I'd been processing for this elongated period of time. It sounded far away, but still somehow near, like I was hearing him through water. As my senses began coming back to me, I realized that his voice was coming from somewhere behind me.

My eyes flew open, and I found that the warmth I was kissing was not Jens, but Jamie.

I should've known. Jens smelled like a warm sugar cookie, not an oatmeal raisin.

I fumbled backwards on the bed in confusion. I tried to jerk myself up, but my muscles were out of practice. I groaned when my neck cracked without my permission. "What the... Where am I?" Before I could get an answer, I started coughing. My throat felt tight and parched from disuse.

An arm banded around my back and inched me slowly upwards. A hand was put to my dry lips and I was instructed to drink. I wrapped my lips around the heel of someone's hand and drank more than was possible. After I had my fill, I dipped my face in the little pool to bring life and lucidity further toward my senses. "W-What happened?"

I opened my eyes and saw Charles Mace, my newly discovered brother in front of me. His hand was wet from feeding the water to me using his many magics I still did not understand. His long fingers brushed the blonde hair from my face with tenderness that made me relax and Jens tense simultaneously.

"You laplanded with Jamie," Mace explained, his face etched with relief. "You've both been out for three days."

"What?"

The only voice I wanted to hear in that moment whispered in my ear, "Shh. You don't need to worry about anything right now. Just chill and let yourself wake up."

I was leaned up against his chest, and the comfort of that was indescribable. My eyes began to focus again, and I saw that we were in some sort of thatched-roof hut with a mud floor. Mid-afternoon light crept in through the half-open doorway. Other than the straw bed and a large steel basin bathtub, there was nothing else in the hut. "Are we in… Where is this? Haiti?" I guessed, moving my fingers around to build up my circulation.

Jens shook his head and inched me up further so I could breathe better. "Nope. Still in Undraland. We're in Nightdwarf territory. Most of their civilization is underground. They lent us this aboveground house until you and Jamie get better."

"Jamie?" I glanced down next to me and saw Jamie's motionless form. He had a bit of color back and was breathing steadily now, thank goodness. I buried my forehead in my palm to cover my shame. "Oh! I thought he was you! I kissed his neck. Now it's all awkward. Could we not tell him I did that?"

Jens chuckled, shaking my torso gently with the motion. "You don't have to worry. Your Tomten prince's still out. I know you dream about me constantly."

"Oh, shut up." I rolled my shoulders and finally had the wherewithal to sit up on my own. I looked down at my bare legs and grimaced. I was not dressed in my clothes, but in a bag-like itchy dress that fell to my shins. "Why am I always waking up in a dress?"

Jens grinned, rubbing circles in my back. "Don't worry. I had Tor clean you up and dress you while you were out. I know how smitten you are with Jamie, what with you kissing his neck and all, so we gave you matching outfits."

Sure enough, Jamie was wearing the exact same thing. I mean, exact same, only the fit was not as baggy on his larger build, and the dress barely fell to the knee on him.

"I sincerely hope you're joking," I grumbled.

"You know I am. Britt took care of you two and washed your clothes for you."

Jamie's dress was cut open at the chest, showcasing several bandages wrapped around his torso. Then it started coming back to me.

The bear.

No, not bear. A Werebear. Pesta's own creation of sending harvested evil souls back out into the world to do her bidding. She was tracking me, sending out souls to kill me, while the bodies those souls came from were checked out and pretty much lobotomized in her Land of Be. "Where you can just Be" was the slogan. The retired Undrans had their little lifetime siesta, meanwhile she broke her word by weaponizing the forfeited souls. She had been allowed to use only bears to experience the world she had been banned from. Now she migrated to using other animals – a fact the many magical kingdoms of this surreal world were as yet unable to accept. She had murdered my parents and taken my dad's bones to start a portal for humans, opening up another race to use for her own devices. She wanted me for the rake she guessed was passed down and still in my possession. She also wanted my bones to finish the human portal, so a new race would be open for her perusal. The rake was the only weapon that could be used to destroy her portals. That was our mission.

I rubbed my temples as the information overload sizzled in my brain. "Tor got through to the portal and destroyed it?"

"We never even got close," Jens replied, chagrinned. "Our injuries were because we were running invisible through a battlefield. It was too well-guarded."

"Did any of the Daydwarves see you?"

Jens shook his head. "I don't think so. We were welcomed here with open arms, so no. To them we're your entourage, accompanying the 'human female' Queen Lucy around to the different regions."

Mace spoke up. "They're throwing a big party tonight to honor you."

"Huh? Um, okay. That's awfully nice."

"Might be good if you could walk by then," Mace hinted. "How do you feel?"

"Like I've been hit with a ton of bricks. What happened to me? Did I get some weird leprechaun flu?"

Jens snorted. "Leprechauns. You and that imagination." Then he shifted awkwardly behind me. "How did you guys escape the Were?"

"Henry Mancini!" I exclaimed, whipping my head around to the door. "Where's my dog?"

"Foss has your wolf," Mace answered. "Did you know it's not a dog? Might not be the safest choice for a pet. Your Tom should know better."

"Shut up, Mace," Jens growled.

"Henry Mancini would never hurt me. He's okay though?"

Jens nodded. "What happened to the Were, Loos?"

Moisture welled up in my eyes before I could stop it. I pictured my hand clutching Jamie's machete, terrified at the notion of using it, but knowing it would be worse if I didn't. "He hurt Jamie, so I... stabbed the bear in the belly. Twice, I think, with Jamie's knife." I couldn't bring myself to look at the men; I was so ashamed. "The second time I didn't drive it d-deep enough, so Jamie helped me finish him off." At this, I broke down into quiet sobs. "I'm sorry! I'm so sorry! I didn't want to kill anybody!"

Jens patted my back and nodded gravely at Mace.

My brother kissed the top of my head and drew me to his chest, away from Jens. "There, there. It's what you were supposed to do. You're lucky you both survived."

"He hit Henry Mancini!" I wailed. "He attacked my dog and Jamie! Peaceful resistance wasn't working!"

Jens got up abruptly and left the hut with no explanation, plunging me into guilt-ridden despair over killing a living being. Charles wrapped his arms tighter around me as I sobbed like a baby. "You can't peacefully resist a normal bear, much less a Were. Lucy, it's okay. You're safe."

"It's not okay! Killing is wrong! Martin Luther King would have found a way!"

I spent the next fifteen minutes crying on Mace's shoulder while he tried unsuccessfully to understand my grief.

When Jens returned, it was with a hard expression that I wanted to cower from as he towered over me. "Give us a minute, Mace," he ordered. There was no mistaking the sharpness in his command.

Charles released me, wiping the lines of tears from my cheeks before rising from the bed. "You'll be alright, *kära*."

Jens stiffened at this and stared Charles down as he exited the hut. When it was just the two of us and Jamie's unconscious body, he crossed his arms over his chest and puffed his breast out authoritatively. "I don't like him," he ruled.

I wiped the last tear away and scoffed. "You have a hard time getting along with people? I don't believe it." I shook my head and brought my knees to my chest on the bed so I could rest my head on them. "You don't have to like him. You're completely free to make things as difficult as you need to."

"You know that's not what this is about. He called you *kära*!"

"Do you hear yourself? So what? Foss calls me rat. *Kära* is a far sight better than Tor calling me human female all the time. Queen Lucy. Lady Kincaid. So what? Because Charles is nice to me, now he must be the devil? Be more obvious, why don't you." My hand rested on Jamie's shoulder, and I lowered my voice so as not to wake him.

"Obvious? Talk about what's right in front of your face. *Kära* is like 'hey baby' here. It's a lovey term of endearment for lovers in love, with the love stuff." Jens's cheeks were turning pink. He looked like just pushing out the word love was strangling him.

I shook my head. "Don't do this."

"What? Look out for you?"

My hands flew out and animated my frustration. "Don't make things difficult like this. Charles is my brother now. I actually have a chance at making a family for myself again. Don't be a baby and fill my head with semantics to try and drive a wedge between us. I don't need protection from my own blood!"

Jens was so aggravated that his pitch rose to get his point across with more passion. "He does the hug and lurk!"

"The what?"

"You know!" He mimed a hug with his shoulders hunched inward. "When he hugs you, he doesn't let go when a normal person would. He hugs, and then he lurks. The hug and lurk. Come on! It's plain as day that he's in love with you."

"Well, maybe you should yell at me about it!" I shouted back. "I can't believe you're doing this! I finally get... and then you... and I don't care what you say! There's nothing wrong with Charles or the way he looks at me."

"Ah-ha!" Jens yelled, pointer finger raised in triumph. "I never said anything about the way he looks at you. You did notice something off about him. You just won't admit it because then I would be right! And we can't have that, can we?"

I threw my head back in exasperation. "Oh! You are so arrogant! The world doesn't revolve around whether or not you're right, Jens. Charles is perfectly fine. I'm lucky I get a chance to have a family again! And frankly, you don't get a say in this. Your job is to protect me, not swagger around like a jealous fool. Newsflash, you're not my boyfriend!"

He struggled with which angry words to spit out at me, his face shifting from pink to red.

I didn't want to hear it. I stood and stomped past him with my nose in the air.

"Lucy, wait! I'm not done talking to you."

"Oh, yes you are!" I marched out into the fresh sunlight, but I couldn't fully enjoy it because of stupid Jens. I didn't know where I was going with no shoes on, but one thing was certain, that hut was too crowded for the both of us.

Read Nøkken, the next book in the series

Find your next great read and sign up for the newsletter at www.maryetwomey.com

Mary also writes contemporary romance under the name Tuesday Embers.
View her books at www.tuesdayembers.com

2/23

2/23

CPSIA information can be obtained
at www.ICGtesting.com
Printed in the USA
LVHW051108020123
736297LV00016B/267

9 781508 634546